I0668637

HOPE RESTRAINED
(Estate Series – Book 2)

By M.S. Willis

OTHER BOOKS BY M.S. WILLIS

Control Series

Book One – Control

Book Two – Conflict

Book Three – Conquer

Estate Series

Book One – Madeleine Abducted

Book Two – Joseph Fallen

Coming in 2014

Honor Bound (Estate #4)

Grace Restored (Estate #5)

Table of Contents

Hope Restrained is dedicated to the first fan characters of the series, Erica and Crystal. Good luck to you.

Prologue

Evil. It's a concept you believe you understand – a thing that you can declare, without hesitation, as bad. Within evil, there is no light, there is no hope and there is no redemption. That is the rule, and it is one that most people hold as truth. This is a story that will make you question the basic tenets of what you think you know. It is an introduction to grey areas and it is a place where decisions have to be made and where evil must be measured.

There are situations where a person is given a choice and where the only available options are between atrocity and the unthinkable. It is a place where you must decide between honor and betrayal and where your chances of survival are slim to none.

She is an assassin; a strong woman who was raised to be a weapon. She is a brilliant mind and a beautiful soul that was tarnished at birth simply because of circumstances outside of her control. Brought up within a rival criminal network, her life was overshadowed by The Estate. It was a place to be avoided and a path never to be crossed.

However, fate is never kind and even when a woman walks carefully to elude the darkness she knows surrounds her, sometimes circumstances

1

force her to directly into the belly of the beast. It was kill or be killed and hers was a mission of life or death.

Her name is Hope Delacroix, and when she entered the walls of The Estate stronghold, she wasn't going in as a slave...

She was going in as a warrior.

Chapter One

Honor sat still against the corner of the wall. Her vision diluted and hazed and her thoughts only making sense when the fog lifted for brief terror-filled moments. Huddled over herself, tears dripped down her face. The screams, blood-filled and agonizing, echoed through her skull while recycled images stalked her thoughts, never leaving her, never allowing her escape. Battering and relentless, they tore at her soul when the hands of men tore at her body. She could leave her body behind, she could escape the flesh if only her mind hadn't been shattered by the bits and pieces - flashes of crimson stains, sparks of burning pain. Terror knew nothing of this Hell, no word strong enough to describe the waking nightmare, the never-ending cruelty.

A door opened and light flooded in attempting to touch her skin before callously being denied the chance as the door was once again closed.

He walked towards her, his features liquid and unsettled as she attempted to see beyond the way light played along his skin.

"My angel..." Her words were slurred, her voice so fragile, it barely cut through the silence in the room.

He covered her mouth, the warmth of his hand seeping into her cold, chapped lips. The salt of his skin met the broken areas on her face, but she savored his

3

touch, despite the reminder of the violence committed against her. She knew better than to talk – he always wanted her silent.

"I've come to take you away my pet – but only if you are ready for me this time." His voice rolled across her senses, the words trapped within a tunnel, the meaning lost to her understanding. She just wanted him to keep talking, to stay with her, to never go away. He was her angel, he'd told her so. He'd said he'd take her away if she was good, if she learned to behave. Every time she failed he had no choice but to leave her alone with the monsters. She hadn't been ready before, the pain too much to keep quiet. She prayed that she could behave, could be good so he would take her as he'd promised.

His hand brushed down her cheek, his mouth covering hers as the warmth of his hand moved lower to cover her breast. She moaned into his mouth, welcoming his touch. Lifting her from the floor by her arms, he held her when she stood on shaky legs, her body cold from the lack of clothes and the sudden touch of air across her skin. She was putty, each muscle refusing to cooperate because of the poisons running through her blood.

He walked her to a table in the center of the room and she pulled back to remember the things she'd seen done to women on its surface, the things that had been done to her.

"Do you resist me?" Dark and cold, his words terrifying despite the beauty of his voice.

She cringed. "No angel."

4

Lifting her, he bent her over the icy metal surface, immediately securing her hands to the shackles on top and her feet in the short chains connected to the legs of the table. Her legs spread wide, she was bared to him, unable to move or resist his demands. Her head rested perfectly on the other end, a small indented piece trapping her chin in place at the edge.

She felt his large body over hers, his hand gripping into her hair and tears traveling down her cheeks at the pain his grip caused.

When he forced himself inside, she screamed out, her body too abused to handle the contact, her sobs so thick, she choked on them as they poured from her mouth. He tsked behind her, unmoving, before slowly pulling out. Her heart sank into her stomach, hating herself for having failed.

Moving around the table, her eyes followed him once he came within her peripheral view. He moved in front of her, placing his hand on her head. She cried louder, her disgrace wearing heavily upon her body and soul.

"I'm disappointed with you, pet. I gave you another opportunity and you failed." He paused, letting it sink in that she wouldn't be saved. "Open your mouth so you can clean off your shame."

He grasped the hair at the top of her head and pulled up, opening her impossibly wide before cleaning himself within the wet heat of her mouth. "Maybe if you are good the next time, I won't have to leave you to be punished again."

5

When he'd released, she swallowed down the taste of her failure before he removed himself from her mouth and left the room while her tears ran in rivulets towards the table to which he'd left her strapped.

Chapter Two

The wind howled as Hope Delacroix stood surveying the perimeter of the shadowed house. While tearing at the base of her black leather trench, the angry wind also beat against the branches above her, unrelenting as the wood creaked and groaned. Slowly, methodically, she willed the rate of her breath, calming her body. Her head tilted slightly as she listened for other noises outside of the wind rushing past her ear. Sweat prickled along her skin despite the cold.

Maybe, it had been an accident.

It was a thought that only served to render false comfort.

She'd gone missing three weeks prior. Three long, aggravating weeks during which Hope had paced the streets, desperately seeking out any clue that could be found in the dank and dirty alleyways that acted like a maze within the city.

She knew her sister had been taken, some instinct within her telling her that darkness was creeping along the edges of her life; small tendrils of which reached out, wrapping around her despite her efforts to avoid its gaze. She wasn't surprised to receive a call from a man claiming to be the abductor, but what did surprise her was the identity of that man. Not his name – no - she didn't believe he was honest when he identified himself. It was the network to which he belonged that had been the terrifying shock to her system.

The Estate. It was a dark power, created by evil and demented so thoroughly that it lorded over other criminal networks, imparting fear of a wrong word or wrong move. There were rumors that Joseph Carmichael had sold his soul to the devil to gain the wealth and power he had over so short a period of time. But those who'd been in the Estate - the few who'd survived and made it out with their tongues and minds intact - they laughed at the rumor. From what they'd seen inside those large foreboding walls of the compound, Joseph Carmichael hadn't sold his soul - he was the devil himself.

She remembered a rumor two years prior that Joseph had been killed. At first, she didn't believe it - but, when those rumors persisted, when a year had passed and the dealings of The Estate had lessened, she grew nervous. Trepidation crept along her bones as she wondered: what was so powerful it could destroy Joseph?

Now, standing outside a two-story mansion within the Estate compound, she flicked a knife in her right hand and rested her left on the butt of a gun she had tucked into the waistband of her pants. There was no movement outside except for the stirring of leaves in the violent wind at her feet. The windows of the house were blacked out, preventing her from seeing inside. She'd wished for an easy solution; break in, find her sister, get out. But she knew the likelihood of success was low.

Jumping the walls hadn't been difficult. She chuckled to think that she was probably the first person to attempt entering The Estate uninvited. The compound had a reputation for swallowing bodies - once a person entered those gates, very rarely were they seen again. What was the use of keeping people out, when it was almost guaranteed they'd never leave?

But she'd had no choice, her sister was too precious, too good to be left victim to the beast. And now, Hope had to enter that house.

Creeping forward slowly, she stepped softly across the dried leaves that blanketed the ground — a silent stalker covered in the blanket of night. The wind continued tearing at her hair and her coat slapped the backs of her calves — the sound, reminiscent of skin against skin. Her boots felt heavy on her feet and she forced her heart to beat slowly, methodically, when she breached the shadows around the building.

Fear trickled along her spine. She knew it could never be this easy, that there were eyes watching her, silently laughing, thinking she believed she was alone. However, she knew better than to be so ignorant to believe they hadn't already noticed her; they were too well organized to be ambushed. Despite that knowledge, she had to try. Fighting had been ingrained in the life she led as an assassin.

9

She'd begun her training when she was still in braids. While her sister played with dolls and paint, Hope was given blades and sticks. She was different than her twin, darker somehow, and the adults had simultaneously admired her and feared her. They'd noticed her differences early on, and after the discovery, they'd fed and fostered her odd *proclivities*.

But her sister, Honor... she was always the light, almost as if they'd split apart when their mother had carried them; the light and dark sides of one soul, so opposite of one another that they couldn't be contained in a single body. Hope was the older twin, always protective of the innocence of Honor. She adored her, and at times grew jealous of Honor's talent in art, music and writing – all the things that were beautiful and pure in the world around them. And whereas Honor was skilled in things of beauty, Hope was skilled in death and pain.

When she'd learned that Honor had disappeared, she'd lost her mind, sleeping only two fitful hours a day so that she'd have more time to search every square inch of the city. Hope felt lost without Honor – darker, somehow. Without her, there was nothing to pull Hope back from the darkness that consumed her.

Rounding the corner of the house, Hope's eyes looked up into the face of a camera that clicked quietly, following her movements, a hidden eye watching her and tracking her path. When she heard a branch break beneath the foot of another person, she gripped her blade tighter against her palm. Turning slowly, her gaze fell on five men, all armed, guns drawn with her body in their sights. Flicking the knife in her hand, she smiled. Despite her hesitancy; it was time.

"Hello boys." She kept her voice calm, genial, in an attempt to hide the terror and determination coursing through her veins. She knew she appeared an easy target – a beautiful woman, tall –yet slim. It was too much for their testosterone driven egos to believe that she could hold her own against them. But that was exactly why Hope was so good at what she did.

The men sneered, confident in their belief that they had her cornered. The tallest of the group spoke first.

"Hope Delacroix. We've been waiting for your arrival."

She noticed how the man's hand shook slightly as he spoke. The corner of her lip curled up to discover his anxiety. "Nervous?"

Stepping forward she flipped the side of her trench to expose the skin of her abdomen. Her typical uniform of black leather pants connected to straps that wrapped her body to conceal her breasts. The design was not only intended to prevent her clothes from becoming a hindrance when she fought, but also to distract her opponent.

"There's nothing to fear with me." The knife flicked again, turning slowly, effortlessly in her hand. "I've just come to join the party."

11

His hand raised and her eyes shot to see the recorder that he held. A dimple appeared on his shadowed cheek when he grinned and pressed the button on the recorder.

"Hope." It was her sister's choked word and Hope's body tensed in reaction to the sound. "Please." She groaned, pain evident in her voice. "Help me, please." Rage bloomed within Hope's chest to hear it, but she had to breathe steady, had to remain calm in the face of the only thing in the world that could destroy her.

He released the button. "Did you want to cooperate Ms. Delacroix, or shall I tell my boss that you declined his invitation?"

Her eyes narrowed, but she kept her expression open, malleable. She'd been trained to never reveal weakness.

Holding out her arm, she indicated towards the front of the house. "Shall we?"

The men didn't move, keeping their guns trained on her face and body, their expressions filled with uncertainty and caution.

The tall man stepped forward, lowering his gun, and reached out to indicate as well. "Ladies first."

Hope eyed him, a sweet smile still adorning her face. She turned her head away from the man and stepped towards the house. She listened to the rest of his group lower their weapons, relaxing now that she'd complied. When they'd neared the front entrance, the man behind her stepped faster, quickly grabbing her left arm to force her up the steps.

His scream was loud – but lasted only a second.

Spinning rapidly, Hope had caught his throat with the serrated edge of her blade, had pushed the tip inside, using the motion of her spinning body to rip it outwards, severing the tissue and the bone – the blood spraying out across her golden skin. His body dropped quickly and silently to the ground, just as four guns cocked in unison at her back.

Reaching up, she wiped the blood from her face and turned to look at the men.

They tensed when she held up her hand to show them the blood smeared across her skin. "Are you upset about this?" She laughed. "Don't worry. As long as you don't make the same mistake, you will be allowed to continue breathing." Her brow arched. "We can be friends as long as you remember to never touch me."

Spinning on her heel, she took a deep and calming breath before stepping up the large staircase and entering the dark and shadowed mansion.

. . .

"You're insane. That's nothing more than a suicide mission. Not even I am capable of pulling something like that off." Her eyes locked on the

13

man who stood before her. At his feet, knelt her sister, a mirror image of herself, now marked and bruised from her captivity over the previous three weeks. Honor didn't look up and Hope assumed it was because her sister understood the importance that she remain as emotionless as possible.

His voice was slow and assured when he smiled and responded, "You, my beautiful girl, are the *only* person who can succeed. Everybody is well aware of your status within the smaller networks. If any person can compete against Aaron Carmichael – it's you."

"What happens if I don't kill him? No man has attempted to assassinate Aaron and survived. He enjoys his job too much, feeds off of it, from what I hear."

He chuckled. "Then it appears you two have something in common." The sudden transformation of his expression from jovial to stern was unnerving. "I suggest you succeed, Ms. Delacroix." His hand flinched and the chain wrapped around her sister's neck tightened. "Her life depends on it."

She looked down into Honor's face. She wasn't in pain, but she was so heavily drugged that even if she had been horribly injured, she wouldn't have been aware.

Hope's hand twitched, her desire to snap his neck while shoving her blade deep inside him, overpowering the calm façade she wore. They'd not bothered to strip her of her weapons when

14

she'd entered, realizing she wouldn't act in a way that could kill her twin. Pacing, she continued rolling her blade in her hand, her other hand fisting in anticipation of a kill. Surveying the room, she noticed how the men stood about, guns drawn, booted feet held at shoulder width in postures intended for a fight. Her sister was barely able to hold herself in an upright and kneeling position on the floor - her body appeared frail, her spirit already broken. What had these men done to her? Hope could only assume the worst, but kept her expression bored and blank.

"You need something from me – that much is apparent. Why help you if you'll only destroy her in the process? Each day she remains here could be her last. Your treatment of her is obvious."

He mocked her when he smiled. "I believe you've just discovered your incentive to move quickly, Ms. Delacroix. The longer you take, the longer she is made to suffer. Once you accomplish your task, you are free to take her home. I have enough toys to keep me adequately entertained. I won't miss giving up this one should you comply."

Her eyes searched the room and she took note of the women that were chained or bound in some manner. Naked and obviously used, they were withdrawn – most likely drugged like her sister. "I can see that."

"Although, I wouldn't mind playing with twins. You don't have to take her home immediately. She's not much to play with, having

15

broken so easily. I suspect you could be more suitable for a man of my tastes."

A humorless laugh escaped her. Hope's eyes leisurely looked over his body and she walked to him slowly, seductively, until she could feel the heat of his body roll across hers. It would be so easy to strike out, to hit him with one fatal blow, but his men outnumbered her and she knew better than to try. With her eyes locked to his, she ran her hand over his abdomen and chest, eventually following his shoulder to his bicep where she squeezed.

"You are strong, I'll give you that." She whispered to him so that only he could hear; the red stain to her lips brushing across his skin as she spoke. "But I doubt you can handle me." She felt him tremble slightly at her touch.

His head rotated slowly until his mouth pressed against her ear. "Come back when you've killed Aaron and we'll find out then just how well I can handle my toys."

Wrapping itself tightly around her blade, her palm ignited in pain as it gripped the razor sharp edge. She wanted to bury the steel in his body, feel the resistance of his skin when she ripped it apart – but that wouldn't save her sister.

"You can count on the fact that I'll return when I'm finished, and then you and I will play." Despite the disgust that prickled along her skin, she placed a soft kiss on his cheek before turning to exit the house.

"One more thing, Ms. Delacroix."

She stopped, turning her head slightly so that she could hear what he had to say.

"There's an Estate meeting in the ballroom this evening. I suggest you clear your calendar so that you may attend. If you fail, we'll keep your sister alive – that is, until she can no longer serve our needs. I want to make sure you understand that fact. I hope it'll act as additional incentive for your success."

She blinked slowly at his words.

Stepping out of the house, Hope calmly shut the door behind her and stepped out into the shadowed woods that led to the mansion at the center of the compound.

Chapter Two

"Mr. Black, the decorator has arrived to tour the west wing. Shall I have one of the maids show her around?"

Xander looked up from the book he had laid out across the table. Pinching the bridge of his nose in frustration, he opened his sapphire blue eyes to look at the face of a lower guard. "No." Irritation saturated his exhaled breath. "She's early, isn't she?"

The guard shrugged his shoulders in response. Rolling his eyes, Xander waved him away, annoyed with the daily bullshit he had to endure in his position within The Estate. It had been two years since Joseph's death – two years that they'd worked to destroy the habits and tastes for hedonism and depravity that had been built by Joseph's insanity. However, progress was slow. There was no quick remedy to dismantling a network as extensive as the one in which they'd been raised. And for those two years, Xander had taken over running the staff within the building, keeping a tight hold and constant watch over every person who had access to Aaron and Maddy.

Standing up, he rolled his shoulders back and walked out into the stone floored hallways. Finally reaching the foyer, his eyes met with the petite woman who'd been hired to refurbish the west wing of the mansion that had sat barren and

18

empty since Joseph was killed. Over the years, fabricated rumors and stories spread through the mansion of ghosts walking the wing, a belief that Joseph had never really left when his body had been burned.

It was bullshit. Complete lunacy that Xander had attempted to disregard until it became impossible to ignore the whispers in the hallways, the quick change of subject when he approached a group of men. Aaron found the rumors humorous, shrugging them off with no regard; but Xander felt that the time had come to put them to rest.

Approaching the woman, he noticed how her entire body stilled in his presence. She appeared nervous and frightened. With her long brown hair, shorter stature and hourglass figure, she resembled Maddy. If he didn't know already that Maddy was an only child, he wouldn't have been surprised to find that they were sisters. He felt an instant warmth towards the woman, if for nothing more than her striking resemblance to the woman who had pulled Aaron from the depths of his darkness.

"Welcome to The Estate, Ms...?"

"Oh!" Her voice was at an unusually high octave and she cleared her throat quickly before continuing. "...I apologize, um, my name is Erica. 'Ms.' is reserved for women far older than me."

A smile tugged at his lips and he nodded his understanding. "Of course, Erica. Thank you for coming on such short notice, our other decorator

19

had an emergency and could not complete the job. We would have been in a bit of a bind if it hadn't been for you."

A blush spread over her cheeks. "Really, it was no problem. I was available."

Xander offered his arm, and once Erica had accepted, he led her up the corridor to the ballroom. The doors groaned as they were opened and she tripped over the transition in the flooring.

Steadying her, Xander asked, "Are you okay?"

Her green eyes were wide when she looked up at him and he noticed how gold flecks added depth to the color. "I am. I...I apologize. I'm a bit nervous in your presence. Aaron and you are very well known throughout the city. I assumed another staff member would be showing me around."

He attempted to appear genial. The last thing he needed was for this one to meet with an unfortunate *accident* like the previous three. Although, for the most part, the halls, apartments and common areas had been cleared, every once in a while a surprise was hidden beneath a rug or within a wall. Pictures and other evidence of the activities within the corridors had been found. Typically, they were discovered in an area within which the decorator had not been permitted. Xander had to take action to prevent the information from causing any future issues.

"Yes, well, there are very specific instructions for your position. I like to ensure that you are completely aware of my expectations and rules. If any of them are broken once I'm confident that you know them, I won't feel as bad for having to order your termination." He smiled.

By the expression on her face, it was apparent she hadn't missed the veiled threat. When they approached the door, his chest rubbed up against her back as he reached to open the door for her. She jumped in response.

Lowering his head close enough that his breath could brush across her cheek, he said, "I apologize, I didn't mean to scare you." Chuckling, he pulled away and motioned for her to walk into the wing. She stared at him before finally shaking herself of whatever emotion had overtaken her and walked forward, the sound of her heels clicking throughout the empty halls.

"I don't have much time to give you the tour, so I will allow you to wander certain areas on your own. The commons areas and apartments down the first four hallways are yours to do with as you will. Any rooms beyond the fourth hallway and the master suite located at the end of the hall are strictly off limits." His voice grew louder when he stressed those last words.

She turned to him, confusion furrowing her brow. "Why not complete the entire wing?"

His eyes locked to hers when he instructed, "Do not ask questions. Operate within the limits

21

I've given you and do not break my rules. I'm certain you will not like the results."

Shock was evident in her reaction, but eventually, she appeared to accept his conditions and he smiled in response. "Good. A guard will be waiting for you by the main doors to the ballroom. You have two hours to do whatever preliminary tasks you require. After that time, I'm afraid you will need to leave. If you have any questions, the guard can take you to a person who can assist."

Reaching out, he took her shaky hands within his. "Please, try not to be nervous while in the mansion. I'm aware of the reputation of The Estate within the city and I can promise you, we are not as dangerous as some believe. As long as you comply with the rules set for you, there will be no problems."

She smiled. He noticed how her eyes twinkled up at him, and he could feel how her pulse raced beneath her skin. "You have very pretty eyes, Erica." Her uneasy smile brightened as her cheeks once again blushed red.

"Now, if you'll excuse me, I have other matters to which I must attend."

Pivoting on his heel, he walked quickly to exit the wing, knowing without having to look back that she continued staring at him as he left.

. . .

"Isn't this the third decorator?"

22

"The fourth."

Aaron's head swiveled up to look at Xander from the papers splayed across the surface on his desk. Chuckling, he commented, "Do I even want to know what happened to the last one?"

"You don't."

Nodding his understanding, Aaron stood up from his desk to cross the room and exit into the living room of his suite. "It doesn't matter. I trust that you have the staff under tight control. Regardless, we have far more pressing issues to handle. Specifically, tonight's meeting."

Sitting down in one of the wing-backed chairs by the desk, Xander settled in, exhausted already. "How in the hell did Joseph and Emory have time for dealing with the daily bullshit with this place and still have time to destroy so many lives?"

Aaron chuckled. "My father was a very intelligent man, Xander. Never forget that. I'm sure it was more than the two of them running the show. Unfortunately, they've all been killed, so we'll have to work a little harder to catch up. Now, as I was saying, tonight's meeting will be difficult. Regarding the unit causing problems within the network, I haven't been able to precisely identify who it is. Have your sources come up with anything?"

Xander rubbed at his tired eyes. "No. But there are rumors that women are being brought onto the compound once again. We've visited each house on the compound and haven't yet found anything."

Leaning against the wall, Aaron eyed his guard warily. "Who is performing the searches?"

"Jason's unit and Patrick's unit. I'm sure both men are very thorough. I've run a few searches myself – much to the chagrin of the unit leaders, I should add. They are not pleased with the changes we've made. Keeping them in check has been a full time job lately."

"Well, they are criminals. I intend to announce some more changes tonight. I expect that whoever is the cause behind the recent rumors will be obviously distraught with my announcements. I want you to keep an eye open and note the reaction of the men in the room."

Xander nodded. "We only have a short time before we need to be in there, is Cricket getting ready?"

Aaron shook his head in amusement. "She's going to slaughter you one of these days for referring to her with that nickname. She's in the back room. You should go get her. I need to go through some documents once more before starting tonight's meeting."

After standing from his chair, Xander quickly exited the room, crossed the living room and entered the corridor leading to Aaron and Maddy's bedroom. "Cricket! It's almost time for tonight's meeting, are you dressed?"

Even though he'd seen her naked countless times when she'd been a slave, over the two years that they'd taken control of The Estate, he'd made it a habit of granting her modesty. Not that he minded. She'd become a little sister to him and he had no desire to see her naked.

"Xander! Come here please. I need your help."

Entering the room, his eyes fell on her small frame as she reached around attempting to button the back of her dress. Her face was scrunched in concentration and he laughed at the sight of it. "Problems?"

Dramatically lowering her arms, Maddy scowled up at him to see the humor in his expression. "I understand that Aaron wants to shower me in everything *luxurious*, but does it have to be so hard to put on?"

Approaching her, Xander spun his finger indicating for her to turn around. His fingers worked quickly over the buttons until, finally, the red silk dress hung perfectly over her small frame. "Even if the dress is difficult, you look absolutely stunning wearing it. I'm not sure how Aaron handles parading you in front of the network."

Smiling shyly, she responded, "He'd kill any man that touched me and they all know it. Sometimes I suspect he hopes for someone to make the attempt. I don't condone the darkness in him Xander, but I believe it builds up when he

25

hasn't had an opportunity to feed it. He needs an outlet- one far darker than I can provide."

Xander's face softened in understanding. "He was the executioner for a long time, Cricket. It's how he was raised. Some habits are difficult to let go, especially when they are enjoyable." Grabbing her chin, he tilted her sorrowful face up. "But you are his light – eventually, you will drive out every shadowed corner that exists within him."

Her blue eyes sparkled. "Thank you." Shaking herself free of his hold, she added, "Now stop calling me Cricket."

She turned to exit the door into the corridor and he chuckled behind her. "Never."

Reaching the living room, Xander saw that Aaron stood by the front doors ready to leave for the ballroom. Aaron waited for Xander and Maddy to take their positions at his back.

"Maddy, I want you to remain close to me or Xander for the evening. I fear I'm about to upset a number of people. For your safety, I don't want you to wander far." Aaron looked back at her, his face soft despite the sternness of warning.

She smiled back at him, her cheeks highlighted in pink when she answered, "Of course – Master."

Aaron's lips twitched from a threatened smile before he turned to exit the room and move down the corridors.

26

As usual, when they entered the ballroom, a hushed silence fell over the large group of men who were seated at tables throughout the space. Aaron nodded in the direction of the group acknowledging the men, and turned to climb the stairs to the stage. Maddy followed, her face directed downward, still mimicking the role that she'd been abducted to play. When they'd reached the top step, Maddy's long dress bunched under her foot, tripping her. Aaron turned instantly, both he and Xander crouching down in their attempt to catch her. The sick crunch that sounded behind them preceded the floors of the stage shaking when the guard's body hit the ground.

Instantly looking up, Xander noticed blood seeping from the man's head. He turned to immediately look out over the audience. A black clothed figure moved rapidly within the shadows of the room and, without hesitation, Xander pushed up to chase him towards the doors of the west wing. Every other man froze in shock where they stood and the room was quiet except for the sounds of Xander's boots thundering against the ground. His heart hammered against his chest – a mixture of rage and urgency. How the fuck did this guy get into the mansion?

The man disappeared through the doors just as Xander crossed the room, blowing past the closing doors before they latched closed. The rapid beat to his heavy steps echoed through the emptied halls, the figure still within his sights. When they reached the fifth hallway, the man he chased appeared confused, looking right and left, in search of the exit. He went left and Xander smiled knowing he'd chosen a dead end.

Rounding the corner, Xander slowed his pace, walking past each door, reaching out to ensure they were still locked. Behind him, he could hear as more men tore into the hallway, their steps beating against the ground in their haste. When Xander rounded the final corner, the bone of his jaw cracked with the force of the intruders fist. The man drew a gun, holding it to Xander's head just as three blasts sounded from the interior of the corridor.

The man fell back, and Xander looked up, rubbing his jaw as his noticed the man reaching to cup his own shoulder. He pressed back against the wall where he'd fallen and a line of blood smeared down where he'd slid along the painted finish.

Standing finally, Xander approached the crouched figure, keeping enough distance between them so as to prevent the intruder from kicking out at his legs.

Within seconds, Aaron, Jason and another guard stood at Xander's side – Jason and the guard's guns aimed towards the masked man and Aaron's knife held in his palm.

"Remove your mask." Xander's instructions were spoken slowly, forcefully.

The intruder didn't move – was so still, in fact, that Xander straightened his spine in preparation for a fight. Two clicks sounded as Jason and the guard readied their guns. Aaron took a step forward, his anticipation of the kill too pressing to remain patient. Xander reached out, stopping Aaron when he attempted to pass.

"Wait."

Aaron turned to argue, but the intruder shuffled up into a seated position, blood pouring from his shoulder to the floor. Xander stepped forward, grasping the top of the mask in his fist. Pulling at the material, it peeled away revealing the identity of the intruder.

The four men froze when they discovered that it had been a woman who'd attempted the kill.

She looked up suddenly, the gold color of her eyes swirling with hatred and pain. Her long brown hair, previously tucked and concealed beneath the mask, now fell around her shoulders. Silently, she looked between the men, her gaze searching their faces, stopping briefly on each one. When she looked back to Xander she kicked out, catching Aaron on the shin with her boot. He lunged forward, but Xander grabbed him just before his knife could sink into the woman's chest.

"No! We can't kill her."

Aaron's eyes burned into Xander when he yelled, "She attempted to kill Maddy..."

"Xander's right."

Aaron and Xander turned to look in the direction of Maddy's voice, while Jason and the guard held their guns on the female assassin.

29

When Maddy approached them, she reached up to run her palm along Aaron's cheek. "Please, Aaron, let her live for now. Don't you want to know why she's here?"

Chapter Three

Hope's shoulder was on fire and her eyes locked on the brown haired man who'd first chased her. Holding his stare, she was surprised when she heard the woman's voice, so soft and docile, Hope couldn't believe the men listened as they had. When the woman approached, Hope finally looked away from the men to fall upon the petite beauty. Her dress spilled along her frame, rubies and garnets crushed into a liquid and painted across her skin.

Reaching up, the woman caressed the face of Aaron Carmichael. Hope assumed she was another criminal, or possibly a *lady* of the Estate – one of the pampered bitches who spread their legs for the men within the network.

To Hope's astonishment, Aaron appeared to calm when the woman touched him. Hope's eyes looked over the group of men that stood before her, but flicked back to Aaron when he finally spoke. "Take her to the cell. We'll interrogate her after tonight's meeting. Xander, stay with her. Jason can escort Madeleine and I to the ballroom." Xander nodded and grabbed Hope by her injured arm. When she winced, he smiled.

"Does that hurt? Imagine how it will feel if you struggle against me." His hands searched her body slowly, forcefully, in search of weapons she had stashed. Pulling away the three knives she had

31

tucked into her clothing and retrieving her gun from the floor where it had been shot from her hand.

She sneered up at him, but allowed him to lead her away from the group. She couldn't let herself be taken captive – her sister's life depended on her freedom. A desperate rage bloomed within her body and she knew she had to keep fighting to escape. Her heart started a frantic hammer, but she breathed slowly, calming the reaction of her body to the futility of the situation. She had nothing to lose if she fought – fighting was just as futile as giving up, you end up dead regardless.

It would be impossible to defeat all three men with her injury and having her weapons stripped, but one man alone – with him she'd stand a chance. They moved quietly down the corridor, and when she'd heard the doors close behind the other men who'd reentered the ballroom, she struck out quickly with her uninjured arm, the bone of her forearm impacting with Xander's nose.

"Fuck!" He released her in response to the pain and she took the quick second of freedom to drop to the floor, swinging her leg out to catch the back of his feet. Her injured shoulder twisted and it felt like a spear had been driven down her arm. She grit her teeth against the pain, realizing that there was no time to stop.

When Xander fell to the ground, she heard the back of his skull crack against the stone tile and used his stunned moment to retrieve the thin knife she had tucked in her clothes. Bringing the knife down, the blade sliced into his thigh, but his reaction was a second too fast for her to avoid. His fist impacted with her chest, knocking the wind from her lungs. While gasping, she rolled backwards, just out of reach of his hand when he attempted to grab her.

"You are starting to really piss me off!" He lunged towards her, but Hope was able to sidestep him and use the few seconds it took for him to stand up to sprint down the hallway towards what she hoped was the exit outside. Blood rushed through her veins and she couldn't hear anything over the white noise in her skull and the pounding of her and Xander's boots through the empty corridors; each of her steps were mirrored by his. Her heart raced, her body moving gracefully and strong – a weapon itself in the way she moved. He lunged for her as they rounded the last corner. Twisting to avoid him, she felt the movement of the air from where his hand had passed.

Steeling herself for the fight that would not be avoided, she struck out again, but with her injured arm, she didn't have the strength or speed necessary to battle someone his size. He'd been anticipating the strike, moving quickly to avoid the blow. Normally, she'd counter, but her shoulder prevented the move. Reaching out, Xander grabbed her injured arm, taking advantage of its weakness to spin her so that her back was against him. When he had her tucked against him, his chest collided against her from his labored breath, the heat of which rolled along her neck causing the fine hairs to stand on end. He was so close, she

33

could smell his cologne. It was something foreign, a spice or musk.

Lunging forward, she simultaneously kicked back with her leg. Her foot impacted with his knee, pushing him away and causing him to release her. Quickly, she turned to face him and shoved her hands against his body while he was still off balance from her kick. He fell, but reached out, grabbing her and pulling her down alongside him. The jolt through her body stunned her, the pain of her shoulder impacting with the ground instantly crippling her, but exciting her at the same time. She'd been trained to enjoy it, to crave it. Pain would not be the factor that slowed her down.

He rolled on her within seconds, his hands coming down heavily on her arms, his legs and feet pinning her shoulders, abdomen and hips. Sweat slid down his jawline as he scowled down at her. She struggled against him, desperate to free herself from the impossible hold in which he'd trapped her. His body pressed into hers, the pain of his hold floating in exquisite waves throughout her body. The mixture of adrenaline and endorphins was a heady sensation that rushed through her veins when she fought.

"I've had enough of your bullshit." Seething with anger, his words were broken and strained from his heavy breathing. "I apologize for having to do this, seeing that you are, technically, a woman and all." Before she could react, he reached behind his body to pull the gun he had tucked into his waistband bringing it around quickly and striking it

34

against her temple. She felt the pain of the hit only briefly before a black tunnel overtook her.

. . .

As soon as she was unconscious, Xander rolled off of her and leaned up against the wall while he inspected his injured leg. The pain was excruciating and he couldn't believe he'd been so stupid as to miss the thin blade. Growing up with Aaron, Xander was well aware how many weapons could be hidden on a person's body. "Fucking bitch!" He kicked out with his other foot, striking her in the side of her unconscious body. He hated this woman – for her attempt on Aaron's life and for stabbing him – but, still, he couldn't help but be intrigued by her skill as a fighter. He knew he was a tough opponent for most men; but for a woman? He wouldn't have believed it if he hadn't just been part of it.

Pushing himself up, he calmed himself before grabbing her legs and picking them up off the floor. He chuckled while looking at her limp body. "I'd be a gentleman and carry you if you hadn't stabbed me in the leg. Unfortunately, you're just going to have to deal with being dragged." He laughed to himself again and pulled her through the corridors to a small holding cell which had horrified him to discover after Joseph's demise, but now one for which he could be thankful. When he entered the room, he immediately placed her by a wall. Four shackles were attached to chains in a bizarre pulley system. The pulleys were then attached to four individual cranks. When he'd first found this cell, it had taken him a minute to figure

35

out the purpose behind it, but, after remembering Joseph's tastes, he was disgusted to think about what could be done with the elaborate setup.

With the chains, Joseph had created marionette puppets out of the person unlucky enough to wear them. They could be positioned in whatever fashion he would have wanted, the pain inflicted either by the position they were set in, or in what was done to them while they were chained. And, judging by the condition of the room when it had been discovered, what had been done to those poor souls was ghastly and horrific. Even after the room had been scrubbed down with bleach, the stains from the blood could not be removed. Rust color splotches marked the floor, the walls – even the ceiling. Normally, Xander would use any other room, just to avoid the latent energy contained within this cell, but in his current situation, this cell was exactly what he needed.

Tugging the pulleys out from the wall, he was able to secure one shackle to each of her wrists. She was dead weight due to having been knocked out, so he used the cranks for the chains to drag her across the floor and up so that she was hanging from the wall. He lifted her enough that her feet barely touched the ground. She winced in her sleep when the arm of her injured shoulder was forced above her head, but she didn't wake as a result of it. He smiled to know he'd caused her pain, the bitch deserved it after attempting to take the life of his friend. Walking towards her, he went through her clothing again in search of weapons or identification. She moaned when his hands ran over her hips, her thighs, and higher over her

36

stomach and chest. Xander bit back his reaction to the sound, not wanting to feel anything for this woman beyond his hatred for what she'd done. But he found himself staring at her, his eyes studying her body. Her hair fell in dark waves down her back, perfectly framing an angelic face. Every muscle of her arms, legs and torso were sculpted and toned, but not so much that she was bulky. Her body curved slightly in all the right places, but she was still lean and fit. She was a fighter of some sort, but the to what extent, Xander didn't know.

She was clean and he cursed under his breath that he'd have to extract the information from her rather than it being as simple as reading an I.D.

After taking one last look, he turned to exit the cell on his way to speak with Aaron about what should be done with their guest.

. . .

"Stop laughing, Aaron, it isn't fucking funny! I'm telling you, that bitch is a skilled fighter. We need to find out why she's here and who sent her. There could be more coming and we can't allow our guards to be down if that occurs."

Chortling in an attempt to stifle his laughter, Aaron eventually gained control of himself before responding. "I find it hard to believe you were so badly beaten by a woman. You've been fighting me since we were kids, I've never actually had the opportunity to stab you. You know better that to leave yourself open."

Xander rolled his eyes while breathing out a frustrated breath. He winced from the antiseptic that Maddy brushed across the skin of his leg before responding, "I didn't expect it. I was surprised by her strength. Whoever trained her was, obviously, very good at what he did. But a woman?"

Aaron nodded and sat on the corner of the wing-backed chair facing the couch. "I've heard of a female assassin within a smaller network. We have limited information on her, but I know there was a rumor that she could compete against me."

"Why would Joseph let something like that slip by?"

"She was never a problem, from what I know. Unless she did anything that threatened The Estate, Joseph wouldn't have concerned himself with her; but, none of that matters. She's attempted something now and we have to deal with this quickly. It pisses me off that someone has dared strike out at The Estate." Aaron stood up, pacing back and forth, rubbing his hand across his chin while he thought.

"All done." Maddy packed up the small medical kit they kept in the apartment and smiled up at Xander. Turning to look at Aaron, her voice was almost a whisper when she asked, "What are you two going to do with her? I assume if she's been trained, she's a threat, but will you treat her

38

differently than you would a man who'd made such an attempt?"

"No." Xander's response was solid and immediate. "That bitch deserves what's coming to her, Cricket, and I don't want you concerning yourself with her." Standing, he pulled his pants back up, now that Maddy was no longer tending to the wound. He looked down at the hole from where the woman had stabbed him. "Fuck. And these were my favorite pair."

"Xander, I want you to do whatever is necessary to gain information from her. After that, you are ordered to kill her. She attempted my life, or possibly, the life of Maddy. I don't give a shit what her reason is, she will not leave the compound alive, do you understand me?"

Xander looked up at Aaron, noticing how his eyes narrowed from his rage. He nodded. "She'll be dead before the morning. You have nothing to be concerned about there."

"Must we kill her?"

Soft and delicate, Maddy whispered her question. Standing, she stared at Aaron, crossing the room so that she could touch him. "I'm tired of the constant slaughter. We're trying to bring down this network, but it seems like everything we do only serves to make it stronger. Maybe, we should let whoever sent her send more, let them start a war that kills off the network while we run as far from it as we can."

39

Aaron's face softened. "It's not possible, Mouse. If anybody is going to be targeted within the network, it will be you, Xander, or me. There wouldn't be a war, because there is no loyalty – not to anything that is worth their lives. They are loyal to the network, to the money and the power, but not to me specifically. The Estate members will follow whoever controls it. If more are sent and I'm killed, they'll take control, The Estate will exist indefinitely."

Xander pitied Maddy when he saw her face fall at Aaron's words. He knew she hated living in this place, knew she still felt trapped, held within a waking nightmare. However, she wanted it destroyed and the only way to accomplish that task was to remain a part of the very thing they hated the most.

"Use any method necessary to get the information we need, Xander." Aaron looked up from Maddy, anger evident in his eyes. "We can't look at her like a woman brought in, we have to look at her as a threat. I expect her to be treated as such."

Nodding his understanding, Xander strode across the room towards the door.

"Do those methods include rape?"

He stopped, his head dropping before he slowly turned to look at Maddy. Her eyes were red from unshed tears.

Aaron reached out, pulling her towards him. Tipping her chin up, he looked at her for a few seconds before responding. "Maddy, she's not like you. She's like us. You need to recognize that. We'll do whatever we have to do to keep you safe. I hope it doesn't come to that, but it can be an effective method of breaking a person down."

"Are men raped as well?" The incredulity in her tone was surprising.

"I can tell you that Xander and I have not participated in that type of method; but, I can't say that I haven't heard of it being done."

Her head fell against his chest and Aaron wrapped his arms around her to comfort her. Aaron spoke again just before Xander left to return to the holding cell.

"I'm sorry, Maddy. We are not good men."

Chapter Four

It felt like her shoulder was on fire when Hope woke. Her head pounded where she had been struck and her wrists stung from where they'd been cut by the metal shackles. She knew instantly that she was in a cell of some sort, a prisoner of The Estate.

Shaking away her disorientation, she slid her feet across the ground so that she could push up on her toes to remove the strain from her arms. Her head fell back against the wall when her bodyweight was better supported. Opening her eyes, she strained to see in the dark. Above her, was a glass domed roof, the moon and stars of the night sky clearly visible and providing enough illumination that she could make out the small table in the center of the room and an elaborate system of chains that ran across the walls.

Her heart tapped against the inside of her chest, slowly, rhythmically, as she forced herself to not panic – to remain clear headed despite her situation. When she could put her full weight on her toes, she tugged on the shackles, the movement sending a sharp wave of pain down her arms. Her body shuddered at the sensation. Since she'd been young, she reacted to pain differently than most people – she'd enjoyed it. Not so much the sensation of the pain itself, but the rush that coursed through her body afterwards. It caused her heart to pound a little harder and her skin to tingle as if from a lover's touch. It numbed her, but also made her feel alive, human – not the pragmatic machine she'd been trained to be.

A small click echoed through the room just before the door opened. Light flooded in from the hallway and Hope clenched her eyes when it washed across her face.

"Oh good. You're awake."

She could tell immediately from the voice that it was the man from the hallway. The door shut and she peeked open her eyes to see his outline standing near the door. Even in the darkness of the room, he was an intimidating presence. He was wide in his shoulders, but his waistline was thin. The material of his shirt bunched around the defined muscle of his arm and he stood with his hands folded behind his back, his feet parted to shoulder width. His hair and complexion were dark, but his eyes...those were caught in the moonlight and they shone out, a brilliant sapphire blue.

"I'd ask how you're feeling, however, I'm sure I already have a good idea." He slowly walked forward, the sounds of his boots against the stone ground echoing louder with each approaching step. "You're lucky you're still alive. Under normal circumstances, Aaron would have removed your head for a stunt like that. The only reason you are still breathing is because I need to know why you're here."

He stopped when he stood a few feet from her. "Now, are we going to play nice, or does this have to be painful."

She didn't even flinch at his implied threat. She'd been raised to endure whatever torture he could inflict. They'd called it a gift – her penchant for pain, and they'd nurtured it so that it would benefit Hope when she fought or in case of capture.

Inching closer, he held her stare. "What is your name and, more importantly, why did you just attempt to kill Aaron Carmichael?" She could see his muscles tighten, rage settling across his shoulders when he'd moved within inches of her. Raising his arms, he placed a hand on the wall by each side of her face.

A shiver ran down her spine, but she shook it off and silently turned her head to break eye contact. She felt his hand wrap itself within her hair and pull.

"Answer me!" His nostrils flared, the heat of his enraged command brushing across her cheek. Her scalp burned where her hair was knotted in his fist.

She winced in reaction to the pain, hissing when he pulled her face to his.

He stared at her for several minutes, his eyes darting over her features, memorizing each shadow on her skin. She held still, desperately attempting to steady the beat of her heart, to deny him any sign of fear.

Pushing off the wall, he distanced himself. Folding his hands at his back, he paced the length of the room. When he finally stopped, he turned to her with a smile adorning his face.

"You're well trained. I'll give you that." Slowly, he stepped towards her, his movement graceful as a prowling tiger. "But, I'm sure there are ways to make you speak."

His finger flicked up to run along her jawline, down her neck and along the center of her chest, stopping just above where the leather intersected between her breasts.

She wasn't surprised by his first implied threat. If nothing else, she could rely on a man's loyalty to his cock. However, she was glad for him to have made it.

She cleared her throat, preparing to play a role that had bought her freedom many times before. "Like what you see?" She smiled when his shocked eyes rose to her face. "Unchain me and we can work something out." She hated this game, but it had been useful in escaping other situations. She never went far with any man, just enough to get him to free her of her binds. All of the men died within seconds of making that mistake.

He leaned into her, the stubble of his chin rubbing against her temple. Whispering, he teased, "You'd like that wouldn't you?" He pushed away again, moving to the table in the center of the room to sit against it. "Unfortunately for you, I'm well taken care of in that department. I'm sorry to

45

crush your hopes and dreams, but I'll decline." He smirked at her.

She didn't respond, refusal a blanket across the thoughts she couldn't reveal. Allowing her eyes to roam over the empty walls of the room in which she was held, Hope wouldn't allow herself to look at his face. He was handsome, a fact that could not be argued, but he was also the person preventing her from returning to that other bastard's house. They would kill her sister, would destroy the only person she'd admired in her life and she couldn't allow that to happen.

Her eyes shot back to him when he spoke.

"Tell me your name."

She stared at him, her lip curling in rebellion and disgust. "What does my name matter?"

"It doesn't." With a blank expression, his words were spoken with a matter of fact tone. "However, the identity of the person who sent you does."

"And what makes you so sure I was sent by someone? Maybe I've simply heard the rumors that Aaron Carmichael has become his father. Or, maybe it's just time for The Estate to be destroyed along with the evil that created it."

He smiled, his voice booming when he responded, "You're an assassin. That much is obvious!" Reaching up, he rubbed at his jaw where she'd hit him. "No woman hits like that and hasn't been trained."

A humorless laugh broke free of her throat. "Growing up in the shadow of The Estate is enough incentive for all women to be trained. Do you think nobody knows what goes on here? We notice the disappearance of our families, our friends. We can smell the bodies as they're burned."

He smiled. "You've done your homework. Congratulations." Mockery weighed down his last word. He paused, his eyes twinkling as they moved over her. The timbre of his voice deepened when he calmly stated, "I can promise you, I will discover who you are, and while I'm at it, I'll also discover who the fuck sent you. If you make my life easier by giving up the information now, I'll make sure you are no longer breathing when you become one of those burning bodies."

She was amused by his threat. "You can set me on fire right here, big guy, and end this bullshit game right now." She winked. "I'll never tell you a fucking thing."

His chair flipped backwards when he stood, the thick wood striking the ground loudly as it fell. Within a second he was across the room, the tip of his nose pressed to hers. His hand squeezed her cheeks painfully from where he'd grabbed her face to force her eyes in his direction.

"We will find a way to make you talk - as soon as I find out who the fuck you are." Slamming her head back so that it hit the wall, he turned and exited the room swiftly, leaving her chained. Her skin burned along her face from where he'd

47

grabbed her. The room was silent except for the sound of rain hitting the glass ceiling of the circular room. She looked up, her eyes taking in the darkness of the night sky. The stars were no longer visible and the moonlight barely breached the clouds.

When the door opened again, Hope slowly looked down and found that the woman from the hallway had entered. She was surprised, but kept her expression blank. The pain in her shoulder had finally gone numb, and the blood stopped flowing due to her arms being held above her head.

"I want to see if we can remove the bullet from your shoulder." Her voice was melodic, soft, but carrying a hint of strength unexpected of a woman so small.

Hope looked her over, noticing how she'd changed from the red dress into black pants and a simple green shirt. Their hair was similar in color, but, whereas Hope was tall and thin, this woman was short but curved in every place that mattered.

"I didn't think you'd be much of a talker." The woman sat down where Xander had previously sat. "I wasn't much of one either when I first arrived, so I can understand - although I'm sure it is for far different reasons."

Hope studied the woman's face. Even though it had been years, she recognized her. "You're the musician who went missing. I saw you on the news for days. I figured you were as good as dead when they found nothing except for a rose left in the parking lot outside of the theater."

The woman smiled. "I'm surprised they left the rose behind. That sounds a bit sloppy for Joseph." She let out a faint sigh, "And yes, at one time, I was her. But that was years ago and things change."

Hope had to keep the woman talking in case there was a chance she could play on her sympathies. "What did they do to you?"

Her blues eyes blinked and she smiled. "To whom are you referring? Aaron and Xander, or The Estate as a whole?"

"Is there a difference?" Hope's voice dripped with the hatred she felt. She'd lived her entire life fearing The Estate's reach. Living in shadows, she'd been careful not to draw the attention of its members. Somehow, despite her efforts, it found her anyway.

"My name is Maddy, by the way." She smiled warmly. There was nothing but kindness in her eyes as she reached for a box on the table.

"And this is where I'm supposed to be polite and tell you mine?"

"Not if you don't want to. Xander will find that out. He's very resourceful. I'm only here to remove the lead from your body. We'd hate for you to get an infection. Aaron is particular about that."

"He likes to keep his slaves healthy?" Hope laughed. "That's new."

The woman's eyes flicked up from the supplies she was gathering for a brief second. A blush fell across her cheeks from an unspoken thought. Eventually, after seemingly gathering what she required, she looked up again. "You're not being kept as a slave."

She stood from the table and crossed the distance, antiseptic and a cloth held in her hands. "I'm going to clean you up first, then we'll see what we can do about the bullet."

"Surgery will be difficult, don't you think?" She shook the chains. "Given that I'm chained and all."

The woman angled her head when she asked, "Would you like me to remove them?"

Suspicion tore through Hope's body at the suggestion. She wouldn't kill the woman if freed, but she would silence her in order to escape. Playing on Maddy's sympathies, she responded, "Yes - please. I'm afraid of what they will do to me, afraid that they'll..." She let her eyes fall, desperate to appear scared and nonthreatening. Looking up again, she continued, "...I'm afraid they'll hurt me or rape me. Please help me get free."

Straightening her head on her shoulders, Maddy took a few more steps, smiled and shrugged. "No problem. I'll ask Xander for the key when I'm done cleaning you up." Another smile.

Hope's shock turned to frustration. "He'll never give them to you."

"I know, but if you're going to make impossible demands, I'll offer impossible responses." She looked up into Hope's eyes. "I'm not stupid. I've lived in this place for three years. Don't you think I would have learned by now how your kind operates?" She pulled the coat away from Hope's shoulder to inspect and clean the wound.

Hope flinched from the sting of the antiseptic on her skin, but stood still, allowing Maddy to tend to the wound. The bullet hadn't struck anything vital, but infection would render her arm useless. She needed her body to heal if she had any chance of escape.

"I'd ask why you attempted to kill Aaron, but I think I have a pretty good idea. Not many people would attempt the executioner's life. You're very brave - or stupid."

Hope looked down, confusion furrowed her brows and her eyes narrowed on Maddy. "You sound like you like it here. I saw how you touched him in the hall. You must be the type who likes being treated like a disposable toy."

Maddy chuckled. She continued cleaning Hope's skin when she responded, "It doesn't matter what I like, only what he likes."

Rolling her eyes, Hope suddenly recognized the weak spirit in front of her; completely pliable and easily conquered.

It was almost like Maddy knew what Hope had been thinking. "You remind me of him. Your darkness, I recognize the hatred and the rage. I wouldn't be surprised to find that you enjoy your kills as much as he enjoys his. People like you need someone to look out for you, to pull you back from whatever black depth to which you've fallen. It would be a futile task if that person didn't use something that brought you joy, don't you think?" She looked pointedly at Hope but then smiled softly. "There. You're clean, however I don't think I'll be able to remove the bullet without assistance. Does your arm hurt?"

Hope rested her head against the wall. "I don't know. My arms have gone numb from the chains."

"Oh, good. We won't need to drug you then."

Disbelief crept across Hope's thoughts. "What the fuck is wrong with you people? How the fuck are you standing here like a fucking saint when you're surrounded by death?!"

The door opened and Xander entered the room carrying a file in his hand. He looked surprised to find Maddy in the room, but his expression quickly returned to a blank canvas. Placing the folder on the table, he pushed it in Maddy's direction. After packing up the supplies, she took the folder from the table and thumbed through the contents. Hope couldn't understand why she was being treated with such high regard.

"I find it ironic that your name is Hope...especially considering that you have none." His voice was amused, yet stern – a hidden warning within the mocking words.

Her eyes narrowed. "You know my name. *Congratulations*."

"Actually, I know more than your name." He leaned back against the surface of the table, his hands folded in front of him. Maddy put the folder down and reached up to touch his shoulder. The minute her hand connected with his body, his expression softened and he turned to look at her.

"Go easy on her, Xander. She's a woman who finds herself in the same situation that we all have experienced at one point."

He smiled at her, taking her hand in his to remove it from his shoulder. "You shouldn't be here, Cricket. She's a lot more dangerous than you realize." Looking up, he met Hope's stare. "Hope is a trained assassin, aren't you? I suspected as much based on your behavior, but now I can say without a doubt who you are." Looking back at Maddy, he motioned towards the door. "You should leave. I have a lot to discuss with our guest."

Maddy silently nodded and left the room. Xander stood and stalked towards Hope. She noticed a slight limp to his stride and grinned.

53

"How's the leg?"

Xander stopped, looking quickly at his leg before glancing back to her. "It's better than your shoulder, I'm sure." A crooked smile peeked out on his face, his humor evident in the glint to his eye.

Hope didn't respond, allowing him to approach. Despite being chained, she wouldn't relent or accept defeat. Too much weighed on her. Fearing that the men who took her sister had already learned of her failure, she was desperate to escape – but if she couldn't, she wanted to inflict as much damage as she could on the bastard that stood before her. When Xander had stepped within range, she pushed off the wall with one foot, kicking out at his injured leg with the other.

He caught her foot. Angling his head, he grinned mischievously. His voice sounded like a growl when he teased, "Now, now, Ms. Delacroix, I've already discovered the strength of these..." His eyes burned a path up her calf and inner thighs. "...long legs of yours." Tightening his grip, his fingers dug into the muscle of her calf. Out of reflex, she attempted to pull away but he tsked.

"I also learned that you have more weapons on you than I'd expected. Given your profession, I'm not surprised." Stepping out, he trapped her other foot with his. Pushing forward he bent her leg up towards her body causing the muscle in her thigh to burn from the strain. Once he had her pinned, he used his hands to untie her boot. "I'll

54

have to perform a more thorough search to ensure I'm not injured again. I'm sure you understand."

Contemptuously, Hope laughed. He was pressed so close to her, she could feel his heat brush across her skin. His cologne wrapped itself around her senses, mixed with another distinct scent – musk or sandalwood. Taking shallow breaths, she willed her body calm but noticed that her heart still beat wildly against the walls of her chest.

Lifting one hand from her leg, he pressed it against the artery in her throat. "Your pulse is racing. Is it from fear or excitement?" Chuckling, he returned his hand to her leg, running it up the ankle and calf slowly, his fingers digging into the muscle as they passed. Despite the shiver the coursed through her body, she remained blank, expressionless while he performed his search. Her anger grew to know that he was stripping her of her clothes in an attempt to strip her of her dignity. She wouldn't let it work.

Angling her head down, she pressed her forehead to his. "It's good to see that my *hopes and dreams* will be fulfilled after all."

His blue eyes shot to hers and the stubbled skin of his jaw pulled across his face when he grinned. "I suggest you remain calm, *Sunshine*, we're just getting started."

55

Chapter Five

After examining one leg, Xander lowered it, trapping her foot under his, and bringing her other leg up to remove the boot and search for additional weapons. Although, he performed this search already while she'd been passed out, he did so again while she was conscious to show her who held the control between them.

She scowled at him as he ran his hand up her leg.

He smirked in response.

An assassin. She was a fucking assassin, and one who, for the most part, had kept her distance from any dealings with the Estate. Xander couldn't understand why, now, she chose to attack. The file they had on her wasn't thick, but what he did know was that Hope was raised within a much smaller and less powerful network. The only reason she'd even been noticed was because of the rumors that if there was someone out there who could compete against Aaron, it was her. They'd never been able to obtain anything more than a grainy image, but given her skill, Xander had taken a shot in the dark to connect this woman to the one discussed in the documents he'd found.

Her name had been familiar to Xander when he'd first discovered her identity. He'd heard of the woman who, like Aaron, seemingly enjoyed her profession too much. And he remembered a story about a woman bathing in the blood of her targets – who could calmly and quietly tear a man apart without so much as flinching at the act.

"It appears your legs are free of unexpected surprises, but what about the rest of you?" His blue eyes shot up to look at her, the corner of his mouth twitching from his attempt to hide a salacious grin.

She rolled her eyes. "Strip me naked and fuck me or shut up. I'm already tired of your threats."

He stood up slowly, his eyes searching her face for any sign of fear...there was nothing. He marveled at her ability to remain so calm and uncaring about what he'd been doing to her. He hated to admit it to himself, but he was confused by her lack of concern. "Eager, aren't you?"

"Remove my chains and I'll show you just how eager I am." Shaking them above her head, she added, "But I can't do much without my hands."

He laughed. "How many times has that worked? Obviously, you're alive and were previously free to run about...how many times have you fucked your way out of a tight situation?"

Her eyes blinked slowly, the deep mahogany of her lashes contrasting sharply with the gold tint of her eyes – but she didn't respond.

"Interesting." Xander realized they both were playing games. Obviously rape wasn't a threat, but pain — nobody was willing to endure that for very long.

With her foot still trapped beneath his and her other leg held against her body, he reached down to grab the lower shackles. Securing one around the ankle of her raised leg, he pulled the chain, tightening it so that, he could secure the other. Once accomplished, he stepped back to look at her body, now completely immobilized by the chains.

"Have you figured out what this room is yet? Really, it's absolute genius on the part of the person who designed it."

He watched as her eyesight traveled over the walls — her eyes narrowing to find the system of pulleys and bars.

"You do realize, I can have you in every position I want without having to release your binds, and there's not a damn thing you can do about it. I have no need to risk setting you free." Walking back to the table he grabbed a pair of sharp medical scissors from the kit Maddy had left behind. He stalked back to her, raising up the scissors and receiving no reaction from her at all. He touched the cold, sharp tip to her skin, dragging it across her, splitting the skin, a faint pink line welting up and drops of blood welled from where he'd allow the metal to travel. He expected her to scream, to grimace, or to reveal some fucking sign that he'd found her weakness. What he didn't

58

expect was for her eyes to roll back and for her body to shudder under his touch.

The gold of her eyes shone out at him when she finally lifted her lids. "Pain won't work for you either, I'm afraid. What else you got?" He watched as those words rolled out from between her full lips; her tongue flicking out to run the crease of her mouth, her pupils dilating in response to the pain.

"Fuck. You are exquisite." He couldn't help his growled outburst. Her reaction was, quite possibly, the most erotic thing he'd witnessed.

He stepped back, completely knocked off balance by the seeping desire within his mind and body. She was his enemy, a woman who'd attempted to kill the only people he cared about – but, she was unlike any woman he'd ever come across. His curiosity was peaked and his pants tightened despite his hatred towards her.

Suddenly torn between needing information and wanting to sink his cock deep inside her, he stood motionless except for the movement of his eyes across her body. "I'm not sure whether I should fuck you or kill you. Either way, I believe you would enjoy it."

"The second part, maybe." Her eyes narrowed, her voice was breathless. "But I don't enjoy being fucked by a man so pathetic he needs a woman to be tied up to do so."

He smiled, a dimple popping out on his chin from the motion. "Oh, I do appreciate my women bound, but that's only if they request it."

She rolled her eyes again and allowed her head to fall back against the wall behind her. Her chest pushed out from the position and his eyes caressed the places where he wanted his hands to travel. Shaking himself of his lust, he asked, "I know who you are now, but what I can't understand is why, after so many years of avoiding The Estate, why, now, do you not only attack, but come onto the compound to do so. The only reason I can imagine is that you were hired. Tell me who sent you, and I'll end this quickly."

"Beg. Maybe if I see you on your knees, I'll feel a little more giving." Her words were becoming more strained and he noticed the erratic movement of her chest with her labored breath. He surmised that it was the position in which she was held. He knew that given enough time with their arms held above their head, a person would begin to struggle to inflate their lungs and drag in the air that they needed.

He walked over to the levers and lowered the position of the chains so that her arms were held out to her sides instead of above her head – still tight enough to restrain movement, but not as tortuous as the previous position. Looking down, he noticed the puddle of blood that pooled beneath her, the smooth surface disturbed each time a crimson drop fell. Her shoulder had started bleeding again from the movement of her arm. Between the loss of blood, lack of water and

60

difficulty to breathe, it was obvious she was fighting to remain conscious.

"We'll need to fix your shoulder." He spoke slowly, noticing that she only appeared to partially understand what he was saying, her head rolled slightly atop her shoulders and he grew concerned. "I'll return shortly."

Quickly exiting the room, he traveled the corridors in search of Maddy and Aaron. Finding them in their quarters, he looked between the concerned look on Maddy's face and Aaron's typical blank expression.

His words were urgent. "We won't get very far with her if we don't do something about her shoulder. She's bleeding badly."

"Again?" Maddy's voice interrupted his thoughts.

Aaron immediately looked down at her, rage brushing across the green of his eyes. "You were in there? What were you thinking?!"

She spoke quietly when she confessed, "I know. Xander explained her profession to me, but she was chained. There was no way she could have hurt me."

Looking up at Xander, Aaron's expression became murderous. Stalking forward he stopped just inches from where Xander stood. Xander rolled his shoulders back, not allowing Aaron to intimidate him. Aaron's words were spoken slowly, menacingly when he asked, "What the fuck

61

do I care about her injury? I'm sure it won't be a problem once she's ash! What does bother me, however, is that you allowed Maddy anywhere near her!"

Breathing out an annoyed sigh, Xander responded, "I went to see if I could find any information on her from the files kept in Joseph's office. Maddy snuck in when I wasn't in the room." He glared at Aaron until finally, Aaron backed down. "I found her name and some information regarding her origins and network, but not much. She's definitely the woman about which you'd heard rumors. However, until now, she'd been careful to keep her distance. I want to know why, now, she decides to attack. We need her to tell us her purpose for being here. She may have been hired and now that she's been caught, I'm certain there will be more sent."

Aaron stepped back. "Who would be so stupid or mad to attack us at our own compound?"

"You said it earlier, Aaron. We would be the first targets of any potential attacks. Lately, none of us have left the compound. Where else would they have the chance?"

When it didn't appear that his argument had helped to sway his friend, Xander continued to press on. "I need more time with her. She's not as easily broken as most. She's all but demanded that I rape her and pain only serves to turn her on."

A brow arched over the green of Aaron's eye and he smirked. "That would make your job more difficult, I imagine."

Xander's resultant laughter was a short burst. "Yeah, she reminds me of the bastard I grew up with, maybe you know him."

"Shit." Aaron cursed under his breath and walked to the bar. Grabbing the crystal decanter, he poured himself a glass of scotch, choking it down quickly before pouring another. Maddy sat quietly on the couch, her attention on the two men. When she finally spoke, they turned their faces toward her.

"It would take threatening a person she loved. But, even then, she might be able to ignore something as loathsome as that if it serves her purpose." Looking directly at Aaron, she commented, "You were able to watch your father almost rape me, you were able to whip me to the point where my skin split open and you were able to kill indiscriminately in front of me...may have killed me, if it was ordered. If she's as determined in her task as you were in yours, I'm not sure that there is anything that will force her to talk."

Aaron visibly flinched from the reminder of Maddy's presentations. "But I acted eventually, the alliance wasn't even fully prepared..."

"Only when the thing you were losing became more valuable than the task you were hoping to accomplish," she interrupted.

"I'm not following you, Maddy." Aaron walked towards her, Xander following closely behind.

"She's like you, Aaron. I picked up on it almost immediately when I walked into that room. I know the look of fear, of pain and suffering; she had none. There was no emotion in her at all. You were like that once as well, but as soon as I brought out even a small amount of emotion in you, I became more important than your desire to destroy Joseph."

Xander's jaw dropped when he realized what Maddy was saying. "You want me to seduce her to get the information? She just tried to kill the man you love and you're suggesting that I should bring her some fucking roses? That's insane, Cricket."

Her head swiveled in his direction. "Is it? How well has threatening her worked out for you? Some people are more willing to talk if you give them something they like rather than fighting against them." She nodded her head to indicate in Aaron's direction and winked. Aaron scowled behind her.

Xander grinned. It always amused him when the lion bared her claws; so much strength for such a tiny person. Returning his attention to Aaron, he continued, "Regardless of the methods I employ, my point is that I need more time if you want information from her. However, if you want her death to be immediate, I'll return now and take care of the problem."

64

"Take more time, Xander. I trust that you know what you're doing." Aaron's words were exasperated.

Xander nodded. "Then I'll need some assistance in repairing the damage to her shoulder."

"Call Adair. His unit should have more than enough drugs to knock her out. I'll assist you so that you can retrieve the bullet and sew up the wound."

Pulling his phone from his pocket, Xander responded, "I'll make the call."

Chapter Six

Her head felt fuzzy and she noticed when she woke up that she was no longer vertical. Blinking her eyes rapidly, she attempted to bring the room into focus. Her brain was wrapped in confusion and her movements were lethargic and uncoordinated. Her heartbeat pounded in her head, slow and labored, punctuating the white noise in her ears. She tried to lift her head, but it was too heavy and she knew immediately that she'd been drugged.

"Fuck." It was all she could mutter. Her throat was dry and her voice barely escaped as a whisper. The exposed skin of her back was cold from where she was laid on the floor and her hands were locked into a shackled belt around her hips. Struggling to see, she blinked again and again, but she couldn't bring the room into focus.

"Good morning, sunshine. I was wondering when you would finally wake up." His words echoed as if he were standing in a tunnel.

She let out an annoyed sigh.

"Are you thirsty?"

She nodded her head slowly, too disoriented to communicate and too thirsty to refuse. She heard his steps as he approached her and felt his hand come under her head, softly helping her into a seated position. The rim of a glass met her mouth and ice cold water rushed down her heated tongue and throat. She choked trying to drink it too quickly. He pulled the glass away.

"Let's try that again when you've woken up a little more." Grabbing her sides, he turned her and positioned her so that she could lean up against the wall. A shot of pain raced down her arm when she put too much weight on her shoulder.

"We removed the bullet and stitched up your wound. You were losing consciousness from the blood loss."

"Should ... have let me die. Would have saved us both ... a headache later on."

Admiring her tenacity, he chuckled in response to her broken words. "It's a good sign that your sparkling personality has returned. Means we can get back to business sooner rather than later."

Her head still pounded with each beat of her heart and her muscles tightened when she felt him sit against the wall next to her. "I hope you don't mind, but you're not talking very loudly and it's easier to understand you from down here." The side of his body brushed up against her. She pulled at the shackles on the belt and groaned when she realized they wouldn't budge.

"We need to give your shoulder time to heal, but can't leave you free to roam about either.

67

Luckily, we have all sorts of useful toys with which we can keep you restrained." His words dripped with humor, but Hope wasn't amused.

Allowing her head to fall back against the wall, the sharp crack of pain against her skull helped dull the irritation she had with Xander's company.

"Do you want to try and drink something again?"

She nodded. She fucking despised him, but she couldn't allow herself to weaken any further. She didn't have to be in perfect condition to escape, but she couldn't allow herself to become crippled either.

He brought the glass to her lips, placing his hand at the back of her head to steady it on her shoulders. When she'd finished the glass he took it away.

After sitting quietly on the floor for several moments, she could blink open her eyes. Her vision was still hazy, but she saw that sunlight now flooded the room from the glass ceiling. Her heart sank to see it – to know that her sister had spent another night with those men. The only thing Hope could do was pray that Honor was still alive.

She didn't want to acknowledge him, but she needed to know how long it had been since her capture. "What time is it?"

"One in the afternoon. You've slept a long time since we performed the surgery. I was starting to worry we gone overboard with the drugs."

It grew quiet again, the silence settling between them; nothing more than the sounds of their breathing could be heard and Hope struggled to regain complete consciousness. The glass clinked against the stone when Xander grabbed it and moved to stand up.

"Give me some information, Hope. Let me make this easier on you." She heard the sound of the glass being placed on the table. "I can't express just how pathetic a woman like you looks bound and on the floor. Well – pathetic for an assassin, not as pathetic for a woman. That image is actually quite endearing."

"Fuck you." She forced the words out. Whatever they'd given her must have been strong because the residual effects were almost crippling.

He was beside her suddenly, his hand rubbing along her cheek and jawline until his thumb rested against her parted lips. He brought his mouth down so that it brushed against her ear. His voice was a breathy whisper when he admitted, "Have it your way; but you should know, I'm not exactly opposed to the idea of *fucking* you any longer."

She didn't react because, inside, Hope was already crushed. The frustration of restraint started to affect her while images of her sister chained and sitting at that bastard's feet replayed in her head. Fury settled along her spine, her heart

69

rate picking up, her muscles tensing and flexing – her mind regaining clarity and shedding the fog of whatever they'd forced inside her body. She considered telling him, but knew he'd kill her and would end up killing her sister as well when attacking the people who'd turned against him in that house. Tears burned at the back of her eyes to realize that even if she could escape, and even if Honor were still alive, she'd have to kill every single person in that fucking house to save her, or to avenge her. Given the number of men she'd seen, the odds were next to impossible. She realized that her situation was futile – that death would best be served quickly.

She looked up, Xander's outline finely becoming more sharp, his features becoming clear. "Just fucking do whatever is you're going to do and get it over with. If you think I give a fuck about whoever is out to kill Aaron and his little slut..."

His hand was around her neck in a second, his forehead pressed against hers and the blue of his eyes glaring down at her. "I'd rethink what you were about to say if I were you."

Her angered boiled in her veins, the control she always had slowly slipping with how helpless she'd become. Bound, injured and drugged – a combination that rendered defeat. She had nothing to lose.

"I'll make a deal with you." Opening her eyes more, she saw his brow furrow in interest and felt his hand loosen around her neck so that she could speak easier. "I'm not going to willingly tell

70

you what I know. I realize that by doing so, I'm signing my own death warrant. You don't want to kill me without getting the information you need and your normal forms of torture won't work on me —at least the ones you are willing to do." She could tell already that he wasn't as ruthless as the other men she'd known – the men who'd trained her and broken her before any other man had the chance.

Xander pulled away, his eyes still trained on her face.

"Unchain me and fight me for it. You win – I tell you what you want to know before you kill me. I win – I kill you."

The corner of his lip twitching made it obvious that he was attempting to hold back a grin. "In your condition?"

Hope smiled. "It'll make it an even fight. If I was at full strength, you'd be dead before you could fight back."

His finger came up to run along her jaw and she jerked her head away from his touch. "By my recollection, I've already defeated you at full strength; considering you are in chains and I am not."

Rolling her eyes, she argued, "That was four against one." She glared up at him, anger snaking through her veins. "And as I recall, I had a gun pressed up against your skull. If it wasn't for your friends, you'd no longer have a head."

"Touché." He winked.

When he stood up, she craned her neck to keep him within her sight. He stared down at her for a minute before saying, "I won't go easy on you. It will be a fight to the death."

Her eyes narrowed. "It's good to know you understand the rules."

After staring at her for another quiet moment, he acquiesced, "Fine. But I'm not fighting you in the condition that you're in."

Her eyes widened in disbelief. "Why?"

He smiled. "No offense, sunshine, but you smell."

"And what the fuck does that have to do with anything?"

His hoods lidded over his darkening gaze. "Because, if I win, I'll be taking more than information before you die." He turned suddenly, walking out of the room and allowing the door to slam shut behind him.

She stared at the door trying to decipher whether he'd been serious or not. His threats didn't concern her – he'd never win. But if she could escape..."

When the door opened again an hour later, Xander stepped in; a chained collar grasped in his fist and a mischievous grin plastered across his face. "Bath time."

72

Chapter Seven

Her gold eyes flicked up at him and he smiled to see her scowl in reaction to the leash. Technically, it wasn't necessary, she wouldn't be able to free herself of the belt, but he wanted nothing more than to break her down physically and mentally. Sure, he'd fight the bitch – but not before getting his fun out of it first. Holding up the leash, he smiled. "Can't be too careful. I wouldn't want you to injure me before we have a chance to work this out."

She sneered. "You're sick, you know that?"

He chuckled in response. "You have no idea."

And she didn't. Remembering back to when Maddy was first brought to the mansion, Xander recalled how he'd been a little too excited to see her chained. He would never admit it to Aaron or Maddy, and the situation had certainly changed over the past two years...but he couldn't deny that, initially, the power and her submission had enticed him. However, Maddy didn't excite him as much as the woman on the floor before him. No. Hope was like a wild animal, one so majestic and rare, that to possess her was a testament to the owner's power.

Stepping forward, he allowed his eyes to wander over Hope's body. Her hair hung down to her hips and framed her thin face. It was striking, to say the least. But when she opened those eyes, when the gold color shone out and contrasted against the dark color of her eyelashes and hair, that was when he lost himself to her beauty. Her body called to him; the lean line of her frame and the tone to the muscles that lined it. She wasn't curvy, but perfectly proportioned. It was a fighter's body hidden within feminine skin. His mouth watered to taste it – to taste her; and he felt himself slipping into a dark chasm of longing and need.

She looked up at him when he approached and he smiled to see the hatred written across her features. The fact that she so obviously loathed him only made his goal of taming her stronger – a need so intense, that he wasn't sure he could resist taking it too far.

"Bend forward as much as you can. I want you facing the floor when I place this on you." His grin was wicked "Put your ass in the air for me."

Sneering, she responded, "You're not seriously going to put that fucking thing on me? Just let me out of these chains and let's get this over with."

He spoke slowly and without emotion. "You stated your conditions, I stated mine. It's time to remove your stink." The corner of his lip twisted up in humor to see her eyes narrow further at his insult.

75

She didn't bend forward as he'd requested and he grabbed her by her hair and forced her to face down. Appreciating the docility forced on her by the belt, he snapped the collar in place only to grab her hair again to pull her back up. Before letting go, he wrapped his fingers tighter in her thick hair, pulling it just so he could watch and appreciate the way her body reacted to the small amount of pain it produced. He wanted to see more.

Quickly tugging on the chain, he ordered, "Stand up."

Her gold eyes blinked slowly, her full mouth twisting in indignation. Playfully, he gave the chain two more tugs. His amusement wasn't easily contained. When she didn't budge, he looked down on her with an expression of absolute boredom. "We're never going to get to the end of this if you don't cooperate now."

"I cannot fucking wait to rip your smug head from your body."

He smiled and tugged again.

Pushing herself up on her knees, Xander kept his eyes trained to her body. Even chained, she moved gracefully. He tossed his keys down at her knees. "You're welcome to unlock the shackles at your feet."

She sighed and open her hands to indicate how they were bound to the belt. Her expression mocked him, her understanding finally settling in that he was just toying with her. He bent down on one knee and retrieved the keys from the floor. He swirled a hand in front of her. "Turn around." She complied almost immediately and an eyebrow cocked on his face to see it. After unlatching the shackles at her ankles, he winced to see how they'd cut into the skin. The air hit her wounds and he watched as her spine straightened from the pain.

"We'll have to be sure to clean those. I'd hate for them to become infected."

"Doesn't really matter. You intend to kill me anyway."

Standing above her, he tugged on the chain again to instruct her to turn around and climb to her feet. "Yes. But, in case you win, I'd hate to lose my life just for you to crawl off somewhere and die like a wounded dog."

Her eyes shot to his. "Has anybody told you how fucking aggravating you are?"

He thought of Maddy and grinned. "I've heard."

One more tug and he led her out of the cell and down a side hallway that led behind the ballroom and into the right wing. When he neared the suite he'd made for himself after Joseph had been killed, he pulled a key from his pocket and unlocked the large wooden doors. The suite wasn't as large as Aaron's but Xander enjoyed having his own space in the mansion after so many years of having nothing more than a small room inside Aaron's.

"I apologize for the mess, but I haven't had much time to clean up since you've arrived." He looked over his shoulder and watched Hope's head swivel to look around the room. Her eyes casually glanced over the books and papers strewn about, but would stop every so often on something she found that interested her. Leading her through the space, he turned right down a hallway that led to the master bedroom and bath. Hope stopped in her tracks to see it.

. . .

The walls were painted a blood red, the dark color broken up by tapestries depicting mystical scenes and symbols. The furniture was a dark wood with clean lines and the white linens added the only light color to the room. The room was illuminated with candles. Sconces hung on the walls and some floated in bowls set on the tables and chests around the room. She scoffed.

He looked back at her in response and continued leading her through the room. When they entered the bathroom, her eyes found that the bathtub took up the majority of the room, the water appearing to vanish over the sides. The room was also dimly lit with flickering shadows and flame. He stopped, locking her chain to a pipe that ran along the wall.

She stood still, the remnants of the drugs causing her to sway where she stood. She was tired and hungry, her body weak from the lack of food and her injuries. When he turned back to her, she noticed how his mouth twisted and his

78

eyes were dark and hooded. She took a step back, momentarily forgetting to hide her reaction and his lips finally turned up into the grin he'd been suppressing.

"The tub has steps down into it. Should make things easier considering you don't have use of your arms at the moment." He reached up, pushing the collar higher up her neck so he could untie the straps of fabric that crossed over her chest. Lowering the straps, she shivered at being exposed, but also because of the way his sapphire eyes burned into hers. His face was set in some unreadable expression and Hope was angered by how her body reacted to his stare. Her eyes dipped down to look at the movement of his mouth when he spoke again.

"I'm afraid these clothes are going to need to be burned. Your blood is all over them."

Fury and scorn coursed through body, her skin prickling at the way she been exposed. When he moved closer, still holding her stare, and began to unbutton her pants, she forced her rage aside, desperate to regain control over herself. She had to remain clearheaded to escape, and she couldn't allow herself to allow emotion to blanket her actions and decisions. He knelt to rip the material down her legs and she considered breaking his nose with her knee. Fighting, however, was not in her best interest as a result of the belt in which he'd secured her.

He stood up, leaving her pants bunched around her ankles. Walking behind her, she heard him pick up something and drag it across the floor. When he approached her from behind, he stood close enough that the material of his clothes tickled the exposed skin of her body and his lips brushed her ear when he instructed, "Sit down."

The back of the chair he held pushed into her legs and she fell back into it. He stepped around, kneeling again to remove the material from around her feet. When he looked back up at her shadow danced across the violent beauty of his face and Hope attempted to blink away her attraction.

Breathe in...Breath out...

Willing her body not to react, she felt disoriented by the drugs, the flush across her skin a result of the wisps of euphoria that still danced lightly across her mind. Her eyes opened and then widened to see the intensity of his stare. His eyes were the color of a deep sea, churning with violent, impassioned thoughts. Her lip parted slightly and her body tightened in reaction to his gaze.

His hand ran up her leg, curving around her calf before moving around to run along the top of her thigh. He traced his thumb along the sensitive skin beneath, his fingernail scratching and teasing as it traveled. Her body quivered at his touch, the hint of pain driving incessant pulses of anticipation through a body she was having difficulty controlling.

He pushed up, standing above her casting a shadow over every inch of her skin. He curled the chain around his hand, tugging gently until she stood up on shaky legs. Reaching out, he balanced

80

her, his eyes hooding further to see her body sway. Slowly, so slowly, she breathed, an attempt to calm the rate of her heart that pounded like thunder in her head. He stepped backwards, his eyes still locked to hers. Light and shadow danced across his cheekbones, the dip of his cheeks and over the cut of his square jaw. She closed her eyes again – her body betraying her when she couldn't afford to let herself fall. Her sister was too precious, the only thing good and pure in Hope's life. But even when her mind fought violently against the hormones crashing across her brain, and when thought battled against instinct, she knew was losing. She looked down, desperate to hide from his eyes. She watched as her bare feet moved over the stone floor, until he stopped. The water beside her circulated through the tubs, the jets creating bubbles that broke at the surface, the sound competing against the sound of rushing blood through her head.

"Watch your step, I'd hate for you to fall without a means of catching yourself." His voice was a deep timbre, vibrating against her skin with each syllable that left his sculpted lips.

She looked up.

His eyes were shadowed as he stared at the belt around her waist. He allowed his eyes to slowly turn up, to study and burn into memory every feature of her body, until his arrogant look met the surprise in her expression.

She couldn't look at him long, choosing instead to rotate her body. Looking down at the bath, she smelled gentle fragments of spiced scent that wafted up from the water. Her toe dipped down into the steaming liquid when she stepped down, burning along her skin as she pushed her foot further. The entire length of her body bucked when her ankle met the heated pool and a ringing sounded in her ears when the pleasurable jolt traveled up her legs, wrapping around her torso to snake up the back of her neck. His calloused hand reached out to steady her, the rough texture making it evident he handled weapons often. Her own hands bore those patches of skin wore hard by the handle of a blade or a gun.

With her body becoming immersed, the warmth of the water seeped into her body, the ripples around her pink as it washed away the blood. She dipped down allowing it to glide over her shoulder, hissing and biting her lip as the crimson stain was erased from her skin. Her head fell back and her hair became weighted, the strain to her neck only adding to the ecstasy she felt in that moment. Allowing herself to sink beneath the surface, she contemplated staying there, losing herself in oblivion, in numbness and an absence of awareness. But she couldn't leave Honor behind, couldn't at least try to get to her sister before they killed her. Hope's head broke the surface of the water and she pushed up, allowing it to fall in rivulets down her skin.

"Turn around." She felt the collar pull and she turned quickly, attempting to keep from being pulled completely back. The collar spun on her neck, the part to which the chain connected stopping on that center of her throat.

His grin was crooked and cruel. "God, you are a treasure. It's a shame we're not better friends."

She blinked the drops from her lashes.

The heat from the bath was making her light headed, the steam stealing the oxygen from the air, leading her down a tunnel, making her mind groggy and her body loose. He spoke again, the words disjointed and distant, but the tug on the chain brought her forward, her legs cooperating only to keep him from pulling her forward and into the water.

Her vision fogged over, the details of the room being lost within a blanket of steam. The illumination of the flames fought against the heated gossamer clouds. Reaching the stairs, she looked up into a perfectly blank expression, Xander's thoughts hidden behind eyes that flashed blue from the light that was able to penetrate. Her head felt heavy and her knees buckled beneath her weight. He reached out to grasp her arms, just as blackness overtook her.

Chapter Eight

He caught her just as her body collapsed. Her skin was pink from the heat of the water and his hands slid along the soft and dripping wet surface of her body. Picking her up, he laughed to himself thinking that she'd been a bit too high to handle the temperature of the bath.

While carrying her to his bed, he couldn't stop thinking about the view of her body when she'd stepped in the bath. He'd watched intently when she'd descended, noting the way her body shook when her wounds had been touched. It took all he had not to rip off his clothes and climb in behind her. Her ass was perfectly toned, the contour one that had been formed by hours of running, of walking or fighting. When she dipped beneath and when her body broke the surface, he groaned at the way her ebony hair plastered itself across her shoulders and down her back. But beyond even those moments, was when she turned around and her skin prickled and flushed while her breasts tightened. Battle scars slashed heavy and white across her tan skin – prideful reminders of the men she'd fought. She was decadence hidden within a recalcitrant package, a force to be conquered and a predator to be tamed.

Laying her body atop the silk comforter, he instantly noticed how her skin glowed against the blinding white of the fabric. His mouth salivating, his teeth aching to bite down into the smooth flesh of her body, he retrieved a key from his pants, unlocked the shackles at her wrists and pulled the belt from her limp body. He pondered the convenience that she'd passed out again, but brushed it from his thoughts, sliding her body up the bed, securing her arms and legs. He hated to continue using the sharp metallic rings on her wrists and ankles, but anything less and he knew she'd find a way to escape her binds.

He looked over her body, completely bare except for a scrap of material between her thighs. It would be so easy to take her right then and there, but he didn't want to simply fuck her body. No. He wanted to warp her mind so that she begged him to fuck her, so that she believed him as necessary to her as breathing. He regretted that he'd have to fight her, but she was the type who needed to be truly dominated, the type who needed to be defeated in order to be owned.

Moving up the bed, he ran his fingertip across the center of her abdomen, his eyes fixed on the way the muscle flexed beneath his touch. He increased the pressure of his path up through the center of her breasts and over her neck, his other fingers brushing against the slow pulse below the skin.

"Wake up, sunshine. Don't leave me yet." He tapped her cheek playfully and her eyes moved beneath her lids, eventually fluttering open to reveal a groggy cloud within the gold. She looked sated and satisfied, completely lost to a sea of obscurity.

"Come back, beautiful. We were just getting started."

She blinked up at him, attempting to move her arm to rub the sleep from her tired eyes. When the chained had been stretched taut and her hand couldn't go farther, she groaned and rolled so that her face was pressed against the pillow."

Turning, he went back into the bathroom to get a glass of water, filling the cup, he took a vial of clear liquid from his pocket, adding a few drops. It wasn't fair for him to keep her drugged, however he wanted her shoulder to have time to heal before she moved in a way that might injure it further. He'd lied to tell her that the last dose had been given when they'd removed the bullet, but he didn't feel guilty for having done so.

When he approached her again, he placed the glass on the table, reaching his hand beneath her back and pulling her up into a seated position. The chains had just enough slack that she could move about semi-freely; another good reason to keep her sedated.

"Drink this. It will make you feel better."

Her mouth and throat worked hungrily at the liquid, her tongue sweeping out against the glass, desperate for the last drops of moisture. He pulled it away and set it back on the table.

Her head rolled in his direction, the sluggish movement youthful and endearing. "Is this the part where I'm supposed to beg you not to fuck me?" Her gold eyes flicked open but remained hooded.

86

"Where I say I'll tell you everything if you'll just spare me my dignity?"

He thought about her words. Smiling, he replied, "Well, it would make things easier."

"Fuck you." The corners of her lips curled. "You're wasting your time, unless it's for your own benefits more so than for making me talk." Her speech was slow, slurred, but he appreciated the intelligence that remained hidden behind the fog he'd created in her head. However, his dissatisfaction with her continued fight rubbed irritatingly across his nerves.

Slipping his hand between her legs, he slid upwards against the skin, pinching it between his thumb and finger while the other fingertips gripped into the muscle of her thigh. Her head rolled back, her body arching slightly in response to the hints of pleasurable pain he was forcing through her. Reaching the apex of her thighs, he pulled up, barely brushing against the flesh, his eyes taking in how her body responded to every soft touch.

Running his hand over the slight curve to her stomach, he stopped at her ribs, tracing his fingertip along her breast. His words came out in a throaty whisper. "I don't need to fuck you to get inside you, Hope. I know what you like, what excites your body despite your hatred of me. I know your dirty little secret, the one you use to your advantage."

Her eyes widened as much as the haze would allow and she looked at him, focused on the

87

features of his face and appeared to study him; every expression, every movement. He enjoyed these moments; ones where she was between doses, when hints of her drive and personality peeked through the fog until the next wave of euphoria returned her to oblivion. He pressed his hand up until it covered her breast and, after taking the soft skin on the side between his fingers, he bent down to bite on the hardened tip while pinching at the side. His tongue laved across the tip and she arched up almost instantly, the flexibility of her body apparent in the way it bent towards him. While continuing to work at her breast, to apply just enough pressure to awaken the nerve that ran to her core, he looked up at her. Her lip curled up, her teeth grit together. Her hands wrapped into the chains to which they were secured and she writhed, silently begging for more, for a sharper high – a stronger hit to her system in order to induce the rush of blood and endorphins that came after it. His body shivered over her, his own rushing blood creating in him an inferno of desperate want. He enjoyed overtaking her, empowered by not only dominating her, but for sending her to heights he wasn't sure she'd reached before.

When he released her breast, he pushed up to sit over her, wiping the moisture from his mouth before placing his hand on the bed next to her head. Her hair was spread across the sheets, the silk of it wrapping around his fingers. He tugged and watched as aftershocks of pleasure rolled across her prickled skin. Bringing his mouth to her ear, he knew she could feel the heat of his body wash over her – the power to the beat of his heart where he pressed his chest against hers.

"Your strength is also your weakness. You're able to endure because you like the pain, but you like it a bit too much don't you?" He bit down on her earlobe, felt her chest collide against his from the movement of her body. "I'm sure no man lived long enough to discover that secret; but I did, and I intend to use it to my advantage as well." Pushing up, he looked down into the enraged gold. "You can kill me tomorrow if you win – but I can promise you that if I win, I'll fuck the shit out of you before you tell me what I want to know."

Removing his weight from her, he held himself above her and watched as she settled from the pain he'd granted. Her lips curled slightly and parted from her heavy breath. He heard the chains shake from the movement of her arms and legs, her ass grinding down into the mattress, moving in a manner meant to seduce and entice. It was carnal and it was raw – a woman overtaken by her body's darkest needs.

Her mouth moved, but her words were barely discernable. The pink tip of her tongue flicked out to run along her lip. He tracked its movement, gripped his hand into the mattress to ease the ache of want it ignited inside him.

"Again."

It was faint and he almost believed he didn't hear it, but when she repeated it, stronger, slower, he looked at her and smiled.

He responded to her just as slow and assured. "Will you beg?" His eyes searched hers. Every so often, light would spark off the gold making them appear metallic.

Her eyes rolled back slightly, before she blinked and refocused on his face. "Again."

Dark laughter rolled within his chest. She wasn't begging, but she wasn't giving up either. He was suddenly glad he wasn't a better man; refusing because she was drugged would have been difficult if he had been. Trailing one hand down her stomach, he kept his gaze locked to hers. The tips of his fingers slipped beneath the thin patch of material and she shook her head. "No...not..."

"Shhhh. I know what you need." It was a resolute vow that he whispered to her.

And he did. It was exactly like Maddy had said; you could recognize it - Hope's darkness. Her body reacted to pain and torment like it was a lover's touch. She craved it; was starved for it. Nothing could take her to the same peaks. She needed it to remain sane.

Moving down her body, he trailed his lips over her abdomen, allowing his teeth to graze across the skin. Ripping the last bit of material from her body, he didn't take his time to run his finger down along the skin, discovering how ready her body had become. A growl emanated from his chest and he breathed in deeply the smell of her skin. When he reached her hip, he bit down on the skin, her body bucking up in response to the feel of his teeth on her the delicate nerve endings. His fingers dug into the tight muscle of her ass and thigh, and he shuddered to feel it move within his grip, to tighten. Her body was perfection; strong and lean, every tendon, every muscle and fiber within her developed and honed to fight. His hands gripped her legs, forcing them apart, bearing her to his eyes, his hands, his mouth. She moaned above him, the effects of the drugs heightening her reactions making her hyperaware of every brush of his hand across her body, every drag of his fingernail against her skin. Unable to resist, he covered her, allowing the heat of his mouth to sink into the sensitized flesh, allowing his tongue to flick out and tease the skin.

Her taste was divinity, ambrosia intended for men far more worthy than him – quite possibly too good for any man at all. He lapped at it, desperate to fill his mouth with her essence, her need. Holding her down, his hands preventing her hips from moving beneath him, completely overpowering her efforts to demand more. The chains rattled and he looked up to see her hands grasping desperately to the sheets, her breasts swollen and throbbing for his touch, for his abuse.

Slipping one finger within the heat of her body, his groaned in appreciation of the muscles rippling down, gripping at him at tightly as his other gripped in the skin of her leg.

"Fuck." He breathed out the word without being able to stop himself. Working her body, plunging his hand deeply, only to tease and twist her up inside, he asked, "Is every part of your body

91

so fucking strong?" He'd never felt anything like it, her grip becoming almost painful when he finally slipped a second finger inside.

The sounds that escaped her lips were driving him to a point of painful frustration. The material of his pants had become offensive and tight across his cock. She was a trigger ready to be pulled and he wanted to bury himself inside, to feel and experience her body as it milked him, devoured him when she was lost inside a rapturous deluge of heat, ecstasy and carnal need.

Pulling away, he reached up, pinching the small bundle of nerves at the top, applying enough pressure that would make most women scream, but Hope seemed to absorb it, her skin flushing red and white, stretching taut across her twisting frame. She was wound too tight, small quakes rolling through her, her breath escaping her in moans between the way she panted erratically. Fuck, if she wasn't the model of perfection, then Xander didn't believe it could ever truly exist.

Kissing along the inside of her thigh, he squeezed down on the small bundle while at the same time, sinking his teeth into the delicate skin of her inner leg. When the minute hint of iron met his tongue, when he had to stop himself from biting down harder to taste more, she screamed. He slammed his finger back inside to feel the exquisite strength of her core while her body tensed above him. The chains rattled across the sheets and her chest seized with her stolen breath. He released her leg, looked up to watch her face twist with blissful passion and dangerous heights.

92

And he lost his ability to resist.

His hands made quick work of his shirt and pants, tearing the cloth from his body, his muscles tense across his bones and his cock so fucking hard that he feared just lightly touching it would send him crashing through into the same agonizing release he'd just witnessed her endure. He crawled back over her, his hands coming down on her arm, his mouth trailing over her neck, nipping and biting until he covered her mouth with his, his tongue demanding dominance over hers, his teeth scraping over her swollen lips. He growled out a command into her mouth, refusing to release the contact.

"Beg for it."

He positioned himself at the opening to her body, teased her by sliding within, but never truly filling her or stretching out the muscles that throbbed hungrily for him to bury himself inside. He wanted to break her, to shame her, to make her plead for him to take her and control her – to fucking own her.

He brought his mouth to her ear, bit down on the lobe sending small hints of the wave that would wash over her if he bit harder. Blowing lightly against her heated and sweat-soaked skin, he commanded her again.

"Beg for me, Hope…"

Chapter Nine

Bit and pieces flashed in her mind: the deep brown of his hair, the violent edge to his cheekbone and jaw, the way the muscles of his body rippled along his frame when he moved, reminiscent of a prowling threat, a hunter who stalks in the shadows.

He hovered above her, his chest colliding against the tips of her breasts and wave after wave of sensation drove itself through her; the smallest touch eliciting anticipation of his painful strike. Every inch of her skin was desperate and on fire, the nerves so awake that his breath brushing over her body felt like ice.

"Beg for me, Hope."

The words were jumbled, echoing from deep within something far from where she lay, but she wanted him back, closer, touching her, driving her. She floated inside a bubble of fire and ice, of day and night. Thought was obsolete and meaningless, the only things necessary were pleasure...and pain. She'd beg, now that she'd been pushed to a point of abandon and carelessness, she'd beg for more, for it never to end. Her strength was her weakness, and now that he'd discovered it, he forced her body to betray her, to mock her for how feeble her mind had become.

"Please." Her plea was muffled by her intoxication and she opened her eyes to see his wicked grin. He didn't look real. He wore his strength and command over her like he would clothing, every inch of his skin sticky with masculinity and raw power. Drops of sweat dripped down his brow, sliding along his skin, breaking apart against the stubble of his jaw. She'd trembled when he'd raked his cheek along the inside of her thigh and she wanted to feel it over her breasts as his teeth bit into the tips.

"Please what?" He laughed softly and his words vibrated through his chest, tickling her skin where he touched her. Every few seconds he would run his length between her thighs, tempting and teasing her – promising to fill her so full, her own body would break apart around him and her mind would shatter within her skull.

"Break me...please"

His eyes widened in reaction to her words, surprise flitting across his features before his pupils dilated and his eyes appeared black. Small streams of light flickered across their skin, absorbed by shadow as they moved. In one swift push forward, he stretched her to limits she'd never known; the delicate skin torn by his girth, the salt of his skin seeping into the fissures, the light caress of discomfort and torment. It was enough to sedate her, to cripple her, to stop every bodily function so that she only knew the sensation of him sinking inside. His hand curled into the hair at the base of her skull and fire ran across her skin, her head pulled back, her neck stretched and taut. When his

95

teeth sank into the skin, already stretched to a point of tearing, she exploded around him, a volcano erupting within her body, the slice of steel and brush of velvet. His fingers raked down along the skin of her back as her body violently arched into him, she needed more, another push, another fix of the numbing effect of the pain. She wanted to become lost within his tempestuous storm – dominated, controlled, a puppet tied to strings made of glass and razors, of satin and fur.

He breathed out hard above her, the brush of his breath relieving the inescapable heat of her inflamed skin. Her body writhed and contorted, each muscle flexing and relaxing, she'd become nothing more than a tool of pleasure, a soul in need of torment.

A scream built in her chest until it pressed up into her throat, eventually tearing from her mouth into his. He pulled her hair tighter, bent her neck back impossibly farther until forcing her to release around him and over him. Still trembling within the waves of exquisite oblivion, she heard him and felt him growl, his teeth sinking once again into her skin as he powered forward one last time.

. . .

Her eyes rolled back in her head and he gripped her hair so tight, it cut into the skin of his hands. Her neck was bent so far back, he knew that with the tiniest flick of his wrist he could snap her spine – and she wanted more, needed more. She was a woman designed to ache for the sadist hidden inside him.

Reaching his own peak, he released inside her, claiming her as his pet, his prize. He watched her face contort, waves of pleasure rushing down her body, small quakes still shaking her beneath him. His palm slid down her cheek, fingers digging trails along her neck until he could wrap his hand around, push his thumb into her pulse, feel her heart thunder through her body for him.

Placing soft kisses on her face, he watched her become lost to obscurity – a nirvana created in her mind from the rush of blood poisoned by passion, fueled by the drugs and forced by his hand. Allowing his forehead to lay atop hers, he grinned to see her eyes move beneath the lids, to hear the small moans escaping her lips while she lay trapped in the euphoric state in which he'd placed her and had allowed her to go.

The next noise he heard was like a shot to the heart and to the head. The front doors were being beaten against by someone's fist.

"Fuck!" Pushing up from the bed, he grabbed a towel and wrapped it around his waist to answer the door. He swung it open, the movement so fast and violent that his rage was pouring out into his strength. "What!"

Emerald green blinked back at him, a blank expression on Aaron's face except for the hint of fury hidden behind his jewel toned eyes.

"Where is she?"

It took a second for Xander to shake himself of the hormones in his blood and clouding

97

his mind. Stepping back, he allowed Aaron to enter the living room, noticed how Aaron's eyes surveyed the candles peppered throughout the room before turning back to him. "The bitch. Where. The fuck. Is she?"

Xander tensed, his back straightening in response to the question. "She's here."

Aaron's eyes slowly opened and closed, his disapproval instantly visible across the features of his face. Looking down at Xander's naked state, he commented, "I can see that. What I would now like to know is why she's here."

"We need information."

"Did you get it?"

"No."

They stared at each other, neither man moving or blinking. Aaron was the first to speak again. "Is she bound?"

Xander motioned towards the bedroom. "You're welcome to check. If she can escape those binds, then she deserves her freedom."

Aaron shot Xander a look before stepping into the bedroom. He closed his eyes to find Hope spent and sated, her body spread limply across the bed, nothing on her body except for a collar and a chain. Bringing his hand to his face, he pinched between his eyes, the veins in his neck popping out from rage. When he spoke again, his voice was low and controlled, his words were a warning.

"You were supposed to be getting information out of her, not fucking her senseless!"

Xander couldn't suppress his grin. "I'm taking care of both."

There was no amusement in Aaron's expression when he ordered, "Get dressed and be in my quarters in fifteen minutes. We have some issues to discuss. Jason will be joining us as well."

Xander nodded his understanding and didn't turn with Aaron marched around him and out of the apartment. When the door slammed behind him, Xander let out an annoyed sigh. Cursing under his breath, he moved to his closet, quickly dressing in black sweat pants and a t-shirt. Walking past the bed, he sat down on the side of the mattress, cupping Hope's cheek with his palm. She smiled and pushed her face against the heat of his hand.

Looking down, he whispered, "I'll miss this side of you when you wake, because I know you'll hate me in the morning."

. . .

"You instructed that I make her talk. You weren't specific in those instructions except to say that I should employ any method that I decided would be useful." He paused before quickly adding, "And I believe I was also instructed to seduce her."

"That was Maddy!"

"Whatever."

99

Aaron's face had turned from red to purple at the flippancy of Xander's response. He stepped closer to Xander until both men were nose to nose. Their bodies straight, their muscles tense and their feet set in a position to balance them when they fought. The pitch of Aaron's voice was dangerously low when he asked, "How exactly is drugging her and fucking her going to make her talk? She was unconscious when I saw her. How, exactly, do you intend to pull information out of a limp body?"

Xander stepped back, the knowledge that Aaron was slipping into a rage so deep, that his instinct to destroy would cloud over logical thought. "Calm down, Aaron." He struggled to keep his own anger at bay when she answered, "She'll tell me everything we need to know tomorrow."

They stood in the center of Aaron's living room, the large iron chandelier hanging proud over their heads. Maddy and Jason sat on the couches that surrounded them and Xander forced himself into a relaxed stance, not wanting to trigger Aaron's rage further.

"How can you be sure of that?"

"Because, I've agreed to fight her for it." Xander stepped back again after admitting that small fact. When he looked at the murderous expression plastered across Aaron's face, he took another step back just to be sure he was out of range.

"Okay, you know what?" Maddy stood up and crossed the space to place her hand on Aaron's shoulder. "We should all sit down and talk about this." Aaron's torso slowly twisted on his waist when he turned to look down at the petite beauty by his side. The controlled quality of his speech and movement made it frighteningly clear that he was on the verge of violence.

"Madeleine, you will go back in our room and out of my sight for now. This conversation does not concern you."

Her eyes widened in recognition of his tone. She looked quickly at Xander, fear written across her face. Without arguing, she did as she was told, knowing better than to argue with Aaron when his anger had reached a boiling point. Xander watched her as she disappeared down the hall, wishing he could disappear as well.

Returning his eyes to Aaron, he flinched in reaction to Aaron's razor edged gaze. "I want you to explain to me what you mean by that statement, Xander, and I fucking hope to God that what you say to me is logical and well thought out. I would hate to think that the person I have in charge of the majority of this network is a fucking lunatic!"

"She said she'd fight me for the information. I win, she tells me what I want to know."

"And if she wins?"

"She won't."

101

"How can you know that! She's a trained assassin and from what I've learned since we've captured her, she's a professional at what she does."

"Because I know something about her that I can exploit to my advantage. She won't win, Aaron."

"You're too arrogant and she'll exploit that. This is not some ordinary woman, she is a *trained* killer. Even I would use caution in a fight against her, and you're standing here telling me there's no way she could win. You're not thinking clearly and there's no fucking way I'm allowing this to happen."

Xander's own rage settled over his shoulders to hear Aaron question his decision. "She's injured, starved and dehydrated. Add to that the drugs I've been feeding into her system for the last twenty-four hours and I'm not concerned that she'll somehow defeat me!"

There was a dangerous tension in the air when a third voice drawled, "You two argue like brothers. It's amusing."

Their faces turned in unison towards Jason.

"As entertaining as this is, I'm not sure how any of this is a fucking problem. The bitch is probably some psychopath who thought she'd make her name by taking out Aaron. I doubt she has any information and is toying with you, hoping for a slight chance that she can escape this place. Just fucking kill her now and work the other networks to find out who sent her. You don't need to hear it from her. In fact..." He stood up. "I'll do it for you."

"You'll have to kill me first." Xander immediately stepped towards Jason and Aaron's hand gripped Xander's bicep to keep him from moving farther.

"Calm down, Xander; now."

He stepped back, but only because he wouldn't disobey Aaron's direct order in front of Jason. Even though Jason had proven himself a good ally when they'd taken The Estate from Joseph, and he'd also proven himself useful as a unit leader within the network, he wasn't trusted enough for Xander and Aaron to let down their guards.

"Jason, sit down. Xander will handle this. You're here because I want sweeps run of every house on the compound tonight. Contact Patrick and organize the searches." Aaron turned towards Jason. "And do not fuck this up."

Jason held up his hands and sat down. "I'm not trying to step on anybody's toes, gentlemen. I simply thought it was a reasonable solution." Apparently unaffected by Xander's rage, his voice was relaxed and humble.

Aaron let out a frustrated breath. "Of course, however some of us..." His eyes flicked to Xander quickly before falling back on Jason. "...have other interests in mind at the moment. Once you are finished with the sweeps, if you've found nothing here, then I want the smaller networks questioned, if they won't talk, kill them. I cannot allow anybody to think that The Estate has become weak because of my father's death."

Turning back to Xander, he paused, his green eyes searching Xander's face. Jason was right, they were like brothers, and Aaron could read Xander's thoughts just by the look on his face. "I'll continue this talk with you in private, but you can get it out of your fucking head that I'd allow you to fight that bitch. The instant she took the advantage, I'd cut her fucking throat."

"You won't have to. She won't get that far."

Aaron blinked. "You can't be so sure."

Chapter Ten

A small iron chandelier came into view when Hope peeked open her eyes. The room was dark and she was thankful to not have to endure the light of the sun when first waking up. Her mouth was sticky was dehydration and her head swam and pounded at the same time. She had no strength to move, but she didn't hurt. For once, she couldn't immediately feel the wound on her shoulder.

Pulling her arms and legs, she heard the chains just as quickly as she felt the shackles press into her skin. Opening her eyes wider, she angled her head down to see that she was stripped bare and completely exposed. Fury swept over her spine, her heart pounding harder when she struggled to remember what he'd done. The chains weren't so tight that she couldn't sit up, so she pushed herself up from the mattress, pulling her bents legs to her chest to cover her nudity. Her eyes traveled around the room; bits and pieces of the night before echoing in her mind. Candles, his hands, his mouth...the collar and chain still fastened to her throat. The pounding headache increased, heat traveling her veins from her anger, her desire to kill. He'd raped her. Not able to remember, she hoped she'd damaged him in the process.

She heard him before she saw him, the heavy fall of his shoes against the floor a warning as he approached. Knowing what he'd done had sparked her anger, seeing the arrogant smirk that now graced his face stoked that anger into in a seething fury. Her hands fisted and her fingernails cut into the skin of her palms. Her shoulders and back tensed and she ground her teeth, willing daggers into every vital organ of his body.

"You look absolutely stunning this morning. How are you feeling?"

He was gloating and she wanted to rip the expression right off his handsome face. "You drugged me you fucking bastard!" The words were choked in her parched throat, but she spit them out anyway. If she wasn't in chains, she'd find something around the room to slice him open.

"You're much more agreeable when drugged. You should do it more often. I think we'd get along a lot better that way." He winked.

"You are a pathetic excuse for a man."

He stalked towards her, placing both hands on the mattress so he could press his forehead against hers. "You were the one begging me. I must admit, your body is the most responsive I've ever had the pleasure to enjoy." His lips felt like silk across hers when he kissed her, his tongue peeking out to slide across the crease of her lips.

Red blinding anger burst within her and she pulled away. Bringing her arm over, she hit him in the side of the head with the shackle around her wrist. Her leg wrapped around his, tangling him in the chains he'd used to restrain her.

He cursed quickly before grabbing the chain at her throat, and pulling her over as he fell backwards. His weight was enough to force her to move her leg, and he made quick work of the small length of chain she'd managed to wrap around him. Backing off the bed, he kept the chain on her collar wrapped around his palm and pulled her into a position where her arms were stretched out behind her from the shackles and her torso was bent forward. She was powerless to move and he chuckled above her.

"That's one hell of a way to wish me a good morning. And here I was trying to be playful. Maybe if you apologize and promise you'll behave, I'll release this chain and let you up."

"I'll never fucking *behave* for a man so pathetic he has to drug women in order to rape them."

Keeping the chain taut, he approached her, leaning down and blowing his breath across her angry skin. Pressing his mouth to her ear, he whispered, "You've behaved for me quite well already, the means by which I brought about that result is unimportant, just the fact that I did." Pushing closer, he added, "You begged me to break you, and I still have every fucking intention of doing just that. You should let go of your stubbornness and allow me to do it in a way that benefits us both." Pulling away from her he released the chain and allowed her out of the uncomfortable position. She rolled her shoulder back and he grimaced to think what that had just done to the healing wound.

107

She glared up at him, the cut of his jaw causing flashbacks of the previous night to play in her head; the candlelight across his skin, his teeth buried in her flesh. She looked down at her inner thigh and saw the angry bruise from where he'd bitten her, a shiver rolling through her body to remember what he'd made her feel. Her body fought against her, hatred and contempt mixed with a nagging ache for the torment of his hands.

"I'll make you behave in other ways as well. I'll fight you today and once I win, you'll tell me what I want to fucking know and then I'll do with you as I see fit following that."

"Just unchain me and let's get this over with." The gold of her eyes shot to his, the color blinding hot from her rage.

His expression darkened and his lids hooded. "So eager." He blinked as if bored. "But first, let's take care of some of your body's *other* needs." Grabbing the belt from the table next to him, he held it up to show her. "I'm going to need to put you back in this. If you resist, it'll only delay the freedom you keeping requesting, so I suggest you cooperate."

She glared.

He smiled.

"I'd take you by just the leash, let you crawl on the floor in front of me like the dangerous and exotic animal that you are, but I can't trust that you won't try to kill me too soon. I'd hate for our fight to begin while you're still so weak from lack of water and food. Plus, a good hit to the bladder and things could get messy." He chuckled darkly. "Nobody wants that."

"You're an ass."

"I'm an ass with a valid point. So do yourself a favor and *behave* when I place your hands in this belt." He approached her and bent over to secure the belt around her waist. Releasing one of her hands at a time, he secured them to the belt. She considered lashing out at him, or strangling him with the chain, but if he was releasing her today, there was no point in starting the bullshit now.

He tugged on the chain at her neck. "Let's go."

. . .

"You're insane for doing this, Xander. And if she does succeed against you, despite your arrogant fucking belief that she won't, I will not allow her out of this mansion if she's still breathing. I don't care what *deal* you made with her, I'm not a part of it." Aaron escorted Xander down the mansion corridors to a work out area in the back section of the building. After taking Hope to the bathroom, he'd given her water – undrugged – and some food to settle her stomach and give her some strength. He didn't tell Aaron that part.

"You're sure she's weak?"

"I'm flattered by your vote of confidence in my ability as a fighter. Seriously, stop, you're making me blush." Xander's were spoken drolly, indicative of his annoyance. He'd sparred against Aaron for practically his entire life, not to mention fought and survived hundreds of attacks inside and outside of The Estate compound, there was no reason for Aaron to believe he couldn't win against Hope.

Aaron stopped and turned to Xander. "From what you and Maddy say, she's like me. If that's the case, then when you get in that room, you'll be dealing with a person who feels nothing but a desire to kill. She'll be a machine and she'll take advantage of every weakness you have, probably the biggest one being that you obviously have a thing for her. Will you be able to kill her if it means you'll live?"

"She amuses me – number one – and, number two, it won't come to that." It was the only answer Xander could give. In his mind, there were no other options but to win.

Aaron scoffed. "If she was simply *amusing*, you wouldn't have threatened Jason's life last night." He gave Xander a pointed look. "I'll be outside the doors. I'd tell you to yell if you need help, but if it got to that point, you'd be dead before I could open the door."

Xander patted him on the back. "A simple 'good luck' would have been a nicer thing to say."

Aaron's brow arched over his eye and he pulled the door open. Walking in, Xander heard it close behind him and he stared at Hope who stood near the other end of the large space. She was dressed in the sweat pants and shirt he'd given her when they'd been in his room. They were two sizes too large for her and he wondered how well she'd be able to move while wearing them. Crossing the room with dread weighing on his shoulders, excitement also ignited in other areas of his body. He remembered how she was absolutely sensual in the way she moved, in the way she fought. He looked forward to experiencing it again.

. . .

Hopes eyes tracked Xander as he approached. Dressed in a snug cotton shirt and military style cargo pants tucked into his boots, he walked casually across the floor, looking like he was ready to spar more so than fight for his life.

"Will there be weapons?" She prayed to get her hand on a blade. After she'd woken up that morning, she realized how much time had passed since she'd seen Honor. While she waited for hours in the room to be brought to this gym, she imagined in horror the things being done to her sister. Hope's heart shredded inside her chest and her throat thickened at the idea that things could have gone too far, that Honor couldn't endure, that she could be dead.

"Not sure you can beat me without the use of steel? I thought they would have taught you better than that."

Her eyes narrowed at him, hatred rubbing against her thoughts and nerves, but dotted with

111

heat, with an ache for something he'd done the night before. "It would make things quicker if I could remove your head with one clean slice instead of having to tear it off."

He smiled in response and her body shuddered like it remembered him – his touch, his bite, the feeling of him tearing through her, filling her. She fought to shake it off, remembered that she had only one person that was important, and that person depended on her escape. Images of her sister growing up had been battering at her mind since Honor disappeared. Their childhood hadn't been easy. There had never been much light in their lives, but what did exist was because of Honor. Losing her life now that she was old enough to leave these wretched networks would be a cruelty of fate from which Hope would never recover. She had no choice but to kill the man that stood in front of her.

"Should we establish a rule that you refrain from tearing into me as I'm releasing you from the belt, or is it safe for me to assume that you will attempt to kill me with only one hand free?"

"You're a dick."

"You would know," he growled in response, allowing his eyes to slowly travel over her body.

She was suddenly glad she was going to kill him. His fucking arrogance had pushed on her last nerve. He looked down at the belt and used a key he'd retrieved from his pocket to unlock it from

112

around her waist. All she needed was one hand free and she could end things quickly, use the key herself in order to free the other hand once he was dead or incapacitated. Her response to the small metallic click was instantaneous. She immediately went for his face, hoping to cause enough damage to his eyes to give her time to use the chains to finish him off.

But he was too fast.

Her wrist went from the shackle directly to the iron grip of his hand. He caught her, had anticipated that she would strike out immediately once freed. His other hand gripped around her throat and within a second he had her pressed to a wall with every inch of her body completely immobile beneath his. His forehead pressed tightly to hers.

"Do not think that I'll go easy on you, Hope. I know you will end my life if given half a fucking chance."

Her gold eyes looked up suddenly into the stormy twilight of his.

"I've already had you once, so it wouldn't be a complete loss if you were to suffer a severe enough injury to prevent me from fucking you again. I'm not afraid to hurt you." He let go of her throat and brushed his finger over the tip of her nose. "You never know, you might like it."

An aggravating mixture of rage and lust, hatred and need, coursed through her blood. She was still weak, lethargic; but the added shiver that his touch produced on her skin, or the way his smell ignited something deep within her core, she couldn't allow those feelings to affect the fight – to cloud her thoughts or make her hesitate in her actions.

Breathe in...Breathe out...

Slow, steady, methodical. She calmed her body, her mind. When she no longer struggled against him, he released her and stepped back to unlock the remaining shackle from her wrist. His messy brown hair fell across his forehead and into his eyes, his broad shoulders flexed with each small movement he made with his hands, and when the last metal shackle fell from around her wrist, the back of his hand came up.

The impact with her face was hard to enough to knock her several feet from where she'd been standing.

Chapter Eleven

It was a cheap shot, but one he used to introduce her to the fight. He wasn't lying when he warned her that he wouldn't go easy. He understood that she was lethal – even injured and weak, she was a person who should not be underestimated.

She recovered from the hit quickly, pushing herself back up into a standing position in one fluid and graceful motion. She moved the same way a person would dance, long sweeping motions, with a quiet speed that made you believe she cut the air like a sharpened blade. Her eyes narrowed in his direction, but not from anger. No. She was studying him, plotting how she'd overcome his strength and size. He recognized her behavior, her motions – he'd fought against the same almost every day while growing up.

She stood stock still, the silence in the room pressing against his ears, the rush of blood in his head, the only audible noise. He anticipated that she'd rush forward to attack him, her hands set in a way to render damage where they came in contact with his body; but when she pivoted to turn, when her long legs powered her in the opposite direction and towards the exit doors, his brows shot up and he launched forward to stop her from opening the doors where Aaron waited.

"Fuck!"

His feet pounded across the floor of the gym, his strides barely longer than hers. He noticed how she appeared to hover as she ran, her feet never touching the ground beneath her. When she neared the door, her arm extended out in front of her body ready to throw the door open wide, and ready to open a door that would lead to her death. He sped up, the muscles in his thighs working his body forward. Her fingertips touched the wood, pushing it open just before he wrapped his arms around her, tackling her to the ground. Rolling over each other, he felt her fingernails cut across his face while he attempted to move their bodies into a position where he'd trap her beneath him – where he'd have the advantage. He raised his head in time to see Aaron's green eyes looking in the room just before the door closed.

Once Xander had regained control, he pinned Hope beneath him, using the weight of his body to restrain hers, the strength of his arms to hold hers. She was a slippery bitch, her body able to bend and contort in such a way, that she was able to slide out from his grasp. When her closed fist beat against his temple, he flinched against it and moved to avoid it. She took the shift in his weight as an opportunity to move out from beneath him. She attempted to scramble to her feet and he grabbed her ankle, only for her to twist around and plant the heel of her foot between his eyes.

Pain thundered along his skull from the kick and he was disoriented for the brief second she took to kick out again, catching him in the shoulder. Flame burst out over the skin where he'd been hit, but he rolled over, pushing himself up, keeping low and lunging forward, wrapping himself around her waist, bringing her back to the ground where their weight difference worked to his benefit.

Catching her wrists in his hands, he squeezed knowing the bones of her wrist could snap from his strength. He felt the shiver flow through her body from the pain he inflicted. Pinning her hands above her head, he spread her legs apart with his own, holding them open with his knees while wrapping his feet over hers. She was trapped beneath him, the wound to her shoulder still rendering one of her arms useless against him. Pressing forward he allowed the heat between her legs to slide over him while his eyes hungrily took in the way her body reacted to his touch.

She sneered beneath him, still struggling to free herself of the hold. If he'd intended to kill her, he'd have done so right then, but those were not the plans he had for the feral beauty pinned down by his body. Bringing his face lower, he ran his nose along her skin. "Are you ready to admit defeat, or should I ravage you further?"

A growl emanated from her chest and he smiled to know she wasn't ready to give up, that she may never be ready until she'd been beat fully into submission. A task he had every intention of accomplishing.

He hardened almost instantly to feel her bare breasts brush against his chest from beneath the thin shirt he'd given her to wear, to feel as her labored breath pushed their bodies tighter together. Pressing forward more, he rubbed between her legs and he could see the fight in her eyes to resist the rush of sexual need he was adding to the already physically charged encounter. He let his guard down for a split second to savor her reaction and she bucked up, twisting suddenly so that she threw him off balance. Her body moved like liquid as she moved from beneath, attempting to crawl to a point where she could push up. Turning quickly, he moved over her, his chest pressed to her back, only for his head to be met with the bone of her elbow, the resultant crack shooting like lightning through his skull. He released her only for a second and she stood up, turning immediately, her feet held in a fighting stance her gold eyes glowing with lustful furry. She was fully awake, that much was certain, and despite her weaknesses, she was intent to win. Even as pain pounded through his head, he smiled, always impressed with the willpower, the sheer carnal need within her to not be tamed.

He noticed how she favored her right side, holding her torso in a way that hinted of a cracked rib or torn muscle. If it were his intent to kill, he'd use the injury against his opponent, but not her. He wanted her whole, her body intact, he wanted to deliver the pain and darkness she craved, but not by destroying the perfection of her form.

Her eyes tracked him when he pushed up to his feet. They circled each other, their skill matched, her speed a perfect counter to his strength.

"I think playtime is over, don't you?"

The brows furrowed over her enraged eyes. "It's been fun." The tone of her words could have sliced his skin.

He laughed at her response and lunged forward. Reaching out, he gripped her hair in his hand just as her fist hit heavily against his cheek and her knee impacted with the inside of his thigh. Twisting the silken threads between his fingers, he extended his arm – pulling, dragging and launching her across the room, the force of his throw so hard that her body slid after impacting with the floor. It was time to end this.

She rolled over and crawled away from of him. Her arm was weak from her shoulder and she held her side with her other arm. Her body moved sluggishly and he knew she'd come into this fight already weak. It hadn't been fair, but fairness had never been his intent.

He walked behind her as he teased, "That's right, sunshine – crawl for me."

Giving her time to continue to fight, to continue to push herself up, only to fall back to the ground when the combined injuries had become too much to allow her to move quickly. When he stood above her, he reached down, grabbing her hair again and flipping her over. She looked up at him, the haze of the hell she'd gone through the last few days clouding her gaze. "I've won, Sunshine. It's about time I take my prize."

She hissed out her response. "I fucking hate you."

He smiled. "You won't be saying that much longer."

He dropped one knee to the ground on her right, before lowering down on the left. Straddling her, he watched as she became lost inside a wave of pain. Her skin prickled and flushed and he grabbed her by the throat pulling her into a seated position, pressing her back against the wall behind her. His other hand reached to slide beneath her shirt, up along her skin until he pinched the tip of her breast hard enough to add to the deluge of pain. Her eyes rolled back, her mouth opening in a silent cry. He was rock hard within seconds.

"I've taken you drugged, and now I'm taking you after giving you the opportunity to fight back. I've defeated you, Hope. Accept it." Leaning down, he growled into her ear. "Consider yourself owned, beautiful."

Releasing her breast, he ripped the pants from her body, his hands coming up to find skin swollen and ready for his touch. "I love a girl who gets turned on by a fight." Forcefully, he slipped his fingers over the skin, forcing them inside. She cried out and he lowered his head to bite down into her skin, to mark her, to claim her, to take control over a body he would never let escape.

Her body bucked and quivered beneath him, her hands moving up to wrap within the thickness of his hair. Her fingers twisted in deeper

120

as he nipped along her skin, kissing the sting before moving to the next spot; his hand working in a slow rhythm against her. Her muscles loosened and he let go of her throat to rip his own pants from his body, to grasp her hip, lifting her, then sliding her over him, spearing himself inside her heat. Her head fell back and he reached up, twisting his hands tighter into her hair, pulling her head back, her chest forward, and bending down to bite her breast through the thin cotton of her shirt.

. . .

She didn't want to melt around him. She didn't want her body to grip him, desperate for him to move; but her body was a traitor and her mind was overcome by the mixture of pleasure and pain, adrenaline and endorphins, by the chilling heat of his body mixed with the biting cold of her loss of control.

Like a sedative injected in her system, her body relaxed when the first bits of electricity coursed along her nerves. The sensation of being filled, of being bitten; he'd seized her body and mind, rendering her loose and malleable in his arms. Floating within a cloud of sensation and heat, her lips parted to release a guttural moan, something that her body had produced to relieve her of the waves of passion and pain that consumed her.

Raising his head from her breast, she groaned at the loss, only to open her eyes and notice how he smirked up at her, fully aware how he drove her body without gaining permission from her mind.

"No worries, beautiful girl. I'll give you what you need. But first..." His hips swiveled beneath, stretching her, invading her. "...I'm taking what I want."

With one hand on her, he forced her hips tight to his; his fingers traveling up her back, the tips digging against the bruised and overworked muscles. She responded out of instinct, her body moving in a carnal rhythm, desire sparked by violence and stoked by her ache for darkness and abject need.

His hands gripped into her hair again, pulling her head back and exposing her neck as he trailed his lips across the taut skin, nipping and kissing away the pain it caused. Small moans escaped her lips, but when those sounds grew louder and more wild, he covered her mouth taking not only her body, but her breath as well.

She came apart suddenly and her mind splintered; the shards strewn and scattered. She opened her eyes to see the heat in his, his own mind obviously lost to his domination of her – to the possibility of taming her. It had been systematic – her body, her mind, her ability to defend herself. Methodically, he'd conquered her. And now, as his touch destroyed her, he gave her life at the same time. She awakened in his arms, ripped from the obscurity she sought and thrown into a world of sensation, of ecstasy, of a dream hidden within a nightmare.

His entire body tensed when he found his release and she split apart to feel him swell inside her and his teeth bite down onto her exposed neck. Forcing parts of her darkness out of her, he replaced it with his own. Her mouth opened and a scream burst from her chest and throat. She was marked – she was defeated – and she was now hopelessly and irrevocably owned.

Chapter Twelve

She went limp over him, a consequence of her exhaustion from captivity combined with the physical exertion of the fight. But, it wasn't sleep that found her. He knew that she floated within a dream, her body so responsive to sensation that, finally, her mind had been granted divinity and bliss.

Pulling away was difficult, but he knew that Aaron would come slamming through those doors if the room went completely silent. Placing the sweatpants back on her body, he also dressed himself and picked her up to leave the room. Pushing the wooden door open with his shoulder, he looked at Aaron.

"I won."

An eyebrow arched in mockery on Aaron's face when he responded, "So, I heard."

Xander didn't respond, his intent to return Hope to his room too urgent for polite conversation. He groaned when he heard Aaron following behind him.

"Do not forget, Xander, she has information that we need. Was it absolutely necessary to knock her out after fucking her?!"

Xander stopped in his tracks, allowing Aaron to catch up and walk beside him. When they started forward again, Xander answered, "I didn't knock her out. She passed out." Under his breath, he quickly added, "She has a tendency of doing that around me."

"Get the information, Xander. You've played your bullshit game. I'm not happy about how much fucking time this is taking!"

Stopping and turning to look into infuriated green eyes, Xander responded, "As soon as she wakes up, I'll get whatever information we need."

Aaron stopped in the middle of the corridor, allowing Xander to march off carrying Hope in his arms. Reaching his suite, he opened the doors and quickly traversed the space to his bedroom where he laid Hope on the freshly cleaned sheets, binding her wrists just in case she woke up and he wasn't there to restrain her.

After securing her, Xander went into the bathroom to retrieve hot water, a cloth and a medical kit he kept in order to tend to minor injuries. He cleaned the blood from her body where the wound on her shoulder had ripped and he also cleaned the wounds on her ankles and wrists from the shackles that had also seeped wisps of crimson liquid. Searching her skin, he found areas that had started to swell with the beginnings of a bruise. Cleaning those, he then applied a salve in an attempt to keep the wounds from becoming worse. Once he'd completed what he could, he walked back into the bathroom and examined his own body in the mirror. After looking over the developing bruises and cuts on his face, he stripped

125

off his shirt to find the matching bruises to his arms and chest. Laughing to himself, he was impressed with the amount of damage she'd done to him in so short a period of time. He wondered, if she'd been at full strength, if the fight had been fair, would she have managed to break bones, to tear at his skin, to win against him.

Returning to the bedroom, he looked her over, noticing how the pain of her injuries still affected the way she held herself even when unconscious. He wanted to wake her and take her again, but the stitches in her shoulder had split and he forced himself from the room in search of someone who could help him repair the damage.

. . .

"She's been stitched up again, but there will be a scar. The wound has been reopened too often and the skin torn."

Hope wasn't sure she heard the small, delicate voice that spoke whisper soft somewhere within the room.

"Why are you looking at me like I'm the monster? It was her stubbornness that caused it." Another voice; deeper, more wild – his voice.

There was no response, just the sound of boots as they exited the room and the muted sound of a door closing in the distance. Without opening her eyes, Hope knew someone was still close by, watching her while she slept.

126

Her arms were bound, but she didn't feel the same cold bite of steel encircling her ankles. She moved to relieve the muscle and flesh of her body where it lay against the mattress. Blinking the room into focus, she saw Maddy sitting at a table in the corner of the room. She held a book open in front of her, laughing quietly at something written on the pages. Hope pushed herself up into a sitting position, crossing her legs at the ankles and bending her knees to bring her legs up in front of her chest.

"How are you feeling?" Maddy closed the book and placed it on the table. Her hair flowed down her back like ebony silk. Her blue eyes shone out and caught the small bits of light in the room, sparkling like precious jewels set into the smooth, alabaster skin of a porcelain doll. Her beauty was unreal.

"I've been better." Hope answered after deciding that struggling against Maddy was pointless. "I could really use some water."

Maddy stood quickly and disappeared into the bathroom before reappearing with a filled glass in her hand. Sitting on the edge of the mattress, she handed the glass to her. Hope took it, eyeing the glass while her hand shook from the weight – her body having been pushed to limits that made her weak. Maddy must have noticed her hesitancy.

"It's only water. Drink, it'll make you feel better." Reaching up, Maddy helped steady the glass when Hope brought it to her chapped lips. The liquid flowed over her tongue and throat, cooling the skin and muscle that burned from a lack of moisture. When she'd finished, Maddy placed the glass aside. Both women had nothing to say to one another and after a weighted pause, Maddy finally spoke into the silence.

"He'd be pissed to find me sitting here. Both of them are overprotective to an extreme." Her face scrunched up in annoyance. "Sometimes, I don't know what's worse: this place or being made to feel like I'm fragile and easily broken."

Hope blinked in surprise, her mind not comprehending how Maddy could be calm in the light of everything that had happened. "They kidnapped you. How can speak about them with endearment in your tone?"

Maddy's blue eyes were relentless in their depth. "Joseph Carmichael kidnapped me. Aaron and Xander did what they could to help me. Their methods were not their choice, but the only option they had."

"And what were those methods?" Not being able to hold her curiosity, Hope quickly voiced her question.

"They trained me."

"To fight?"

"To be a slave."

The confusion must have been evident in Hope's expression because Maddy elaborated, "Sometimes, when you are trapped in a situation with no escape, taking a role of weakness protects you. Fighting against a force you have no expectation of defeating will only make the despair that much more devastating. I see Hell in your eyes, Hope. I see a nightmare behind the gold – a nightmare that once existed in mine."

"You're still here," Hope interrupted.

Maddy smiled. "There is beauty in everything, even in the things we hate the most. I am still trapped by The Estate, yes; but I chose to remain here."

"Why?"

"For love. Aaron and Xander are not good men. But, buried somewhere deep within their souls is a brilliant light, one that grows brighter once it's found. It exists within you as well and I think Xander is intent in bringing it out of you. He's become protective of you, although he won't admit it."

"Xander has done nothing but abuse me." Hope's words were saturated with venom, with the hatred and puzzlement that she felt. She found it unnerving that her heart rate could speed, that her skin could tingle, that a warmth could develop inside her even though she wanted nothing more than to hate him.

"Is that all?" Maddy's smile crooked up, her expression speaking to some knowledge or thought unknown to Hope.

Thick silence fell over them again, only lifted by Maddy's next words. "When is the last time any person made you feel something - anything?"

Hope immediately thought of her sister, the only light that existed in the abysmal truth of her life. She didn't want to speak of Honor, her heart gripped with fear that her sister no longer existed. "I don't know what you mean."

Maddy paused a bit before saying, "You don't have to tell me. But think about it for yourself. I assume you feel nothing - that you have to be cold to hunt and kill, to take people's lives for nothing more than money or request. Beyond that, who has made you feel anything? Love, hate, happiness or misery? Who has been able to affect you so much that you feel human and not like a machine?"

"Why does that matter?"

Maddy shook her head, amusement playing over her face. "Why do you think it matters? It must be lonely, never connecting to anything or anyone — a life always moving, always hiding in shadows. I understand the need to grow cold, but if something can create a spark within you, can break through the fog, I think you should give it a chance to show you just how alive you can become."

Hope's brows furrowed over her eyes at Maddy's bewildering words. Before she could respond, the sound of the front door opening announced the presence of another person in the suite and Maddy stood up to return to the seat where she'd originally sat when Hope had awoken.

Heavy boots fell rhythmically across the stone floors and, from the corner of her eye, Hope could see broad shoulders when Xander entered the room. "Cricket, I need you to leave." His words were curt yet forceful, his tone business-like in its formality.

Maddy didn't object, instead she eyed Xander for a moment before quietly grabbing her book and walking from the room. Xander waited for the door to open and close before turning his attention to Hope. "You have information that I need and I've played your silly games. Tell me why you are here."

She was struck by the urgency of his words. "Why should I…"

His hand was around her face, his fingers digging painfully in her cheeks. With a voice low and barely controlled, he interrupted, "I'm tired of your arguments. You asked to be defeated. I've done so. The next option is death. Do NOT think we can't discover the information ourselves." His voice grew frustrated, his eyes squeezing shut before opening again. "I know what network you are from. We will kill them all, one by one, until we have our answer. If you care anything for the people with whom you are connected, you'll tell me what I want to know."

She glared up at him, noticing quickly his unyielding stare. Shaking her face from his grip, she yelled, "And what makes you think it is MY network that attacks you? Maybe you should spend less time raping women and more time checking on your own men!" She couldn't help her sudden release of anger. It was HIS people that forced her into this, HIS people that held her sister.

He looked shocked and angry, but eventually his expression grew bored once again. "It's about fucking time. Tell me more so we can get somewhere."

Frustrated tears leaked from her eyes. She feared he would kill every person in that house, not taking the time to judge them for guilt or innocence before cutting them down. When she didn't respond again, he breathed out an exaggerated breath and sat down beside her. Her chains rattled when she moved as far away from him as possible. Heat burned along her skin to look at him, making her more angry and confused at his presence.

"What is so important that you risk your life to protect it?" His voice was softer, hinting at concern she did not want to believe he felt towards her. When he reached out to touch her arm, she was angry at how her body tingled, how she wanted to lean into him, to feel him cover her body with his. Her thoughts drifted to what Maddy had said before Xander arrived. Yes. He made her feel things she'd never felt before, made her shiver in memory of the peace he'd granted her mind with the pain he'd granted her body. Lost to the realization, she was startled when his words broke through her thoughts.

"Will dying protect the reason you are here?"

She was unable to talk; her mind reeling against his presence, her heart torn apart by the fear that Honor was gone. It disgusted her that her body was reacting with heat towards a man that had done nothing but take advantage – his methods were objectionable and immoral. Yet, somehow, despite her desire to hate him fully, to reject him as thoroughly as she should, she found comfort with him by her side.

Xander grew restless next to her, but appeared sad when he looked away and said, "I have no choice but to allow Aaron to drag the information from you. I doubt you'll survive his methods."

Her eyes shot to his when he looked back in her direction. "If I tell you it was your men who sent me, what will you do?"

"Not that it will be any of your concern, but they'll be executed immediately."

"That's why I've haven't told you. You'd kill indiscriminately. It's well known that The Estate leaves nothing behind in its wake."

"Why do you fucking care?!" The volume in his tone increased sharply.

"Because they have my sister!"

His eyes widened with understanding, and he didn't even flinch in reaction to the way she yelled back at him, mimicking the intensity of his anger. He spoke slowly, pronouncing each word with care. "We're going to start from the beginning. I need every detail you know."

"Why?" She glared up at him again. "So you can find out what you want to know only to kill me and my sister while punishing your men? It seems to me that if I keep my mouth shut, I'll live a longer life."

He smiled and reached out to grab her chin. She attempted to pull away but his grip was too strong.

"You must not remember what I told you in that gym" The hint of a dark thought graced his expression.

Her eyes peeked up at him from beneath her lashes.

"You are owned, Hope. I have far more uses for you alive than I do if you were dead."

"Fuck you."

His eyes darkened and his chiseled jaw pulsed from his clenched teeth. Eventually he tore into the thick silence, by admitting, "That's one of them – yes."

Her heart fluttered in her chest and her mind reacted with uncertainty and dread. Had he taken her body prisoner while at the same time capturing her heart?

His expression grew serious. "Is your sister like you? Does she kill?"

A single tear slipped down her cheek. "No. She's innocent … an artist. She wouldn't hurt a fly."

The murderous expression that manifested on his face took Hope by surprise. His skin reddened and his body quivered with anger. "How long have they had her." His words were like cold steel slicing across the thickness of the air.

"I'm not sure anymore." Softer, she added, "Thanks to you."

He looked at her with twin blue gems floating within the white fire of his eyes. "It's been three days. You should have told me when we first caught you!" Rage lit his eyes impossibly brighter.

"Would you have cared about my reason when you first took me? I'm nothing more than an assassin, a threat. And my sister is of no use to you either. You would have killed her along with everybody else in that house. You may still. If I can get back to her, I have a chance of getting her out, of saving her life."

His face softened, sympathy obvious behind the blue of his eyes. "I'm sorry to say this but more than likely, she's dead already; and if not, she'll want to be."

Fury bloomed in Hope's chest. But her shock at his next words, was like ice through her veins.

"And we wouldn't have killed everyone, we have no desire to take innocent lives. You can choose to believe me or not, it doesn't matter, but this information needs to be given to Aaron. He'll make the final decision regarding what will be done."

She opened her mouth to respond, but placed a finger against it to silence her. "You've lost. It's time you accept your defeat – fighting will only lead to further embarrassment and injury." Uncovering her mouth, he leaned in and placed a light kiss on her lips. "I prefer not to have to punish you further."

Her ability to speak was stolen by what he'd said. Anger tickled along her spine, but something else, something she'd never felt and couldn't recognize grew inside her – simultaneously frightening and exciting her.

He moved away from her and off the bed. "I'm going to call Aaron. I'm sure he'll want to discover what you know as soon as possible."

When he left the room, he took the feeling of strength and control with him and Hope balled over herself wondering how she'd gone from absolute hatred, to a weak kneed response when he was near. She was angry, she didn't know whether she could believe him or if she could trust him, but given that he'd obliged her, that he'd proven his ability to dominate and overpower her, she knew he was the only chance she had to save her twin.

Chapter Thirteen

Honor's body felt broken, her bones and muscles battered and bruised, the scalding water burning the areas where her skin had been torn. She didn't dare smile even though she knew she was being prepared. Whenever they bathed her – her angel came to her, gave her another chance to prove her obedience.

They pulled her from the cement slab, the metal slats of the grate imprinted across her legs where'd she been sat over it. Even though she could barely move, and even though her body had been pushed to a point where she could no longer fight, could no longer resist the actions of the monsters that held her – she smiled. It no longer bore the crimson stain of their punishment. Her skin was washed clean and he would be pleased with her beauty.

Thrown into a corner of the room, they no longer bound her arms and legs; realizing that her body was too frail and her mind was too far gone for her to attempt escape. She knew that her angel was the only person who had the power to remove her from this place. She wanted to please him – HAD to please him. She was tired of the nightmare. She wanted to be good.

She heard a noise at the door, the knob flicking once...twice...three times...until finally the dark wood broke away from the wall and his body filled the broad expanse of the doorway.

She wanted to call to him but knew better than to speak. He liked her to moan, to cry...but never to scream or talk unless told. She hated the pain, hated having to bite her lip against the splitting agony, to taste the bitter iron on her tongue.

"Are you ready for me today, pet? You've been punished enough for your last failure."

She nodded, not daring to make a sound or disappoint him. She knew she was ready, her body numb to the abuse of the monsters, only her angel taking the part of her that led inside.

He lifted her by her arms, supporting the weight of her body where her legs now failed her. She cringed in fear that he'd be angry with her weakness, but he carried her, granting her a reprieve from her shame of not being strong enough to move in front of him.

Placing her over the ice cold, metallic surface, he secured her in chains, exposing her in all places he cared to explore. She was his pet, his to do with as he pleased and to do so without the complaint of her screams.

His hands rubbed along the bruised muscles of her ass. "It'll be a shame to damage this body further. Behave my pet so I can take you away, so I can rebuild you into the most perfect of my possessions.

Slowly he walked around her, eventually moving in front and holding a rubber strap in his hands. "Open your mouth."

139

Placing the strap in her mouth, he instructed, "This will protect your mouth. You can bite down without breaking your teeth. Thank your angel."

Speaking around the strap through her mouth, she responded, "Thank you."

After he fastened two small chains to the ends of the strap where it stuck out at the sides of her mouth, he walked behind her, using the chains to pull at her like the reins on a horse. Her head lifted, the skin of her neck stretched taut and overextended from the position.

He pushed inside, not slowing to give her body a chance to accept his width. She bit down, but didn't scream, however she wasn't yet happy with herself — they reached this point before. It was what came next that scared her.

Moving within her, she heard the skin of his body slapping against her, felt his width rubbing along the walls of her core. Her moans joined his, her mind in a state of elation that she'd behaved, her body trembling at the force of his strokes within her.

"Let me know how you like my gift, pet."

She moaned, the release of the sound causing him to swell within her - her body quivering violently around him as he moved.

Heat blossomed inside, building like an avalanche about to cover her completely, her breath stolen by the peak over which he drove her. Just as she neared the edge, was about to be lost to an oblivion of primal pleasure, he pulled out. She wanted to cry, but

140

bit down her frustration knowing that her complaint would not please him.

His hand rubbed over her ass again, his finger finding the small delicate space. She trembled, knowing what would come.

She felt him position himself, pushing forward one quick time before pushing again, burying himself fully within. The skin ripped and despite biting into the strap, she couldn't contain the scream that burst from her body.

Ignoring her pain, he powered against her until he found the release he sought. When he pulled free, her sobs shook her body more than what he'd just done. She heard his boots across the floor as he came around the table to face her. Once he'd removed the strap from her mouth, she felt where her lips had torn from the thickness of the rubber. He grabbed her hair, pulling her mouth open again.

"Remove your shame, pet. Perhaps next time you'll be ready for me."

Chapter Fourteen

Xander stood by the side of the bed, his eyes raking across Hope's back when he instructed, "I'll need to restrain you for the walk. When I remove the shackles from your wrists, I want you to sit up and put your arms behind you without struggling against me. The wound on your shoulder needs to heal."

Aaron had ordered that Xander present Hope in the ballroom. His body had flinched in reaction to the words, resonant of a time when being summoned meant you were about to be introduced to unspeakable horror.

Hope looked up at him from the bed. Behind the metallic color of her eyes, he could see her struggle with whether she would do as told or continue to fight against him. The warrior had not yet been tamed within her and Xander was pleased that her spirit wasn't so easily broken. She continued to impress him even now that she'd been cornered and broken down. He hoped the glint of rebellion never truly left her eye, it was what attracted him, made him so intoxicated with heat and desire that he could barely control himself when he was near her.

They stared at each other; their eyes exchanging words without breaking the silence in the room. He willed her to do as she was told and she fought against him. The beauty of her eventual submission was more exquisite than Xander could imagine. Slowly, acceptance passed over her expression, her eyes still alight with a small flame not easily extinguished. But her body turned, the long, lean muscles moving over her frame as her hands came behind her, the backs resting on the mattress as she resigned herself to his dominion.

Extracting the key from his pocket, he quickly released her from the chains and replaced those with handcuffs. But even those actions, simply touching her skin as he removed her from one binding just to replace it with another – his body burned with need and he grit his teeth to pull his hands away in order to comply with Aaron's orders.

Once she was secured, he walked around the bed, noting how she sat with her legs bent beneath her, her face turned down and her mahogany hair a curtain hiding the expression she wore. His clothes hung loosely over her shoulders and he wished to dress her in attire more suited to the spirit he knew existed within her. He stood in front of her, watching as she sat reverently and completely still. He didn't want to take her from the room, wasn't sure he wanted to share her splendor with the occupants of the ballroom.

Grabbing her by the elbow, he led her off the bed and to the front door of his suite. Leaning into her, he covered her back with his chest, his breath trailing down her neck when he said, "Behave when in Aaron's presence. He is not as patient as I am, he won't tolerate rebellion and I guarantee you that his methods of 'correction' are not as *generous* as mine."

The walk was familiar; nothing but the sound of his booted steps echoing through the empty corridors as they made their way to the ballroom. Xander felt ill to look upon the foreboding wooden doors when they neared their destination – memories and flashbacks of the nightmares played out on the other side of the doors, the haunting sound as they opened before him and the terrifying sound as they closed at his back.

Entering the space, he noticed the absence of the members of The Estate, the tables sitting empty where an audience once sat. Looking towards the raised platform at the front of the room, he saw Aaron, Maddy and Jason standing together talking; awaiting the arrival of a woman they considered to be their enemy, a person not worthy of respect or remorse.

Aaron turned away from the group first, Maddy taking that as her cue to sit down and Jason taking it as his to exit the stage and take a seat amongst the empty tables of the room.

Xander walked Hope to the center of the room, the same space where Maddy had been presented to Joseph – where she'd been introduced to disgrace and shame on a scale unbelievable to even the most cruel hearted of men. A thick blanket of tension settled over the barely occupied room, the smallest sounds echoing across the walls. Light flickered over Hope's hair

144

and skin and Xander looked up at the crystal chandelier in the room, wondering if it cast its iridescent spark upon her body as a sign of pardon or in condemnation.

"Thank you for joining us, Ms. Delacroix." Aaron's voice rang throughout the room, his tone and demeanor inflexible in its reproach. "Xander has explained that you are ready to tell us the reason behind your attempt on my life." No emotion existed within his words; the absence of which hinted towards the dark anger to which he'd fallen. Xander looked up into the concerned look on Maddy's face – she'd also recognized the deep black that wrapped itself around him. Hope didn't respond, didn't even bother to look up from the floor, the shame of having been defeated resting heavily on her once proud shoulders.

. . .

Dread trickled along her spine when Xander walked her through the empty halls and through two large doors that led to the place where all of this had started. That dread warped and twisted as soon as the doors closed and she listened as each person took their place in the room and her skin crawled at the sound of Aaron's voice, a warning hidden within his words.

Her mouth was suddenly dry, her throat swelling with anger and resentment, with fear and regret. She felt Xander behind her, the warmth of his body rolling over hers, an unsettling comfort. The muscles of her body tensed, her instinct

145

screamed for her to fight, but her mind – her spirit – those felt broken and dissolved.

"I suggest you speak quickly, Ms. Delacroix. I'm losing my patience."

She felt Xander's hand against her back, his touch softly goading her into a response. She raised her face to look at Aaron, her hair falling back from her forehead and cheeks, her eyes opened wide against the brilliant light played across the surfaces of the room.

Her mouth was dry when she finally answered, "You were attacked by your own men. I'm as much a victim in this as you."

Aaron's shoulders rolled back on his frame and his mouth set into a thin line. The emerald green of his eyes shot quickly to Xander and Jason before returning to Hope. "Explain."

She sighed, finally resigning to the fact that she had no choice but to speak. "My sister was abducted three weeks ago. I was contacted by a member of your network demanding that I enter The Estate compound and meet him if I wanted to see her alive again. I complied and I was told that either I killed you or she died. Given that I like her more than I like you, I made my choice."

She could see every muscle on his body tense, but then he relaxed again, not truly affected by the insult. "Who was he?"

"He never gave me a name, or, at least, a real one."

146

"You could have come to us with the information."

"And sit back and watch you slaughter every person in that house, including my sister? Your network is known for the sick and depraved. I doubted you'd concern yourself with the welfare of a forced whore."

"That's a shame, Ms. Delacroix. We might have been able to help you retrieve your sister. As it stands now, I doubt she lives given that you weren't successful in your attempt on my life and that fact has undoubtedly spread throughout the entirety of The Estate."

His words were another blow to her chest, the pain underlain by the question of whether or not he told the truth.

"How many people were in the house when you arrived."

"Fifteen guards – fourteen after I removed one's head. Seven women, all drugged, including my sister."

It was dead quiet in the room as Aaron appeared to think over the information he'd been given. Hope jumped a little when he finally interrupted the silence.

"Jason, I put you in charge of the searches. How did the slaves go unnoticed?"

A man approached the raised stage, his hair a shock of white atop the sun-kissed skin of his body. He was the same height as Hope, but three times as wide. There was something about him that disturbed her; the way he moved, or the way he held his body; she couldn't be sure. He turned to look at Hope as he passed and the eerie silver of his eyes stole her breath momentarily. He stared at her for a moment, looked at her with more familiarity than he should.

Glancing back to Aaron, he answered, "Patrick and I both ran the searches. I can only speak for the houses I personally entered. I guarantee you, slaves were not being kept. I'm unsure how they would have escaped Patrick's notice as well." He looked between Aaron and Hope, before adding, "I'm not sure that what she tells us is entirely accurate, Aaron. It could be a ruse to create a problem within the network, in order to weaken the whole by setting the individual units against each other."

Aaron stood frighteningly still following Jason's suggestion. A snake ready to strike, his green eyes shifted between Hope and Jason. When she didn't cower under his burning gaze, he appeared surprised that, even though she should be terrified of what would happen, she refused to show fear in the face of her biggest threat. She stood taller, rolling her shoulders back in response to the suggestion that she was lying. She couldn't understand how the women had been missed, if searches were conducted, but she would make sure it didn't happen again.

"I'll take you to the house. Right now, if need be. If you intend to remove my sister without harming her, I'll do whatever it takes to assist you." Struggling to keep her voice calm, Hope allowed herself to sink to a dark place, to separate herself from the soul crippling fear that something had happened to Honor – that something could happen now that she'd involved Aaron Carmichael.

His green eyes were impassive when he turned his attention to her. When he spoke again, he did so in a formal and controlled manner. "You've attempted my life once, and now, you expect me to have you at my back? I'm sorry, Ms. Delacroix, but I haven't survived as long as I have by making foolish decisions."

She felt Xander's hand against her, somehow knowing that Aaron's words had upset him. Feeling his anger like a cloud at her back, she shivered against its heat, pulling her from the unfeeling void to which she was attempting to escape.

Since Hope had entered the room, Maddy had been quiet in her chair behind Aaron. However, when Aaron grew quiet, she finally punctured the silence with her delicate voice. "If what she says is true, you should go tonight."

Aaron twisted his body to look her at her, before she continued, "No woman should have to live as a slave."

Hope's jaw dropped and she looked between Aaron and Maddy, not understanding how she was a slave speaking out against the very thing

149

Aaron had done to her. Noticing how Aaron's expression softened at Maddy's words only served to confuse Hope further.

Turning back, he asked, "Are you able to describe the house, location and features?"

Her stomach twisted over itself, she didn't want them going in without her, didn't want them handling her sister not knowing what would be done with her. But what choice did she have? "Yes."

"Xander, I want you to obtain the necessary information from Ms. Delacroix and place her back in the cell. Once that's accomplished, meet me in my suite. Jason, you will be coming with us as well. If what she says is true, I want any men involved killed on sight. The Estate no longer tolerates acts against innocent lives. Dissension will result in death."

Xander's hand wrapped her bicep almost immediately and he pushed her along through the ballroom towards the doors leading into the west wing. When they'd closed behind him, he stopped before pulling her back to his chest. His mouth rested against her ear, creating tremors through her body. "I promise you, no harm will come to your sister. I will make it my personal mission to see to her safety once we enter that house."

Her heart sank. Turning her head to stop his breath from rolling across her like silk, she asked, "And will she become your property as well?"

The blue of eyes churned like a mercurial sea when he responded. "It would distract me from taming you. No offense, sunshine, but it's not a distraction I want at the moment."

The quiver that ran along her spine and down her legs only intensified the fire ignited within her core by his words. Her mind reeled against the reaction.

He must have noticed her struggle because he stepped into her, the size of his body completely covering hers. "I'd take care of what your body craves right now if I didn't have to go correct your fuck up."

Like ice melted to extinguish the building flame, her expression twisted with anger, every muscle in her body tightening in its desire to fight. "How fucking dare you?"

He winked. "I have no problem speaking the truth, especially if it serves to piss you off." He leaned over and nipped at her earlobe before saying, "You're much more responsive when angry."

He didn't give her time to respond before walking her down the corridor and through a doorway she recognized as the room where she'd been held initially. He immediately bound her arms and legs, but left her enough slack in the chain where she could sit or lie down."

Looking her over, his eyes heated at the sight of her bound and rendered helpless. He knelt before her, grabbing her by her hair and pulling her face towards him. His mouth brushed across hers before pushing again - taking control of her body while silencing the confusion, anger, and insurrection that swirled like a storm within her mind.

Pulling away, his voice dropped to a deep timbre when he admitted, "I hope the spark of rebellion never dies inside you. I enjoy stripping you of your fight every time I light you up inside."

Her eyes widened.

"Tell me which house."

The details slipped easily from her lips, her resolve broken far enough that even something as small as a kiss was enough to leave her loose and malleable.

He smiled once she'd confessed. "Good girl."

Standing, he walked to the door, looking back at her one more time before disappearing out into the lit corridor. When the door shut closed again, Hope was left with nothing but the light of the moon and stars shining through the glass ceiling above her.

Chapter Fifteen

"I don't think she'd lie about this, Aaron."

Xander watched as Aaron pulled on his leather trench, strapping steel blades of all shapes and sizes to his body. They'd prepared for battle together many times in the past and, like those times, they'd covered themselves in enough weaponry to take out a hundred men.

"She has every reason to lie." The green of his eyes roiled with barely controlled anger. "And I'm concerned that you've let down your guard with this woman. If we go there tonight and find nothing, she dies immediately when we return. I've been patient to this point, but I won't allow her to twist your head any further."

"I'm perfectly capable of keeping my head in her presence." Xander's body tensed at Aaron's threat, his spine straightening to think of what he'd have to do to protect Hope if Aaron truly intended what he'd said. He didn't want to think that women were being abused once again at the compound, but in this instance, he prayed it was true.

Aaron stared at him before silently turning to exit the room, Xander quickly falling in step at his back. Entering the living room, he saw Maddy pacing nervously in the kitchen while Jason sat relaxed back into the couch. Straightening at

153

Aaron's presence, Jason commented, "I've spoken with Patrick, he will meet us at the house."

Aaron's face swiveled quickly in Jason's direction. "Did I instruct you to do so?"

Jason staggered as he stood, taken back by the cold fury of Aaron's tone. "No."

"Let's hope it was a wise decision for you to contact Patrick, considering it was his search that failed. I suggest that, in the future, you conduct yourself as instructed without making assumptions that I would want you to do anything further."

Jason's entire body froze at the menace in Aaron's tone. Xander remained quiet, knowing full well that Aaron had slipped into his role as the executioner. As dangerous as a hair trigger, Aaron could react unexpectedly to even the slightest perceived insult, attack or disobedience on the part of his men. Jason appeared to understand as well, and his hands immediately rose in defeat.

"I apologize, Aaron. I didn't intend to overstep your authority. I only thought..."

"Then don't fucking think."

Every person in that room stilled, Maddy immediately facing the floor in reaction to Aaron's anger. Xander knew she couldn't help it – that she used it as a means to hide from the depth of Aaron's rage.

Stepping towards the front door, Aaron turned back to look at Xander and Jason as they walked behind him. "Do not forget, if you know these men or are their friends, they have taken part in an attack against The Estate. Regardless of the relationship you have with them, their punishment is death. Do not hesitate or it will be your death as well."

Exiting a side door, the men poured out into the black of night, six boots marching in unison across the ground, hard with winter's frost. Dry leaves blew at their feet as they traversed the woods, eventually finding the house lit up against the shadows and thick fog that surrounded it. Patrick stood in plain sight, feet held at shoulder width, his hands folded behind his back. He didn't notice the men at first so Aaron held up a hand, stopping Xander and Jason before they could break away from the cover of the trees.

Silently motioning them towards Patrick, Aaron indicated that he was going a different way. Xander nodded and walked away, breaking past the tree line and attracting Patrick's attention. He knew Aaron moved around back, becoming nothing but a fast moving shadow, slipping quietly through the night.

"Where's Aaron?"

Jason answered before Xander had the chance. "Change of plans, he wants us to run the search. Said if we find evidence of slaves inside, we are to kill any man that comes into sight."

Patrick's eyes narrowed for a brief second before he forcibly relaxed his expression. Xander noticed the quick slip, but said nothing before motioning for Jason and Patrick to walk ahead. He didn't fully trust either man and refused to have them at his back.

Approaching the door, they moved swiftly up the stairs of the house, Patrick taking the front while Xander and Jason stood behind him in a triangular pattern. The door swung open and the men forced their way inside, Jason apprehending the man who'd attempted to block the door when they'd rushed inside. Splitting up, each man went a different direction, quickly sweeping through the large expanse of the house. Xander kept his eye open for anything that could point to a trap door, or hiding place – a rug out of place, a separation in the wall, anything that could lead to evidence that what Hope was claiming was true. He knew her life depended on what they found tonight. If they found nothing, it would be the end of Aaron's patience with her game.

. . .

The hinges of the door creaked from age and lack of care when Hope saw light creeping inside the room from the hallway. Lifting her head, she watched Maddy's small silhouette move inside, a tray balanced in one hand while she closed the door with the other.

"I've brought food. You need to eat if you hope to heal anytime soon." As usual her melodic voice barely brushed against the silence of the

156

room. Walking softly over the floor, she approached Hope, placing the tray at her feet. Hope straightened her body, her muscles tight and knotted over her body from her uncomfortable position on the floor.

Her stomach growled angrily when she smelled the food on the plate. Maddy pushed it towards her. "It's okay, Hope, just eat. I haven't done anything to it."

Grabbing the fork on the plate, Hope quickly scooped up some white rice and shoveled it into her mouth, not caring that the shaking of her hand spilled most of it. She continued eating, her stomach churning with the introduction of something solid to digest. Maddy sat quietly watching Hope, her expression one of sympathy and remorse. When Hope had trouble swallowing down the food, Maddy handed her a bottle of water that she'd brought in the room with the food.

When the only sound in the room was the scraping of Hope's fork against the plate, Maddy shifted where she sat, her eyes searching the layout of chains in the room before refocusing on Hope. "Will you tell me about your sister?"

The sound of the metal fork falling against the ceramic plate echoed throughout the room. Hope's body tensed at the reminder that within hours she would find out the truth of Honor's fate. She prayed that her sister was alive and not shattered by whatever those men had done to her over the past weeks.

"What would you like to know?"

"Her name for starters." Maddy shrugged.

"Her name is - or was - Honor."

Maddy's eyes widened slightly. "Hope and Honor. Those are both lovely names. Is she older or younger than you."

Hope looked up and found nothing but kindness and innocent interest in Maddy's eyes. "The same age – we're twins. Well..." The sound of laughter was so foreign coming from her, it had been far too long since she'd been able to laugh. "...technically, I'm the older twin." She remembered all the years that she'd teased Honor with that fact, the look of frustration on her sister's face when Hope always told her to 'respect her elders.'

A smile peeked out on Maddy's lips. "You light up when you talk about her."

Hope's lips cracked from the small smile that snuck over her mouth. "Everything that is good can be found in her. She's the only person that can truly see me, that can understand and not judge certain parts about me."

"She's not the only one."

Their eyes met and Maddy's shimmered with honesty. "There's someone else that gets you, even though the time you've spent together hasn't been under the best circumstances."

Hope blinked. "If you're talking about Xander, you do realize the bastard drugged me, raped me, and has pretty much taken advantage of everything he could with me."

It was odd to Hope how Maddy didn't seem offended by what she'd just heard. Growing up in the networks, the acts Hope had described were commonplace, most people didn't even bat an eye to hear of it being done; but Maddy hadn't grown up in the networks and she had been made into one of the worst types of victims: a slave. Death was preferable to a person like Hope.

"You attempted to kill Aaron - to kill Xander, as well. Did you expect him to fall to his knees and beg you to play nice?"

Hope laughed softly.

"Xander did what he had to do. I think you're more upset with the fact that he was able to get to you, more so than the methods he used to accomplish it."

"He's annoying."

Maddy laughed. "Yes, he is."

Hope looked at her, noticed Maddy's endearment for Xander written across her expression. "He won't stop calling me 'sunshine'"

Maddy's face puckered, looking like she'd just bitten into a lemon before she burst out in laughter again. Holding her hand out, she said,

"Hello, Sunshine. It's nice to meet you. My name is Cricket."

"Seriously? That has to be aggravating. Why does he call you that?"

"I have no idea. He won't tell me."

Hope grinned. "I'd stab him for something like that."

Her expression softened. "I can't say I haven't considered it."

The door slammed open and Hope's eyes immediately shot to Xander when he burst into the room.

"Maddy, you need to go back to your suite now." Quickly crossing the room, he grabbed Maddy by her arm and lifted her from where she sat on the floor. "Go to Aaron. Get out of the west wing."

"Where's my sister?" Hope interrupted Xander's obvious panic with her own.

Pushing Maddy towards the door, he ignored Hope. "Go now."

Without another word, Maddy hurried from the room, allowing the door to slam behind her.

"Where's my sister?" Hope looked up, her eyes narrowing from fear.

160

He didn't answer, just knelt down in front of her, pulling cuffs and the leash from the pockets of his long coat. Hope flinched away. "What happened to my sister? Answer me!"

His hand was suddenly wrapped over her face so tight, the bones of her jaw and cheek ached from the pressure. His eyes looked black when he stared at her. "Do not say another fucking word if you want to get out of here alive. I'll tell you what you want to know eventually, but for now, you'll turn the fuck around so that I can put these restraints on you and you won't resist me."

She stilled, her mind reeling with confusion, but her body reacting instantly to the force behind his tone. When she'd submitted, he let go of her face so she could turn around as told.

Chapter Sixteen

Xander led Hope down a dark trail, her feet tripping over roots sticking up from the ground. The chain of the collared leash he'd secured to her neck rattled into the bone chilling wind that blew across their bodies. He attempted to peer through the fog of night, not able to quite remember the path he'd traveled so many times as a child exploring the expanse of the compound. An owl hooted above them, the sound reminding him that predators watched him while he betrayed the man who'd become his brother.

Catching Hope before she could fall, he pulled her against him so that he could whisper to her without the wind carrying his voice to any man who looked for him. "I know you're weak, but you have to move faster. You're an assassin, put those skills to work now, make no sound as you walk." She looked up at him and his eyes burned back down at her.

"Be a shadow, your life depends on it."

Moving quickly across the path he found again, he shook his head. Aaron was out for blood and Xander didn't know how long he could hide before the edge of Aaron's steel ran across the perfection of Hope's body. They'd searched the house and found nothing except for the indignation of the unit leader who lived in the house. Once everything had been searched and when no chains, or blood, or other evidence of Hope's story could be found, Xander watched as Aaron's eyes darkened, as revenge and vehemence coursed through his veins until only a single target remained – Hope. Aaron had entered that house expecting to feed his darkness. Finding nothing, he focused on the only other way he had to fulfill his need for slaughter.

The path had become overgrown through the years, and not many who remained on the property knew of the existence of this path. Xander wondered if any of the men who knew of it still remembered the way. As it was, Xander was walking blind, the canopies of the trees too thick to allow moonlight to trickle down and break up the thick black that surrounded them.

It felt like hours passed before the full moon above them came into view. They were within feet of where the tree line opened up to a small creak that ran across the compound and he sighed in relief the hear the water babbling across the rocks. Hope slowed beside him, her breath billowing out in front of her in steamed clouds that caught the gauzy light of the moon. Tugging on the leash he led her along behind him, turning once he reached the water and moving quickly towards a rock wall that jutted up from the earth – the entrance to its cave hidden by the wild shrubs growing at its base and the vines that hung over its roof.

"Go inside, sit down and don't make a sound until I return." Releasing the leash, he watched as Hope was swallowed by the dark interior of the cave before he returned his attention to the landscape around them. Xander slowly crept back to the other side of the rock wall, listening for any disturbance in the woods from which they came. After ten minutes, he relaxed to hear nothing but the rustling of leaves.

Moving back to the cave, he climbed inside. "Hope?"

"Over here."

He couldn't see her as he moved through the cave, the vines falling from the ceiling brushing over his face and hair. His hand brushed across her skin when he reached the back and found her huddled into a corner.

"Please tell me what's going on." Her voice was whisper soft and shook with the biting cold of the air.

Using his hands to feel along the wall, he searched for something he hoped remained over the many years it had been since he visited the cave. Finding a soft spot, he moved the years of dead vines covered over several times by new layers. He reached in and grasped the handle of the trunk he'd found here when he was a child.

Pulling it out, he opened the lid, grabbing the old musty blanket he knew would be folded inside. It smelled horrendous for the amount of years it had been stored, but it was warm and dry. Quickly moving back to Hope, he placed the blanket over her body attempting to warm her against the winter wind outside.

When her teeth finally stopped chattering so loud it echoed over the stone walls and ceiling, he sat beside her, leaning his head against the wall. "Your sister was not in the house. There was nothing in the house."

"What?" It was a choked question, disbelief and absolute heartache dripping from that single syllable. The tone of her voice making it obvious that she hadn't been lying when she sent them there. "I don't understand. You missed something, a false floor, a hidden door. They had to be there, unless…"

She didn't need to express her fear and Xander had already considered that when Hope failed to kill Aaron, the men had disposed of the women in case she told Aaron who'd sent her. "We missed nothing. I checked personally for any type of hiding place. The house was clean."

She was stunned silent; her gold eyes almost incandescent against the bits of light that breached the cave. Rage swirled behind the gold and her body shook in her attempt to contain the inferno within her mind and body. He listened to her breath out a deep breath, before slowly refilling her lungs to do it again.

"Let me go."

"I can't"

"Let me go. Let me the FUCK go so I can go find my sister." She lunged towards him, attempting to fight her way free despite the fact that her hands were bound at her back. She

165

pushed him back against the wall, dodging his arm as he attempted to grab her, standing up she ran quickly attempting to escape. Xander grabbed the collared chain pulling her back off her feet, her breath knocked from her when she crashed against the ground. Crawling over her, her placed his hand over her mouth and brought his face close to hers to ensure she saw in his eyes the seriousness of his words.

"Aaron Carmichael has ordered your death. If you are caught, you will be presented to him for execution, do you understand NOW why I cannot let you go?!"

She stilled beneath him. He stared at her for a few minutes, ensuring that she was listening to what he had to say next. "Even though I believe your story, Aaron does not. He believes you're attempting to play The Estate against each other. If we don't figure out what to do, he will find you and he will kill you. If your sister is alive, the only way you are going to help her is to stay alive yourself."

"I'll fight the bastard. I'm not afraid of him."

Xander's eyes clenched slowly shut as he attempted to withstand the feeling of his loyalty being torn in two. He would always protect Aaron and Maddy, would die if it was required to save one or both of their lives, but he couldn't let go of Hope either. Opening his eyes again, he answered, "I cannot let that happen."

Her eyes blinked, the gold peeking out from below her dark lashes. "Will you do something for me?"

"What?"

"Get off me. My hands are behind me and this is, quite possibly, the most uncomfortable position you've had me in yet."

A short burst of laughter broke from his mouth, but he rolled his weight off her, sitting up and reaching over to assist her into a sitting position as well.

"What can we do? If they're not at the house, I don't know where else to look." Hope dared asked a question to which she feared there would be no answer.

His tone was emotionless and cold. Slipping quickly into the role of guard and spy, he detailed what he knew, giving her the only options left to find her sister. "The house you described, it's the hub of our drug unit."

"They should be the weakest of your units. Drug runners typically rank low in the majority of the networks. Why would they attempt to kill Aaron when they stand no chance of taking over control of The Estate?"

Xander smiled, delighted to find that she was as bright as she was beautiful. He wasn't too surprised – the mark of any good assassin was the ability to think and to do so quickly.

"I can only think of two reasons, the first being that these particular men were corrupted by Joseph more than we thought. When he was alive, the mansion was a veritable abattoir. It was one of those places where you grew nervous if you didn't hear agonizing screams in the halls. The silence only meant more death..."

"That's common knowledge about this place. I don't understand how that plays into the drug runners' thinking."

"Simple. When Joseph was killed, Aaron ordered that the sexual abuse and depravity stop. We knew there would be some who were so *enchanted* with Joseph's practices that they'd either continue despite our warnings or attempt Aaron's life."

She shook her head in disbelief. "But, Aaron keeps a slave."

Xander grinned. "I would have thought you'd seen past that by now."

"Maddy's not a slave, is she?"

He stared at her for a few seconds, a small trail of moonlight breaching the vines covering the cave and resting over the gold in her eyes. Shaking his head no, he fought against the urge he had to cover her mouth with his, to grip her by her hair and bury himself inside the fire that burned inside her. Her next words interrupted the fantasy.

"What's the second reason?"

Taking a second to remember the topic, he got a grip on himself to answer. "Another change Aaron made in the network was to bring down the unit that dealt with prostitution and human trafficking. The men who lived because they accepted their reassignment were transferred to the house you identified. We're most likely dealing with men who are unwilling to give up their prior habits."

Her shoulders dropped, the knowledge of who held her sister an obvious weight on her body. Light flickered in again allowing Xander to see that she looked down and that a tear fell from her face. When the light died again and when there was nothing more to see of her than a silhouette, she looked back up again. "How can we get her back?"

"There's a warehouse owned by the network that the drug runners' utilize as a base of operation. I suspect that if they removed the women rather than killing them, they would have gone there."

"Then let's go there. Tonight." Steel inlaid the words of a warrior, Hope's voice was firm and resolute.

"We wouldn't get off The Estate property. I'm sure Aaron is plotting my death as well as yours at this very moment. There won't be an inch along the walls not covered by guards."

She was frustrated and her words sped with her anger. "But the walls must end somewhere!"

169

"If you are far enough out to where the walls end, you have a good day of hiking if you want to see civilization again. And by that point, the terrain is too difficult to manage – it's a natural barrier."

"Fuck!" She doubled over, her body shaking from the futility that consumed her. After a few moments, she gained control of herself and sat up. "How do we escape Hell?"

Xander smoothed her hair back with his hand. "We don't. The only thing we can do is wait for Aaron to calm down and hope like hell he doesn't remember that this cave exists on the property before that happens."

"That's why you sent Maddy, isn't it? She calms him."

Xander nodded in response.

It grew quiet, only the nocturnal chorus of animals and insects piercing the heavy silence. Hope moved to sit against the wall and Xander reached out to help her, choosing to sit at her side. An hour or more could have passed before she spoke again.

"If Aaron was so against sexual abuse, why did he let you rape me?" Her voice was a whisper that brushed across his ears.

Xander grinned, not ashamed of what he'd done to tame his beautiful beast. "You were an enemy. Aaron wanted information and he wanted you dead. How I obtained it was my decision."

"So, why did you do it?"

He turned to look at her in the low light of the space. "You asked me to break you, I complied."

The tone of her response gave away the fire that, once again, sparked inside her. "I was drugged."

He chuckled. "But you weren't drugged in the gym."

Her eyes widened and her mouth fell slightly open from shock. Holding her stare, he leaned forward and brushed his lips across hers. "And you aren't drugged now."

His fingers were wrapped into her hair faster than she could react to what he'd implied. Working over her leg, his other hand explored over her body when he leaned in to take her mouth fully with his.

Chapter Seventeen

His mouth melded to hers, his tongue demanding entrance while the fingers he had tangled in her hair held her head in place, allowing him to devour her slowly. Initially caught off guard by her surprise at his earlier words, she didn't see him strike before she was melting under lips skilled in stealing her breath.

Hope's body heated to feel his strong hand traveling over her tired muscles. The grip of his fingers digging into the knotted muscles, sending shooting sparks across her skin, each one relaxed under his hold. Rough from years of weapons use, the skin of his palm moved under her shirt and up her torso, each bruise ringing with pain when he touched it. She was rendered weak almost instantly, the beginnings traces of endorphins flittering through her blood. With her hands locked behind her back, her chest was pushed out, easy access for his agonizingly slow exploration of her body. He teased at the swollen flesh, brushing the tips of his fingers across skin inflamed with need for his touch. She groaned in complaint and he finally took an aggressive hold of her breast, rolling the tip between his fingers and causing her heart to pound harder against her chest.

"Tell me you don't want me now, Hope. Tell me you want me to stop giving you everything you are desperate to feel." He pinched the sensitive peak sending a jolt of painful pleasure slicing along her central nerve, sparking a fire within her core. His lips traveled along her jaw and down her neck, his hand pulling her back by the hair slowly stretching the skin for his kiss and his bite. Her breath pounded out of her, erratic and uncontrolled. Running his nose along the rim of her ear when he whispered, "Do you remember what I told you about your secret, how I would use it against you?"

She didn't respond – couldn't respond. Chuckling wickedly against her skin, he explained, "Your desperate need for pain is the only drug necessary to make you agreeable with anything I wish to do to you." He released her hair, only to grab the collared chain at her neck. Pulling her up from the wall, he kept his eyes locked to hers when he directed her to straddle his lap. "Stand up."

She watched his hand loosen over the chain, giving her just enough slack to stand, but not to move away. His eyes burned into hers, enchanted her to a point where she didn't want to look away and where she wanted to do exactly as he instructed her. She knew, that by doing so, he would reward her by taking her to a place where her thoughts would scatter and would grant her relief from the anger, fear and frustration that plagued her.

His hand gripped her pants at the ankle and she looked down to see his fingers pulling at the fabric, slowly removing the clothing from her body. Once past her hips, the fabric slipped quickly over her legs, bunching over his hand. After releasing

173

the chain, he lifted her leg, one by one, and removed the sweatpants from her body. Sliding his hands up the back of her calves, his eyes trailing along the length of her legs and up further until the sapphire blue locked to her eyes.

The small wisps of light that streamed through the cave danced across his face, illuminating the violent cut of his jaw and the deep tan to his skin. She wanted to reach out and rub her palm against the stubble on his cheek, but the cuffs prevented any exploration between them, except for his.

"Sit down." Gently tugging on the chain he directed her down so that she straddled his legs, her knees bent, her legs spread. She was exposed to him completely, incapable of moving away or fighting him off. Somehow, this man was able to render her completely helpless, yet stoke a flame within her that burned along every nerve ending in her body all at the same time.

Wrapping the chain slowly around his wrist, he smirked to gain use of both hands while still holding her restraint. Gripping the bottom hem of her shirt, he lifted the material slowly, his eyes examining every inch of her skin that came into view. Lifting it over her breasts, she felt her skin tighten and swell when she noticed the open admiration in his eyes. Eventually, those blue jewels moved to her face, locking with her eyes, burning into her.

"I don't know if you realize just how desirable you are. I suspect that, growing up,

174

nobody understood the darkness in you. They may have reacted with fear, contempt – disgust. To me, however, that darkness only makes you a rare jewel, a woman perfectly built for a man like me." When her eyes widened in surprise, he paused. "I intend to tame you completely, Hope, and not just to give to you the things your body craves, but to satisfy my own need by exploring the depths of your darkness, by sinking inside you, only to raise us both into the light. I know you disconnect yourself from everybody and everything, it's so obvious in the way you dance with death, how you throw yourself into a fight without fear of losing your life. But I won't allow you to disconnect yourself from me any longer."

"I want to touch you." The request slipped off her lips in a breathless whisper, surprising her even though she'd been the one to speak it. Her hands squeezed together behind her back from her desire to run them over the rough skin of his cheeks, through the silk strands of his hair, over the steel of his muscle covered by the smooth perfection of skin.

Wickedly, he teased, "I'm not sure I can trust removing your cuffs, how do I know you won't attempt to get away from me."

She grinned. "You'll still have your leash."

A single brow arched seductively over his darkened eye. Releasing his grip on her, he pulled a set of keys from his pocket and reached around her. She heard the metal of the key hit against the lock, the faint snap as he released it from her wrist.

However, she was surprised to hear it close again, and even more surprised to feel Xander pull their hands between them to show that their wrists were now bound together. Folding his hand over hers, he held out his other hand, completely opening himself to her touch. "I'm all yours."

Slowly lowering her hands to his chest, she sucked in a breath when her palms tingled against the warmth of his body. His form was perfection, raw strength barely contained beneath his skin. Moving her hands up, she brought them along the sides of his neck, up further, along his jaw. She savored feeling the rough skin before finally burying her hands into his thick hair, gripping her fingers tighter and watching his eyes slowly close. She didn't notice that he'd taken the leash back in his other hand, so when he tugged gently, pulling her towards him, she smiled before brushing her lips across his. His mouth pushed against her, his tongue sweeping into her mouth only briefly before his teeth nipped at her bottom lip. She pulled away and opened her eyes only to be assaulted by the intensity of his stare.

"You taste like my destruction," she whispered.

His response was spoken on a frustrated growl. "That's funny. I was just thinking the same thing about you."

Within seconds, he turned, pinning her body beneath his. He grabbed her hands, bringing them above her head. His mouth covered hers, his kiss deep, yet painfully slow. The bastard was stoking her slowly, building the heat bit by bit, until her ache for his touch became absolute torture to endure. His fingers gripped around hers, the tips digging between the tendons and bones of her hand.

Trailing his lips down the side of her neck, he teased at the sensitive skin. Small bites sending sparks along her nerves, before his tongue flicked out to smooth away the hurt. She attempted to push against him, to speed along the aggravatingly slow pace of his mouth. He chuckled across her skin, the sound vibrating through his chest and into hers. Pulling his hands away from hers, he reached between them to grab her hips and hold them in place – her hand also pulled between them from where they'd been chained together.

"Calm down, sunshine, we've got several hours to kill before sunlight. I intend to take my time."

Her eyes closed – the weight of being denied instant gratification a suffocating frustration she was unable to bear. Every sense in her body was awakened, electricity coursing through her body, anticipating his every touch, the dull shocks of pain blended perfectly with the warmth blooming inside. The sound was faint, and had she not heard it so many times herself when she'd practiced or fought, she wouldn't have recognized it at all. But, when she heard the small sound of metal sliding against a heavy leather sheath, her eyes opened again – just before she felt the blade softly slide across her skin.

Her entire body jumped at the sensation, the cold bite of steel – the threat of death dangled before her eyes, a temptation and fascination she'd carried with her for as long as she could remember. He pulled the blade down along her side, teasing her; the pressure enough to warn, to scratch the skin, but not enough to draw blood or cause harm.

His voice was a deep timbre when he whispered, "You welcome death."

Her responsive words barely escaped her. She was thoroughly seduced with the feel of the blade against her body, the knowledge that she was completely vulnerable and exposed to his whims. "Anything has to be better than the life I've lived."

Moonlight flickered off the steel, catching her eye when it flashed. When she looked back up, his eyes were locked to hers, deadly heat swirling within the blue. He stared at her for the longest time, both of their hearts beating against their chests, both of them breathing with shallow and erratic breaths. When he finally spoke into the silence that had settled between them, his words consumed her mind entirely, taking from her the ability to think clearly.

"When I'm done with you, I'll ensure you'll never welcome it again. In fact..." His voice lowered impossibly more, his words nothing more than a breathless whisper across her skin. "...The only thing you'll desire from now on, will be me."

178

The tip of the blade pricked the skin of her hip and, although the pain was nothing more than a quick bite against her skin, her anticipation for it caused it to erupt along her body in waves, her mind instantly locked within the comfortable numbness of sensation and need – his voice echoing in her thoughts as she was lost to the incredible force of his touch.

Before him, and before this moment, she'd always needed more pain to make her feel, to bring a small bit of the reminder of life into her psyche. But, because he affected her so deeply, and worshipped her with such admiration and restraint, even the tiniest amount that he gave her became an unbridled passion within her body - as if she'd been stung by a bee, but felt like she'd jumped from a cliff to land on the jagged rocks below. He put her in a place where a simple kiss against her skin was enough to steal her breath and push her towards a plateau of ecstasy so steep, she feared she'd lose herself when he finally forced her over the edge.

She heard the thin knife strike against pebbles when he dropped it to the ground beside their bodies. His palm, rough from the use of weapons, replaced the sting of steel; warm instead of cold, soft instead of sharp. Running his hand along the same path he'd dragged the knife, the salt of his skin seeped into the thin scratch. Her body arched, her mind reeling that the simplest touch could pull her apart.

Almost instantly, every muscle in her body relaxed, completely submitting to the man who held her.

She allowed him to set their grueling rhythm, losing herself within the slow pace rather than fighting against it. Surrendering to the domination of her body and mind, she allowed him to take her to a place within herself she'd never known. It was warm and comforting, something hidden deep inside, far from the daily dance with death. She didn't want to leave this place, not when he was the one responsible for taking her there.

His hands were rough where they traveled across her skin. But the softness of his touch disturbed her. It was a caress, something tender and strange and she grabbed at his hand where it was connected to hers, directing his touch along her body rougher and harder. He resisted, and became still above her.

"Why pain?"

His words were so soft, she wasn't sure she'd heard them correctly. Opening her eyes, she looked at his face, watching him study the scar on her body that he traced with his finger. His face was bathed in shadow and she couldn't see the emotion hidden in his eyes, but she could feel it – the reverence, the care, and the sadness when he looked at her.

Her chest rose and fell with heavy breath and she was disoriented by the sudden interruption of what they'd been doing. Gathering herself together enough to consider his question, she finally answered, "It makes me a better fighter."

"Your profession is why you like it?"

"No." Her honesty in that simple response surprised her – but it had slipped from her tongue faster than she could think to conceal it. "I liked it before I was taught to fight – it was the reason I was taught to fight."

"So why?"

He finally looked up at her face, and she was desperate for a bit of light to chase away the shadow that covered him. "I can't answer for when I was young, I just remember that it felt good. Not so much the pain itself, but the feeling that came after it – the euphoria. I felt something and nothing all at the same time."

"You surrender to it?"

"Yes."

"But, not when you fight?"

"No." She cleared her throat, forcing down her discomfort with his questions. "No, that is something different entirely. I came alive when I fought and the pain only helped me fight harder. I took my anger out on my opponents and didn't care if that fight would be my last. I was good, even when I was young."

"You were trained as a child?"

She shrugged. "My mother died and my father was part of the network. He didn't know what to do with me, couldn't handle my moods after she died, so he allowed them to train me – figured out that it was the only thing that would calm me down. A female assassin was an asset, I could sneak in more places, be less noticeable."

"You are anything but less noticeable." He grinned.

"Says the man whose guard was shot dead beside him," she teased. "If Aaron hadn't moved to catch Maddy, it would have been him."

"I would have killed you for it – would have never given you a chance to so much as blink before putting a bullet in your head. Aaron is my brother."

She was startled, never hearing that Joseph had two sons. "I thought Aaron was an only child, the only heir of The Estate."

A humorless laughed escaped him. "I was … adopted." She felt his body tense suddenly, anger and bitter thoughts settling beneath his skin. "I've lived at The Estate since I was four."

She grieved to hear his admission. Looking up at his face, a beam of light broke through the entrance of the cave, finally illuminating his eyes. The memories and pain she saw hidden behind their depths was familiar – a pain much like her own.

"You didn't grow cold."

The small bit of light, disappeared behind vines blown across the entrance by the wind.

182

Bathed in shadow again, he was quiet for a moment before responding. "I watched Aaron struggle most of my life with his anger, with a darkness that existed inside him. When he sinks to it, he wants nothing more than to kill, to bathe in the blood of the men he destroyed. I remained grounded to keep him grounded."

"I don't know why you cared. All I've wanted is death and escape from this nightmare world. The cities were overrun by crime and my friends disappeared every week. My sister – Honor – she begged our father to get us away from here, to move some place not overshadowed by The Estate. He would never leave, the streets were all he knew."

He didn't respond immediately, but when he spoke again, Hope was surprised by his whispered confession. "We intend to destroy it – The Estate. It's destroyed us all in some way or another."

"We?"

"Aaron, Madeleine and me." After letting out a frustrated breath, he continued, "The Estate is more than just a network; it's evil incarnate - a living, breathing part of the man who created it. It is as much Joseph's child as Aaron, and even after Joseph's death, it continues to teem with the corruption he spread. Almost every man has been infected with his blood lust, with the power hungry rage that he demanded of the men who served him. It's only since Aaron took control that the worst of the depravities ceased."

183

"Yet, they never truly stopped as you'd believed. My sister is proof of that." She felt the fury she'd been pushing back over the past few days begin to resurface. "If they've killed her..."

He placed a finger over her mouth. "If they've killed her, then she is lucky. I know the practices taught to these men. Joseph always ensured Aaron and I had a front row seat to witness just how horrifying he could be."

The lump that formed in her throat stole her ability to swallow down what he'd claimed. "If she is dead, I'll die as well. She was what 'grounded' me."

His smile was barely visible in the low light of the space. "No, my tortured beauty, I won't let that happen. If she is gone, then I will just have to hold on to you and Aaron both."

He leaned down to kiss her, the brush of his lips feather light against hers. It was intimate, affection based on some feeling other than lust or need. It caused her muscles to fall languid beneath her skin and her head to swim with emotions she'd never wanted to feel. His touch was his acceptance of her hatred of herself – his understanding of her needs at a level no person had known her before. He deepened the kiss, his hands running over her, his masterful fingers making it impossible for her to resist. He was her tormentor and protector, her captivity and freedom. She could, for once, let go of her need to fight, to seek pain just to bask in the comforting numbness that came with it. What he gave her,

184

what he did to awaken and bring to life her body and mind, was more exhilarating than anything she'd known before.

It was hours that he took her over, rendering her completely docile to his whims. She became lost within him, waking up from the haze for brief moments, only to have him kiss her, or nip at her skin and replace her back where she was sated and satisfied. He connected with her, like a puzzle piece finally finding it's match. A man who enjoyed to grant small bits of pain and a woman who needed it to feel like she was alive.

After taking her to a place where she could be free of the pain and heartache of her life, where she could forget about fighting and conquest and despair, Xander wrapped his body around her and she fell asleep listening to the strong and rhythmic beat of his heart against his chest.

Chapter Eighteen

Sunlight streamed into the depth of the cave, the shadows of leaves moving within an angry wind that danced across the skin of their naked bodies. Xander pushed up, his bones aching from sleeping on the ground. After releasing the cuff that bound him to Hope, he stretched his arms above him, popping his joints into place and dressing quickly. His eyes flicked over to Hope, her tan skin stretched taut over lean and toned muscles. He'd take her again quickly if it wasn't for the shadow of a man stretched out across the entrance.

Walking out, blue collided with angry green when he locked his stare to Aaron's.

"I'm not even sure what to say to you, *brother*. You've chosen to fuck the enemy, the remnants of your loyalty left inside the bitch. Was it worth it?"

Xander didn't flinch, he'd known Aaron for too long to believe Aaron truly wanted him dead. Rolling his shoulders back he replied, "If you wanted to kill me, I wouldn't be standing here right now. Why wait for me to face you when you could have easily cut our throats while we slept?" He kept his voice calm and bored, knowing full well the man before him was one wrong word away from tearing his head from his shoulders.

Aaron's expression remained blank and his shoulders relaxed even though a blade still spun over his hand. "I take it you assumed Maddy would convince me not to kill Hope; or that I wouldn't remember the location of the only available hiding place on the compound?"

Xander nodded, also relaxing to realize that Aaron's initial threat had been partly in warning. "She's not lying to you. I have no way of proving it, but I know there's more going on than we realize."

Sunlight flashed off the steel of Aaron's blade. He flicked it in his hand once more, before, placing it in the sheath at his back. "After talking with Maddy last night, I went through some papers in the office for a period of time to consider the situation more thoroughly. When I noticed that the house she indicated was one that took on the sex trade members after that unit was brought down, it caught my attention."

"I came to that conclusion last night as well." The tension eased over Xander's body to realize that Aaron was finally thinking clearly.

The two men stared at each other for a few quiet moments before Aaron broke the silence. "I'm still angry that you went against a direct order; especially one that involved a potential threat. Regardless of whatever the two of you have been doing, she remains a threat – at least until we can determine the absolute truth to her claim."

"I've kept her bound and have been careful not to allow her to run loose over the compound."

He paused, looking towards the cave before returning his attention to Aaron.

"There is a warehouse used by the members of the house Hope identified. If there is something going on, and if they have the women she claimed they had, then I suspect the warehouse could be where they would have taken them."

Aaron's entire body tensed suddenly and his eyes locked to the cave. Turning quickly, Xander looked to find Hope standing in the entrance, her face concealed by the shadow from the vines. Pushing them aside to step out, the metallic gold of her eyes met with the unrelenting sunlight. The chain was still around her neck and she had redressed in the shirt and sweat pants Xander had given her. Her eyes locked to Aaron.

Stepping towards her, Xander grabbed the cuff still attached to her wrist and commented, "As you can see, she is still being treated with caution."

"I'm surprised she didn't kill you in your sleep."

Xander turned back to Hope.

She shrugged. "I figured it was your network that got me into this mess, it would be your network to get me out. Who else would be able to help me now that they've moved my sister?"

"Is that the only reason?" Xander's question was spoken low, barely loud enough for even Hope to hear what he'd asked. She looked

188

up at him, some unknown emotion softening her expression.

She didn't respond before Aaron spoke again. "We'll search the warehouse." He looked at Hope, suspicion still burning behind the green of his eyes. "The man who sent you, what did he look like?"

Hope eyed him back, the same suspicion swirling within her eyes. "Tall, maybe your height, brown hair, broad shoulders – very built. In fact, he was one of the largest men I've seen. He also spoke with the same bullshit affluent accent that you use."

Xander attempted to suppress the same grin that Aaron was unable to hide. "Yes, well, there's nothing wrong with conducting yourself with a bit of decorum, despite what you do for a living. Joseph took issue with those he considered uneducated and common *street trash*."

Xander's eyes locked to Aaron, narrowing at the obvious insult he'd just volleyed at Hope. Glancing back at Hope, he noticed she smiled brightly.

"This coming from the man who slaughtered his own father? Seems to me, whereas he had you educated, he failed to teach you respect. In my network, we protect the ones we care for…"

"I never said I cared for him." Aaron interrupted. "Besides, I am not the person who can take credit for Joseph's death."

Hope's brows furrowed in confusion. "Then who?" She turned to look at Xander.

He held up his hands. "I'm innocent as well, although I won't say I wouldn't have done it if he wasn't already dead by the time I got to him."

"Madeleine killed Joseph with a broken string from her instrument."

When Aaron added that bit of information, Hope turned back to him, her eyes widening in surprise. "She seems harmless. How is that even possible? From what I heard, Joseph died fighting. In fact, the rumors of his death indicate he died in battle against you."

"Then I will need to get information out to correct that belief. I'd prefer people know he died as a result of his drug addiction, that he left himself helpless to a small musician. I prefer people understand how anticlimactic his death really was. He doesn't deserve the death of a warrior."

Hope nodded her understanding. "Do you recognize the man I described?"

Xander spoke in Aaron's place. "Was there anything else unusual about him? The description fits several men in the network, we'll need something to narrow it down."

"Besides the fact that he had my sister on a chain?"

Xander arched an eyebrow at her response, but she didn't notice. She appeared to be thinking back, searching the recesses of her memory to pinpoint details that would be of use. "He had one green eye and one blue. I can't be completely sure on that considering how dark the house was when I was in there, but I'm pretty sure that's what I saw."

Xander looked at Aaron who, at the same time, swiveled his head to look back. Their eyes locked in immediate recognition. Turning back to Hope, Xander asked, "Would you be able to identify him from a photograph?"

She nodded 'yes'.

"Have you called off the search for us, Aaron?" Returning his attention to his friend, Xander began to formulate an idea. Unfortunately, it was one that would be almost impossible to pull off, but not entirely; especially if he and Hope were still considered to be enemies of The Estate.

"No."

"Don't call it off. Let's return to the mansion, I want to show Hope some photos in your suite. We'll need to sneak in. I want the entire network believing that we are still within your crosshairs, so to speak."

Obviously understanding where Xander was going with his request, Aaron didn't ask questions before responding, "I'll have Maddy claim to have seen you near the front of the compound, when the guards leave to investigate, we'll sneak into the building."

191

Aaron looked at the cave, something unfamiliar flitting across his expression, before he took a few steps towards the entrance. Hope backed away, still not completely sure that Aaron didn't intend to harm her. Speaking over his shoulder, he mused, "Do you remember when we came here as kids? We'd fight the dragon that lived here until we could steal his precious treasure chest." He chuckled. "How pathetic that all it contained was a blanket and miscellaneous junk." Parting the vines with his hands, he entered the cave and Xander moved to follow behind him.

He watched Aaron approach the trunk before kneeling down to examine it. "Apparently, our old treasure came in handy. I'm surprised you slept on that thing. There's no telling how old it was when we first found it, not to mention the twenty years or so since we did."

Xander shrugged. "It was better than sleeping in the dirt."

Hope stepped up beside Xander, recognition apparent in her expression. "Where did you get that trunk?"

"We found it hidden in a crevice over in the wall. It was hidden behind vines, why?"

"Because it looks like it was made by one of the founders of my network. He's since died, but only members received one. Would you mind if I examined it further?"

192

Xander and Aaron looked at each other, but then Aaron stepped away from it, extending his hand. "Be my guest."

She approached the trunk, pulling out the miscellaneous clothing and other odds and ends it contained – all of which would have been useful to a person camping or surviving off the land. Xander found it odd when she knocked on the bottom of it and smiled.

"Just as I thought, it has a false bottom." She pulled at something within the trunk and reached in. Extracting a journal, she flipped it over in her hand, tracing something on the back of it with her finger. "Who's Connor?"

Aaron stepped towards her and Hope was on her feet facing him within seconds. They looked at each other, distrust hanging heavily between them. Eventually, Aaron slowly extended his hand. "May I see the journal?"

Hope looked surprised that he would ask instead of demand that she hand it to him. Taking from her hand, Aaron flipped through the pages quickly, but stopped when something caught his attention that was stuck between the pages. Pulling it free and unfolding it, he turned it over and his entire body tensed in reaction to what he saw.

Xander stepped forward. "What is it?"

Looking up slowly, Aaron reached over to hand the scrap of paper to Xander. "It's a picture of my mother, I believe."

193

Xander took the sketch and froze as Aaron did to see it. Drawn in pencil, the sketch was almost the exact likeness of Aaron's mother, at least as much as Xander could remember from when they were young. Handing it back, he watched Aaron carefully fold the picture back over itself and place it in the journal. "We won't be able to carry the trunk back with us if we hope to enter the building unnoticed, but I'll keep the journal to look over later."

Xander moved to pack the blanket and other items back in the trunk before sliding it back into the crevice hidden by the thick curtain of vines. "Let's get going."

Hope cleared her throat to get Xander's attention. Holding up the leash, she asked, "Can we remove my chains now that we are all friends?"

He smiled mischievously. "I'm not sure about that, I kind of like it."

Her gold eyes heated, memories dancing behind the metallic color. "I didn't say we should throw it away."

Xander chuckled and Aaron groaned. "I'll leave you two to discuss...your arrangement. I'm going to head back now to move the guards. I want you to hide within the tree line until you see the guards leave. Once that happens, move quickly to my suite. I'm not sure how long you'll have to make it inside unseen."

Chapter Nineteen

A new room, empty walls, a sea of nothing that never seemed to end. The monotony of white only broken by the black iron bars that caged her. Honor remembered screaming, fighting off the monsters that removed her from the place where he would come to her. She feared she'd failed too often and her angel moved on to find a woman more worthy of his touch.

Waking up, she heard muffled groans and cries, the screams no longer tearing her mind apart, but suffocating her with the knowledge that she was not the only woman tested by her angel.

There were many. All bruised and tattered, dirty and awaiting him. Honor's body tensed with jealousy and shame, wondering if one of those who surrounded her would be chosen.

The machines were not new. Wheels, crosses, tables and chairs intended for cruelty, for blood. She'd seen them before, had been strapped to their bone shattering surfaces - beaten, broken, and left raw. They made her worthy of his beauty and love.

The monsters whispered in a corner, the black of their eyes looking back in her direction, white teeth glistening against the low light of the large room. Crouching low, she cornered herself against the back of her square prison. Her eyes darted back and forth, barely able to see beyond the skin that had swollen on her face from their punishment.

Two of the monsters broke away; lewd grins barely discernible on their features when they stepped towards her. Balling over herself, her head shook as she silently begged to be passed.

Each man knelt down to look into her cage, their eyes peering in at her bringing back to life the bits and pieces of what they'd done to her.

"You ready, princess? Behave and we'll present you in a way that will please 'your angel.'" His low laughter was cold, dripping with mockery. She wondered if he believed she'd be unready once again.

Her body trembled.

"Dose her before you remove her." The monsters stood speaking to each other about her as if she was nothing more than an animal.

"Why don't we have some fun with her first? He'll never know. What's another mark on the bitch's body? I've been eyeing this one since she was dragged in."

The only response was a sickening gurgle, crimson liquid dripping down the monster's legs in a flood before his body fell to the ground, splashing the stain of his demise onto Honor's skin.

The screams started again, tearing her mind apart.

"Shut up, all of you, before I give you a fucking reason to scream!"

196

Quiet came over the room — punctured by sobs and tears, the smell of urine a faint trace in the air.

After dragging the body of one away, the other knelt again, the clatter of metal against metal as he unlocked the small door. His mismatched eyes looked in as the bars swung open. "You need to be cleaned. I'd hate for you to be rejected once again."

She didn't want to go with him, but she wanted to be clean for her angel. She would be good this time, would bite through her own lip if it meant holding in any sound that tried to force its way from her body. She wanted to enjoy his touch, felt ashamed that pain overtook her when all that mattered was that he was pleased. He'd take her away from this nightmare if only she could give him what he required.

Crawling forward, she allowed the monster to take her by the arm, feeling a small prick to her skin and knowing the poison he'd given would loosen her — render her open and waiting for his test. He led her to a corner of the large room. "Stand there. Move and you'll be punished."

Knives created from ice; the water beneath her pink and muddled brown, the spray against her skin unrelenting and cutting like fine razors across her body. She grit her teeth while her bones ground against each other, her muscles frenzied and shaking from the violent cold of the water.

When it ceased and she was left dripping where she stood, he approached. Looking her up and down, his mouth twisted into a grin. "He's asked that you be set up before his arrival. Do not fight me." He

197

held out his arm to motion towards the other women held in cages throughout the room. "Don't you want to show them how you are the most worthy?"

She was walked to a table, her arms and legs becoming liquid from the poison that coursed through her veins. She stumbled and the monster grabbed her hips to steady her. Reaching the table, she bent over it, hissed at the cold bite of the metal surface over her skin. He locked her wrists into place beside where her head rested on the table, her chin gripped by the small indentation on the side. A steel bar was placed over the back of her neck and locked down, rendering her immobile. After securing her feet, he moved in front of her and knelt down. Slipping his finger over her swollen and broken lips, he pushed in, the tip running across her tongue before he pulled it back out again. Her stomach turned.

"Fail again and next time, you're mine." Standing up, he motioned towards the cages in the room. "Cover them all with blankets to block their view." He chuckled. "It will let the bitches hear what a true whore sounds like."

When the men had covered the cages of each woman in the room, they left out a side door. Honor sat motionless on the table, not daring to move an inch in case her angel silently watched.

She felt the warmth of his palm on her skin, flinching in surprise at the sudden touch. The low tone of his voice soothed her shock and she smiled against the unforgiving steel of her perch. "Misbehaving already. Do not jump away from me, my pet. This is your last chance to please your angel."

A tear, hot and wet, dripped from her eye. She blinked the others back.

He walked around, placed the strap into her mouth, connecting the small chains he would use to hold her in place. Lifting the steel bar as he passed, he pulled on the chains once positioned behind her. Her body bent backwards, her ass lifted in presentation.

She felt him invade her, pushing into the deep recesses of her body, working her – molding her into the perfect woman. When he pulled free, she felt suddenly empty, a void previously filled with the full width of his promise.

"Good." He purred.

Pushing forward again, he entered another place, the skin tearing at his girth, her teeth biting heavily into the strap in her mouth. But she never made a sound. When he moved, he pulled the chain bending her back further. "Show me you appreciate your gift, pet."

She moaned against the pain, eventually relaxing around him until he growled out his release, pulling free once taking what he wanted.

She heard his boots hit the ground when he circled the table to stand before her. Removing the strap, he placed the steel bar back in place.

Placing his hand on her head softly, he said, "You are chosen. The next time you see me you'll be leaving this place."

199

His hand left her head and she heard his boots again when he walked from the room. The taste of her grateful tears kissed her lips, the salt sweetly stinging where her lip had been split.

Chapter Twenty

"No. Absolutely not. They'll kill you as soon as you enter the building if what Hope is saying is true. You are my lead guard and my spy, they'll never believe you turned on me." Green eyes shone out from a blank expression, no hint of bending on the decision he'd made.

Xander leaned back against the wall of Aaron's office. "You have the entire network searching for me with instructions to return me to you for execution. I assume now is the best time for anybody to believe I'm no longer your most trusted."

The two men stared at each other, neither flexible in the decision they'd made.

Maddy spoke into the silence between them. "Xander may be correct, Aaron. If Patrick is involved in the attempt against you, there may be other units involved as well. If we can discover who it is, you'll have a valid excuse for bringing those units down. It would be another step towards finally destroying the network."

Hope stood by the built in bookshelves in the office, disbelief settling over her shoulders to learn that the three were working to destroy the network from within. Once she and Xander had made it inside, they'd immediately gathered in Aaron's office and Xander revealed the identity of the man she'd described. He'd pulled a photograph and her stomach turned in reaction to the image. Yes. The bastard depicted in the photo was, in fact, the man who'd held Honor's chain.

"Forty-eight hours, Aaron. That's all I need." Xander spoke without emotion, business like in order to convince Aaron that his idea was not without merit.

Aaron quietly considered what Maddy and Xander had said before responding, "Forty-eight hours. That is all I'm willing to give you." He paused, obviously considering another potential issue. "Dependent upon the amount of men involved, I'll need to incorporate Jason's assistance. It would be best to have someone more acquainted with the individual unit members. I know each leader, however, their underlings appear to change daily and I don't want to involve any of the leaders until we have each man identified as to the unit to which they belong."

"I'll need my weapons." Hope interrupted. If their mission was going to be a slaughter, she was determined to take part. Her skills would be useful to the few men who would be coming in with Aaron.

Xander's blue-eyed gaze rested on her face. "You are going in as a slave. They'll never believe I allowed you to keep your weapons. If weapons are found on you, it might tip them off to what we are doing."

"I'm going in as YOUR slave. Keep their grubby hands off my body and they'll never know that I'm armed." Her eyebrow arched in challenge of his concern.

The entire room grew silent in reaction to her words. She looked from Xander's face to Aaron's, and eventually to Maddy's. "Was it something I said?"

"Slaves of The Estate were not permitted to wear clothes." Maddy's delicate voice pierced the air. "You'll be stripped immediately upon entering the building. You'll have to comply if it is to be believable."

Hope's body tensed. The idea of walking in unarmed went against everything she was trained to do in her profession.

Aaron eyed her, a small, knowing grin peeking out at the corner of his mouth – mocking her. "I don't understand your hesitancy, Hope. Being that we are alike in our *habits*, I assume you've been adequately trained in hand to hand combat as much as the use of weapons. However, if you have not..."

"I'm fine." The metallic gold of her eyes stared back, noting the arrogance in Aaron's expression. "If you'd like to find out for yourself, I'm sure that can be arranged." She smiled when she noticed how he immediately fell into a discreet fighting stance at the sharp cut of her tone.

Xander pushed off the wall, moving to step in between the two assassins. "Fighting amongst ourselves won't solve anything."

"Why not?" Hope turned to Xander, her stance also easing into one intended for a fight. "It might do him some good to have his dick ripped from his body and shoved down his throat."

Xander's eyes widened and when she looked back to Aaron, a blade was already at his palm. She grinned in response.

"Please don't. I'm rather fond of his dick and I'd like it to remain where it's useful." The words sounded wrong when spoken; Maddy's small voice ringing out with innocence and kindness despite the crude topic.

Hope, Xander and Aaron turned in unison to stare at her. She shrugged in response.

Looking over the petite brunette, Hope asked. "Are you sure? From what you just told me, he marched you around naked in your role as a slave. What kind of man does that to a woman he cares for?"

Maddy blinked, her dark lashes momentarily covering the sapphire blue of her eyes before she smiled. "He also allowed another man to touch me, a woman to rape me, he whipped me, and he executed other slaves in front of me, leaving their entrails for me to clean from the floor."

Hope's jaw dropped. Complete shock overtook her and she was unable to respond to what Maddy had said.

Maddy walked over to Aaron and wrapped her arm around his. "But sometimes, when you are stuck in an impossible situation, the solution is not always violence and fighting your way out. Sometimes, it takes patience and cunning to free yourself. Remember that when you two go in to that warehouse. It might be the only thing that saves you and your sister's life."

Despite Maddy making light of prior events between them, Hope noticed that Aaron's face looked pained to be reminded of the past. Maddy noticed as well and brought her hand up to rest it against his cheek. "We accomplished what we set out to accomplish at that time," she reminded him quietly. "And even if we have to continue enduring the madness that this network breeds, eventually we'll be free of it and will watch it burn to the ground around us."

Aaron relaxed, but his expression carried an undercurrent of renewed determination. He looked up from Maddy to lock his gaze on Xander. "You will go in fully armed. If possible, carry some of Hope's weapons in with you as well. If you are caught, or if something goes wrong prior to my arrival, give Hope her weapons so that you both can fight your way out."

Xander nodded his understanding. "The first thing we'll need to do is escape the compound.

205

I'll need you to pull the guards away from the perimeter wall."

"It'll be done."

Turning to Hope, Xander held out his hand. "Care to escort me to my room? I'll only be able to carry a few of your weapons as well as mine. I'll let you pick your favorites." He winked.

She smiled in response, uncertainty creeping along her thoughts at how Xander was able to set her at ease. Accepting his hand, she looked back at Aaron and Maddy. Both of their expressions were grim. "Don't worry. I'll make sure that if my sister still lives, both she and Xander will walk away from this intact."

Maddy's brows furrowed deeper. "What about you?"

Hope blinked at her concern, not used to having someone who cared if she returned. "I've wished for death for many years, Maddy. Considering I've never yet had a wish come true in this hell I've called a life, I'm not worried that it will happen now. We will see each other again."

. . .

Run down to a point of looking deserted, the large white warehouse was shadowed by the dark sky, a phantom across the horizon only when the bright moonlight above touched softly upon the metal surface of the building.

Silently, Hope and Xander walked the perimeter of the building, seeking out hidden exits or small areas where they could escape if they were discovered.

"It's closed in tight, I've seen only two doors besides the main door. Retreat would be difficult if things went sour." Xander spoke low so that his words would not carry on the wind that beat violently against their bodies.

Hope straightened her spine, while rolling her shoulders back, stretching her neck out in habit, physically loosening the muscles in her body so that her movement would be smooth and fluid. "Then we'll have no choice but to be believable."

Xander chuckled, the howl of the wind making the sound barely discernable. "I'm interested to see you play the part of a slave, it'll be amusing watching you attempt to keep your mouth shut and do as you're told."

She looked up at him, noticed how his cheek dimpled from the grin pulling at his mouth. Their bodies brushed up against each other from how close they stood and a small pang of desire ran through her at the contact. His expression fell when he looked back at the building. "I want to warn you what you could see in there. If these men are anything like Joseph, you can expect blood and lots of it. I wouldn't be surprised if flayed bodies hung on the walls."

"It's nothing I haven't seen before."

He nodded. "I'm sure. However, if your sister is one of those bodies, will you be able to stop yourself from slaughtering every man in that room?"

His words were cold...callous in the blunt manner in which he spoke them. Hope took a deep breath attempting to goad her heart back into a slow and steady rhythm. She allowed images to flit through her head. Visions of her sister – naked, bound and bruised – at the end of a madman's chain. "I'm prepared for whatever we find."

Xander looked over at her, reached out to tuck a piece of hair behind her ear. The gesture was so soft compared to words of his response, "I'll treat you like a whore. Do not assume that it doesn't infuriate me to do so as much as it will anger you to have it done. I'm sure whatever you have seen, and whatever you think you are prepared to see, is like a dream compared to what I know could be happening behind those walls."

She looked up at him again, her eyes widening in shock.

"You may have grown up in the shadow of The Estate, but I grew up inside it. The rumors and murmurs that manage to escape its walls don't even begin to touch upon the truth of the horror that existed within the mansion." He paused before looking at her again, foggy memories of a distant cruelty obvious behind the blue of his eyes. "Joseph killed my parents and my sister. From what I've heard, I was taken as another punishment

208

inflicted on my father – kept alive so that my parents could never rest."

"Did you witness their deaths?"

Dark memories settled farther behind his eyes and he grew quiet. Finally breaking his silence, he confessed, "I was present when it happened, but I don't remember the details except for bits and pieces."

She leaned into him and his hand moved to rub down her back. "When this is over - regardless of what happens after we go inside – can I stay?"

His body stilled, his eyes locked to hers in disbelief.

She shrugged. "We both have scores to settle with The Estate. If the three of you are truthful in your intent to destroy it, I want to help you."

Silence again before he smiled a wicked grin. "I'm surprised you ask that question."

"Why?"

"Because I thought you would have figured out by now, that I have no absolutely no intention of ever letting you go."

Leaning down, he brushed his lips across hers, their bodies covered by the shadows filling the alley where they stood. She felt the leather of the collar encircle her throat while his lips moved slowly over hers. Once it was locked into place, she felt him tug the chain before he pulled away. "It's time. You need to remove your clothes."

The full weight of their situation finally rested over her body. She would be vulnerable and exposed, an easy target going in without weapons and without clothes to cover her. Maddy's words echoed in her head and Hope took another deep breath.

"Do me a favor." She grabbed his hand, relishing the heat of his skin against hers before looking up at him again. "If you can save my sister, I want you to do it regardless; even if it means my death. She is innocent and she doesn't deserve what's happened to her."

He looked like he wanted to argue, but then understanding flashed behind his eyes. "How will I know it's your sister?"

Hope frowned and turned to look back at the building. "That's simple. She's my identical twin."

Chapter Twenty-One

Xander stood dumbfounded by her words. Already believing her too beautiful to be real, he couldn't fathom that there was another woman alive who looked identical.

Before he could respond, she slipped the clothes from her body, the moonlight brushing across her form. Each of her injuries was dark against the smooth expanse of her skin – the wound to her shoulder where she'd been shot, the bruises that marred her face and chest from where he'd struck her when they'd fought. It was the perfect disguise, anger and violence that marked her skin, making it believable that he'd treated her as nothing more than a whore.

Moving in front of her, he tugged the chain and she fell in step behind him. Before they reached the dimly lit area around the building he stopped and turned to look at her over his shoulder. Even vulnerable, she wore strength – the true heart of a warrior beating within her chest, hungry for the moment when she'd enjoy letting the blood of her enemies run free from their bodies.

He approached a side door, turning the handle to find that the door swung open freely. He tsked at how they'd left the building exposed and at their arrogance in thinking they were impervious to attack. However, their carelessness wasn't unexpected. Very few dared attack any property owned by The Estate and the authorities were paid to not notice their activities.

Slipping through the doorway, he listened to the silent interior. The only sound he could hear was the faint rattle of the chain he had around Hope's throat and the soft sound of her bare feet stepping in behind him. They were in a small storage room in the back of the warehouse, one that didn't appear to have any person inside for a long time. Cobwebs hung from the ceiling and you could barely traverse the floor because of the amount of boxes and other junk that littered the floors. Weaving his way through the maze of obstacles, he approached an interior door and placed his ear against it to see if he could hear activity on the other side. There was nothing and he began to worry that he'd been wrong to think they'd brought the women to this place.

Turning the handle slowly, he pushed against the thick wood, the hinges creaking in protest at the movement. He closed his eyes against the putrid smell that assaulted him suddenly and turned to look at Hope before opening them again. The expression on her face gave away the fact that she knew all too well that it was the smell of death that permeated the air. Looking back out into the expansive space he saw cages lined neatly in five rows, some covered with sheets while others were left open. Other miscellaneous tables and equipment was also strewn throughout the room.

Leaving the storage room, he kept to the wall as he moved through the space. Just enough light shown through the musty windows that lined the top of the building to let him see that the cages were empty. Moving slowly, they searched the entire building to find that nobody was there.

"Check the cages." Releasing her chain, he pulled a gun from its holster to guard the perimeter while Hope walked silently, looking through the steel traps in the center.

"They're empty." She kept moving between the rows, but held her nose as she approached two covered cages. Pulling the sheet up, she doubled over coughing. Xander walked over, the smell causing his body to retch as he moved closer.

"Um, I spoke too soon." She pointed down into the cages she'd uncovered and Xander looked down to notice that one held the decomposing body of a woman and the other held the decomposing body of a man. "It appears our friends have been here for at least two days. The bodies aren't too badly rotted, so it couldn't have been longer than that." Hope paced the edges of the cages, looking in closely. "This one isn't my sister, so that's good news I guess." Peering closer at the body, she winced. "Holy shit, this woman died a painful death."

Xander stepped over to examine the dead woman, not surprised that it appeared she'd bled out. Blood flooded the interior of the cage, her naked lower torso covered more thoroughly than the upper part of her body. Every inch of her skin

213

was marred by bruising or cuts — some healed, some worsened by the way her body was left after death. "Do you recognize her?"

Hope looked up, holding her hand beneath her nose. Moving to the other side, she peered in to look at the face. "For a second there, I thought it was the woman who let me in the mansion, but..." She peered closer, her expression tightening against the stink. "...it's not her. This woman is much taller, and her hair is lighter, I think. It's hard to tell with all the blood."

"A woman let you in the mansion?"

Hope looked up from the body and nodded. "Well, 'let me in' is probably the wrong way to phrase it. She opened up one of the exterior doors and I knocked her out and left her outside when I entered the west wing. I figured I'd be in and out pretty quickly, so by the time she woke up, it wouldn't matter if she ran around to tell you what happened, because I'd be long gone by then."

Xander blinked, his mind remembering back to the night Hope had attempted Aaron's life. "Can you describe her to me?"

She shrugged. "Petite, brown hair, didn't look at her long enough to get an eye color. She looked like Maddy somewhat."

He closed his eyes in recognition of the woman Hope had been describing. Opening them again, he said, "The decorator? Fuck! You knocked out our decorator?"

214

Hope shrugged again. "It gave me access to the building."

Moving to the second cage, Xander eyed her again before looking in at the man's body. Hope moved to his side and asked, "Do you recognize him as one of yours?"

Xander grimaced. "If he still had a face, I might be able to tell. However, it appears they didn't want him to be recognizable when found." He peered down at the skull, bits of flesh left behind from where they'd peeled the skin off entirely. "I'm unsure if they did this before or after he died, but I assume it was before death."

"Why?"

"Because that was a parlor trick thought up by Joseph. He was quite *creative* when it came to punishment." Images flashed in Xander's head; distant and broken memories of a woman screaming – of a baby crying – and of his father's body falling to the ground.

"You people are some sick bastards. We like things much more short and sweet where I come from. Death is one thing, playing in the remains is a whole new level of crazy." Hope moved beside him again, peering down at the man's remains. "So, what do we do now?"

Surveying the warehouse again, Xander stepped back when he heard the faint sound of car doors closing outside the building. "We wait." He grabbed her chain, pulling her close to him. "Kneel down at my feet."

"Why?"

"Because we're about to have company." Pulling his gun from its holster, he aimed it in the direction of the back door. Three men spilled through, their heads moving on their shoulders as they looked over the building. Finally spotting Xander, they raised their guns in his direction.

"And who the fuck do we have here?"

Xander remained still. "I need to see Patrick. Go get him before I kill all three of you and find him myself."

When the men recognized his voice, they raised their guns higher, not able to tell exactly where Xander stood due to the shadowed interior of the building. When they didn't move fast enough, he shot one in the head and the other in the stomach, leaving the center man looking at his friends on the floor. When the man looked back up, Xander stepped into the small bit of moonlight that streamed in through the window.

"Would you like to join them?" His tone was a warning. Every man in the network knew that, whereas Aaron was the fastest with a blade, Xander was the best marksman of The Estate.

"Patrick has nothing to do with our unit." The man attempted to lie, but the chopped quality of his words gave away his dishonesty.

Xander smiled. Cocking his gun, he raised it, noting how the other man immediately stepped back, holding his hands out in front of him in a defensive position.

"I guess that means I'll have to find him myself."

"Wait!" The man dropped his gun to the ground and reached into his pocket to pull out a phone. He appeared to be fumbling over the numbers and Xander fired off a warning shot to speed him along.

The man finally put the phone to his ear. "Tell Patrick he's needed at the warehouse." He paused, listening to whatever the person on the line had to say. "I don't give a fuck how pissed he'll be, tell him he needs to get his ass here now. Xander is here."

Flicking the phone off, the man replaced it in his pocket and looked back out into the expanse attempting to see where Xander had stepped back into shadow.

"Thank you." One shot fired and the bullet met the man between the eyes.

"Well, that was rude. He made the call." Hope spoke sarcastically behind him.

Xander chuckled, knowing full well that she would have done the same thing. "The fewer men Patrick has at his disposal – the better."

. . .

217

The amount of men that came pouring into the building through the back storage door wasn't surprising to Hope. She sat on the cold floor at Xander's feet, waiting patiently to see if Xander could convince the men that he was now on their side. Her body stiffened with rage when the man who'd held her sister's chain came walking through the crowd. Xander lowered his gun, obviously aware that holding it against the amount pointed back at him was useless.

"Xander." Patrick walked towards them, hands casually tucked in his pockets, his voice echoing throughout the large open space. "I'd ask why you thought I had anything to do with the warehouse, however, given the bitch who sits at your feet, I'm not surprised you figured it out. I should have killed her in her cell at the mansion when I had the chance."

"Thought you had a thing for twins, wouldn't have worked if I was dead." She heard the chain shake softly from Xander tightening his grip. Tugging it quickly, he caught her off guard, her body left splayed over the floor from the force of his pull. She looked up at him, her eyes opened wide with fictitious fear.

With a blank expression, he looked down at her. "Speak again, whore, and I may just give you to him so that he can play out his fantasy." There was no emotion to his voice except for the hint of violence. His action had been a warning and she knew she'd fucked up by stepping out of character. Pushing herself from the floor, she brushed off the dirt and crouched once again face down at his feet.

"I see you got the bitch under control – for the most part, at least. I imagine that must have been a fun task. It's a pity I wasn't the one who had the privilege of training her."

Hope's stomach turned at his words and she wanted nothing more than to dig his eyes out with her fingers.

"I can't say it wasn't enjoyable."

Even though Xander spoke the words to play a role, she knew they held truth. She smiled under the curtain of her hair thinking of how much of a bastard he could be.

"Yes, well, given her outburst, it appears she's not as easily trained as her twin." Patrick's tone was mocking. The smile slipped from Hope's face and rage rattled along her spine.

"Enough small talk. It appears we have a common problem. After I figured out that you were behind the attempt on Aaron's life, I came here hoping we could work out a deal." Fury dripped from his words and it was obvious to Hope that Xander was angry at Patrick's reference to her sister.

Patrick's sickening laugh sent chills running over Hope's skin. "I heard you'd fallen out of Aaron's good graces. Such a shame. How does it feel to be on the intended target of the executioner's blade?"

"Cut the shit, Patrick. We both have our reasons to kill Aaron Carmichael – one, so that I remain breathing and two, so that you can continue in your..." He turned to gesture towards the cages. "...habits." He paused before adding, "I have information that can help you kill Aaron and you have the resources I'll need to make that attempt a success."

Stopping in his tracks, Patrick folded his hands behind his back, feet set shoulder width apart. Hope peered out from behind her hair, watching the confrontation unfold. Patrick glanced down at her before returning his gaze to Xander and asking, "What did you do to piss Aaron off to the point of demanding your execution?"

"I refused to give up my new toy. I presumed since he has one, it was only fair that I be allowed my own. Apparently, he didn't agree."

Patrick huffed out an indignant breath. "Then we see things the same way. Many men within the network are angry with the new rules set in place since Joseph's death."

"So, let's do something about them."

Patrick stood staring at Xander for a few minutes, the tension settling around Hope's body like a suffocating blanket. Finally, without speaking again, Patrick raised his hand to his men indicating for them to lower their guns. Hope shoulders sagged with the tiny bit of relief it gave her.

"We have rules; one being that everything is shared." Patrick glanced at Hope again, his vile thoughts written openly in his expression.

Tightening the chain around his hand, Xander responded, "She's mine to touch, only. However, if you require a showing…"

Patrick smiled. "That will have to do. We'll need to leave here. The women have been moved to another location.

Xander nodded before pulling on Hope's chain. She stood up, her naked body exposed to the crowd of men in the room. Xander looked back at her. Although his face carried no expression, she noticed how his eyes teemed with fury at what he'd have to do.

Chapter Twenty-Two

Xander was somewhat surprised when the large SUV returned to The Estate compound. However, once they'd been hidden and snuck past the guards at the gate, the SUV pulled up to Patrick's house on the outskirts of the property and Xander realized how brave the maneuver had been on Patrick's part. Being that he lived within the section where he'd run the searches, Patrick must have been certain that nobody would have thought to check his personal space.

"The bitch will have to be drugged when we get inside. I like to keep the slaves compliant and quiet. You have no idea how annoying their screams and cries can be after a while." Patrick spoke as if they were discussing nothing more than the weather.

"I'm quite familiar." Xander reminded him. "You forget that I was raised within the mansion itself. I'd just learned to block out the noise, I hadn't considered drugging the bitches. Although, to do so, would have been the same as asking for death. Joseph preferred to hear their screams."

"He was something else. Despite the unfortunate rules set in place by Aaron, it has been somewhat easier to breath since Joseph's death. No longer fearing asking for additional money from the network is nice, however, being babysat constantly by Aaron tends to drown at the relief.

222

Hopefully, when I take over The Estate, the men can benefit in both areas."

Xander eyed him while stepping out of the vehicle. Tugging on Hope's chain, he stepped aside so she could climb out, noticing how she was immediately restrained at his side by another man so that they could inject something into her body. He nodded his head toward her and asked, "Will this knock her out completely?"

Patrick smiled. "Not at all, it will just make her a little more lively when you demonstrate her worth. I've been looking forward to hearing her scream."

Xander's hand fisted around Hope's chain and he resisted the urge to pull his gun and spray Patrick's brain over the interior of the truck. He knew they had less than forty-eight hours to determine the identity of the men involved in this ring and he had to *play nice* if he hoped to obtain it before Aaron discovered their location. He wasn't nervous that they'd been removed from the warehouse and knew Aaron would be smart enough to look closely at Patrick when he discovered that Xander and Hope were not there.

Approaching the building, he noticed how Hope tripped over her own feet, the drugs already taking effect. When she fell, he fought to restrain himself from turning to assist her back to her feet. Staying in character, he yanked at the chain, tensing to hear her cry from the force. "Get up, slut. This is just the beginning."

223

Patrick laughed while walking through the doorway. "You'd think she'd be stronger than the others." Glancing back, he smirked. "But I guess it's the same with all whores. You drug them and they offer their asses up in the air like cats in heat. The chains really aren't necessary, but they are helpful to hold the bitch down for the more *violent* encounters."

The interior of the house was dimly lit, the windows blacked out to prevent people from seeing in. The practice wasn't unusual and Xander knew that no man trusted the other within the walls of the compound. The narrow hallways were quiet as they walked and Xander had to take a deep breath when they finally reached their destination in the underbelly basement of the house. The room stretched the length of the house and, much like the warehouse, contained cages large enough for a crouched human. These cages, however, held live women, their frightened eyes also bleak from the effects of the drugs pumped into their systems. Xander scanned their faces, noticing that none of the cages contained Hope's sister. He did recognize one face, however, and instantly felt sorry for the decorator, Erica. Working for The Estate was a hazardous occupation, regardless of the position you took.

Rather than having shackles attached the walls, the men were using tables, crosses and other equipment to restrain the women not held in cages. Their bodies hung heavily from the chains and memories of his many years under Joseph resurfaced – the all too familiar twisting of his stomach to see how the women had been treated.

224

"Take a seat." Patrick held out his arm indicating an arrangement of couches and chairs within the room. "I say we have a drink with some entertainment before getting down to business. We'll leave your toy with you for now, however, after you're done with her, I prefer she be caged like the rest."

Immediately turned his head to lock eyes with Patrick, Xander's contempt rolled in waves through his body. "She stays with me."

Patrick smiled. "Then I'll give you the key to her box. I will not allow an assassin – no matter how incapacitated she may be – to roam freely. If she were to escape, it would lead to some serious issues for us both."

Xander didn't like it, but if he held her key, he could live with it. "I prefer we talk before starting the entertainment. I need to know the extent of your resources. How many units are involved?"

"Three, so far. But, that number is growing." Patrick arched his brow. "I'm not willing to discuss any more details, however, until after you've performed your demonstration." Raising his hand, he motioned towards a metal table situated in the center front of the room. "Please feel free to use our facilities." His lips curled lewdly at the suggestion.

A chill ran down Xander's spine. Turning to look at Hope, he instantly noticed the haze in her eyes. Whatever they'd given her was stronger than what he'd slipped her previously. She staggered on her feet, but didn't appear lethargic. Her breathing had sped, her body glowed from a light sheen of sweat, her pupils were as large as saucers and she rubbed her hands over the skin of her arms, leaving trails where her nails had dragged across it.

"Fine." He pulled on the chain softly and noticed that even the small amount of force had almost thrown Hope to the floor. He took her arm to steady her and lead her towards the front of the room, being sure to make the gesture look like it was done more from annoyance than from concern.

When they approached the table, he recognized it as one that had been removed from Joseph's wing. Taking a deep breath, he resigned himself to what he'd have to do. Years ago, when Aaron had been requested to present Maddy in a similar way by Joseph, Aaron's refusal based on not 'fucking in public' had been a brilliant way to avoid having to perform. Unfortunately, Xander's situation was not as easy. The men had to believe he was as much against Aaron's hatred of depravity as them.

"Bend over." He eased Hope's body over the silver surface of the table, noticing instantly how she flinched at the cold bite of the steel. Kneeling down, he secured her ankles in place and moved to the front of the table to secure her wrists. Once locked, he moved her head so that her chin rested against the notch on the edge. He could hear her teeth chattering in her mouth and he angrily ground his in reaction. The last thing he wanted to do was violate her in front of the men, but this wasn't about what he wanted to do – it was about what he had to do.

"There's a strap hanging from the wall. It's quite useful as reigns to ride the bitch as raw as you'd like." Patrick spoke from the couch that sat fifteen feet from the table. His posture was relaxed back into the cushions, one arm hung casually over a pillow and a glass of a dark liquor was held in his hand.

. . .

When they'd first entered the house, Hope had struggled to focus on the faces of the women held in cages at the back of the room. Desperate to find her sister, she was disappointed when none of the women in the cages had been Honor. The acrid taste of fear filled her mouth, but she refused to believe that Honor was no longer alive.

The longer they'd remained in the room, the harder the drug wore against her thoughts. She couldn't focus her eyes, and it felt like she was floating even when she'd knelt on the floor at Xander's feet. Each candle in the room was nothing more than a fuzzy halo, leaving her lost within a dark space of shadow and nothing more. Even though she could comprehend the words spoken between Xander and Patrick, it sounded like they were in a tunnel, each sound echoing against the other, mingling to a point where she needed to concentrate to follow the conversation. When Xander had finally moved her towards the

227

table, the sudden weight on her legs caused her knees to buckle, her own feet so heavy she tripped over them as she walked. She wanted to scream when he'd bent her over the surface of the table. It was like lying on a block of ice. The cold surface of the table bit at Hope's nerves, just before a numbing sensation fell over the skin. Pins and needles burst all over her body and the feeling was amplified by the drugs that coursed through her veins. Her head swam from the drug; however, despite her rapid loss of control over herself, she could still think somewhat clearly. It was as if they'd made her own body a prison — taking her ability to move, but failing to completely numb her mind against the horrors occurring within the house. Slowly, she sunk further, the poison finally reaching her mind, her thoughts consumed in waves of confusion.

She could hear Xander move around the table securing her in place, each shackle buckled with a soft click of metal against metal.

Patrick spoke again from somewhere she couldn't see. His words sounded odd and foreign — *strap, wall, hang* — fuck! He was saying something but the sequence of the words slipped from her grasp, folding over themselves to a point where she couldn't put them together to form a coherent thought.

White noise washed over her ears as the room went silent and Xander's response brushed across her thoughts, even though she was unable to understand what he'd said. She fought against the fog that was thickening over her mind,

228

desperate to remain aware enough to hopefully learn the fate of her sister. Losing the battle, she felt Xander's hand on her head, felt his thumb move between her lips and pull her bottom jaw down. He slipped something bitter between her lips, so big that it hurt the skin at the sides and she tried to spit it out. He caught it, forcing it back in and securing it tightly to her head. Tears formed at the back of her eyes, but stopped when her attention was drawn to something warm on her skin, something sharp softly being dragged down her spine until he reached her lower back. Her body responded out of instinct, arching upwards to push against whatever he held against her that felt so fucking good. It was sensation times ten because of the drugs, the softest brush against her skin sending waves of excruciating pleasure through her body.

Like a cat in heat...that bastard's vile words replayed in her head, but she realized the bastard was right: if the restraints hadn't held her down, her body would be pushed up, exposed, inviting the intrusion she knew was to come. The faint sound of a zipper pulling, her hips grabbed, the tip of each finger sending a spear of exquisite pain shooting up her nerves, settling lazily against her mind, exciting her more than the drugs had already done. She was suddenly mad, an internal battle inside her to resist what was being done because she didn't want to give those men the entertainment they sought. But, his hands...fuck...his hands, he fed her bits of pain, bits of numbness within her thoughts, a place she could sink into. He woke up the darkness inside her, left her within a familiar place where he knew she could hide.

She went emotionally dead, the hormones mixed with the chemicals mixed with her blood and when he shoved in, when she was suddenly filled, each muscle gripping and her teeth biting down even when her lip split at the sides from the motion – thought was removed and she was left floating within a space far from the pounding rhythm against her body. The hurt, the pain, the feeling of being ripped apart and put back together, and then there was heat, blooming, igniting, sparking along her muscles and bones. And the scream that tore from her throat from the relentless slap of skin against skin, from the tips of his fingers gripping into the flesh of her hips, and from the contrast of the burning heat of her body against the unbearable cold of the steel table – it was a scream she didn't recognize as her own. It was pleasure and pain, fur and razors, intense ecstasy wound around a violent release, and her body swam within it, her ears ringing from the sound that she wouldn't believe had come from her own throat.

He pulled away and she was left empty, the void growing and settling through her stomach and chest, her body shivering against the sudden loss of his connection. In the distance, someone clapped, the sound pounding within her head, anger returning now that his fingers had released their iron grip from her skin. Metal snapped from her ankles, and the thud of his boots sounding from his path back to the front of the table. The strap was pulled from her mouth and she tasted the bitter iron of her own blood where her lips had split at the sides. Her tongue flicked out, the salt of her

230

skin sinking into the wound, returning small bits of the same pain he'd previously given.

Now released, she slid from the table, caught at the waist by the steel band of his arm and she purred against him in response to the heat of his body rolling against her own. Her mind wasn't strong enough to control the her body's reaction and she died inside knowing that she'd given these men exactly what they'd wanted to see.

Chapter Twenty-Three

"Are you ready to talk business?" Xander held Hope up beside him knowing that if he let her go, she'd fall to the ground. He was disgusted with what he'd had to do, his body barely responding to her chained and offered up to him on that cold, metal table. Playing out the role had been difficult, faking a release only to end the encounter. Rage bloomed in his chest at having the men see her unclothed. That rage grew and twisted into fury when he had to lay her across a table intended for torture and pain. But to have to be the one to inflict the harm, to have to embarrass her and treat her as nothing more than meat – that had been the act which pushed him over the edge. He'd never felt anything like it and he remembered clearly the look on Aaron's face many years before when he'd been forced to hurt Maddy. It was a terrifying cruelty – to love someone and to have to treat them with abuse; to be made to tear apart the mind and body of the only thing you found beautiful in the world. That is what Joseph had made Aaron do and that is what Xander was being forced to do now.

Patrick held up a key, the ring dangling from his finger. "Put away your pet and have a seat. Her cage is behind your chair."

His words caused Xander's blood to boil, but he bit back his anger, maintaining a mask of

232

indifference over his face. "Thank you for allowing me to keep her close."

Patrick smiled. "We are nothing if not accommodating. With a trophy like that, I can understand your hesitancy to let her go far."

"I'm sure. I'd love to see her twin. I find it hard to believe that two exist." He fished for information, hoping to discover if Honor lived.

Patrick's lips curled into a wicked grin. "I'm sure we can make that happen." He held up his glass. "But first – let's have a drink."

Xander took the key from Patrick and led Hope to the cage. He grit his teeth when he opened it and forced her inside the box already stained with the sweat and blood of its previous occupant. While locking her inside, he commented, "It appears this has been used before."

Patrick laughed. "Yes, well there are *accidents* that occur. The men can get somewhat aggressive at times. Only makes the entertainment that much more interesting."

Taking his seat in a chair facing Patrick, Xander asked. "Who are the units you've pulled to your side? If it is only three, then our outlook is quite grim. They'll never be able to force their leadership of the network."

"It is building slowly. Most of the units are happy with the money Aaron is able to filter in their direction. They haven't been affected yet by

233

the bullshit rules Aaron is imposing. But they will be, and when that happens, they'll come to our side."

"Who leads the rebellion?"

"I do." Patrick eyed him before reaching to retrieve a glass from the table between them and filling it with dark liquor. Offering it to Xander, he said, "Have a drink, it'll help settle your nerves. I can't imagine what it's like to know you're Aaron's next kill."

Xander took the glass, swirling the liquid around the crystal, watching as Patrick poured himself another. Only after he'd seen Patrick drink from the same bottle, did he bring the glass to his lips and sip. He didn't trust the bastard sitting in front of him.

"Aaron doesn't appreciate being disobeyed. He is very much like his father in that way – brutal in his punishment of even the slightest bit of defiance by his men."

"At least Joseph had style. Aaron is nothing more than an aggravating nuisance. However, now that we have you, we have a wealth of information. I'm sure that we can be beneficial to each other." When the phone rang next to Patrick, he pulled it from his pocket, glancing at the display before downing his drink and excusing himself to answer it.

Xander watched as Patrick walked away, speaking in a hushed whisper so that no other person in the room could hear what was being said. Every once in a while he'd glance at Xander.

Finishing his call, Patrick walked back over, retaking his seat. When he opened his mouth to speak again, he was interrupted by the cries of one of the caged women. Annoyance flashed in his expression before he ordered the guard to silence her. Xander watched as the guard approached her cage, smiling at her before kneeling down to speak. "What's wrong, whore?"

Xander couldn't hear her response. Eventually, the guard stood again. "She says she's thirsty."

Patrick's responsive laugh was sickening. "Well, then give her something to drink."

The guard smiled and moved to retrieve a hose. Her scream bounced against the ceiling and walls when he directed the violence of its blast at her cage. The other captives cried with her, each of their bodies shaking against the bars.

"Shut the fuck up!" Patrick screamed. Standing up from his seat, he pulled a gun from the back of his pants and shot the woman who'd asked for water. The guard turned the hose off, laughing. Xander closed his eyes for a brief second, his head dizzy from the depth of cruelty of these men.

Sitting again, Patrick motioned towards the now dead woman with his hand. "Like I said: There are *accidents.*" Looking back toward to guards at the back of the room, he commanded, "Clean the bitch up before she starts to smell."

235

Two guards approached the cage to carry out his order, removing the body and dragging it to a side door on the other side of the room, a trail of water and blood remaining from their path.

"So, tell me, what information can you offer us that will be useful in our *mutual* objective." Patrick poured a third glass while he questioned Xander.

Taking another sip, Xander answered, "It depends on your intentions. If it is to solely kill Aaron, that's simple. However, if you intend on taking over The Estate when he falls, that is a much more delicate and involved task." He gave just enough information to sound useful, but not enough to come close to betraying his friend.

"It seemed simple enough after Joseph was killed. In this network, it's every man for himself, they'll align with me just as easily as they did Aaron as long as I give them what they need."

"You'll need the business. If Aaron dies, there will be no one left to manage the daily operation of the company that launders our funds."

"Do we?" Patrick grinned. "Who is watching us anymore that will give a damn? The authorities have been on The Estate payroll for years. Even if the business falls, nobody will care about dirty money. This town has been overrun by us for years and there is nobody that can stop us."

"Even Joseph was not arrogant enough to believe that." Sweat beaded down the skin of

236

Xander's neck, the room becoming uncomfortably hot.

"Joseph was drugged the last several years of his life. Everybody knew it was Emory who led the network – and that bastard couldn't care less about the business. It's a shame he was killed. He would have been quite useful to us." His words echoed even though they were spoken quietly and Xander attempted to shake himself of the odd sensations creeping along his spine.

"You look tired all of a sudden. Perhaps you'd like another drink." A knowing grin stretched across Patrick's face, making it apparent he knew that Xander was feeling unwell.

Xander looked behind him at Hope laid out in her cage. Sweat ran down her skin, dripping to the metal base from her forehead. Her eyes rolled behind their lids and she panted as she breathed. She looked like he felt and he knew instantly that he'd been drugged.

"You must have built up a tolerance. You drank from the same bottle, yet you appear unaffected." His words started to slur when he returned his gaze to Patrick's arrogant expression.

Patrick's smile grew wider. "It was not the liquor that was laced. It was your glass." He swirled his own drink before musing, "I'm surprised you drank at all. I could have sworn you were more intelligent than to do something as stupid as that."

"We are on the same side."

237

Patrick looked up from his glass. "Are we now?" Chuckling, he admitted, "Our reach is farther than you think. I happen to know you are not as hated by Aaron as you claim. However, you are still useful, so you'll have to excuse me for lying to get you back here." He smiled. "You might be just the thing we need to trap Aaron finally. I assume he'll be looking for you at the warehouse. It's a shame he won't be able to find you."

"Fuck you." It was all he could say. The drugs were rushing through his veins, poisoning his body and mind, his comprehension slipping when he crashed into a deeper void of confusion and lethargy.

"I'm not into men, however, I'm sure some of my men won't mind taking you up on your offer."

Two guards approached Xander from behind, grabbing his arms, one placing a gun to his head and the other immediately chaining him to the chair. Once he was secured, Patrick stood up and walked over to take the key to Hope's cage from Xander's pocket.

Holding it up, he said, "Now the real fun begins. If you are nice, I'll even let you stay long enough to watch."

Chapter Twenty-Four

Red, with rust or blood or both. Her eyes opened just enough so she could see the stain. It was everywhere – in her hair, on her skin, on the bars and floors. She sat back; tired, her body barely moving when she became uncomfortable or cramped.

Like animals, they were caged and they cried silently; the sounds of their bodies softly beating against the bars from their sobs. Hope fought the euphoria, the numbness and blanket of confusion, her blood still polluted with the drug they'd forced. Waves of intoxication crashed against her stealing her breath and it felt like, in those instances, she would drown. She pushed through, breathing slowly…in and out. Her heart rate would slow and her blood would stop speeding through her body.

She could barely comprehend what the two men said, but when she saw them grab Xander, lock him down to his chair, something bloomed in her, an emotion that removed the tunnel over her vision, that cleared the haze just enough that she knew to be scared – on edge – alert. She pushed past the next wave, breathing steady, willing her heart to slow back to a normal pace.

Footsteps, slow and rhythmic, she opened her eyes to see them approach. The guard walked through the rows, laughing, kicking at the metal.

Keys hung from his hand and he swung them, mocking the women trapped inside the small cells.

"Who will it be?"

Despite the fact that they could easily be seen between the bars, they backed up, cornering themselves, shrinking so as not to be chosen.

"This one."

He knelt down in front of a cage, and the woman scrambled away, pressing herself against the back. Another woman screamed, an agonizing wail that made Hope's ears feel like they would bleed – made it feel like her heart was being ripped from her chest.

"Crystal! No!" The second woman reached out, desperate to stop the guard from removing her friend.

He kicked at her hand, her arm bending back until a sickening crunch punctured the air and the woman screamed again while pulling her arm back to cradle it against her naked chest.

He laughed when he dragged her out by her hair, the air ringing as her hands slid from one bar to another. She fought and Hope's heart beat faster to watch it, her own instincts kicking in – adrenaline pushing it's way through her. But even that small loss of control brought the wave rushing back, overtaking her, leaving her lost in blissful ignorance of the nightmare of her surroundings.

She didn't push back again until they'd taken the girl to the front of the room. She could barely see, it was too far for her hazed vision and Xander's body blocked parts of the scene. The table, she recognized the table and her body shivered to remember how cold it had been – it felt like razors scratching the skin, pins and needles everywhere.

The woman was laid across, strapped in, and she fought – bucking against the men while they taunted her. They walked around, one in front, one in back. Violated, abused, mistreated – the woman was being used. The men moved, forcing themselves inside, but then one of the guards screamed, the sound flooding the room. Hope forced herself to look, noticing the blood that ran from the guard's hands. He pulled away from the girl and Hope saw the blood on her mouth.

Hope smiled to realize that even strapped down and shackled, that woman still fought.

"Fucking bitch bit me!"

The other guard turned suddenly, grabbing something from the table and moving to stand in front of the woman. "You like to bite?"

Pliers – he held pliers and Hope closed her eyes again fearing what was to come.

She opened her eyes again when the blood curling scream sounded. Holding her hands over her ears, she fought to mute the sound, but it was invasive and all consuming.

Teeth fell to the ground and the horrendous scream would never end. Balling over herself she attempted to hide from the horror that played out in front of her. In her life, she'd seen pain, she'd seen death and she'd seen heartache – but never had she'd seen the face of the beast itself – a thing so vile and depraved that just by looking at it, your soul was charred, a pattern burnt and scored into the deepest part of yourself. It was an inescapable prison, created and molded to fit within the body of the witness. It was repulsive and addicting at the same time.

Eventually, the screams eased into bitter, heartbreaking sobs, Hope opened her eyes to be met with the pool of crimson gathered beneath the woman – noticed how the guard who'd been bitten had replaced himself in his pants and now marched towards the woman, a long thin pole in his hands, spinning in front of him like the propeller of a plane or the blades of fan that could tear a body apart. He laughed at her pain, smiled proudly at the blood stained hand of the other guard, the pile of bits of white bone weaved within the maroon pool spreading at their feet.

The woman looked up at them as much as she could with her head strapped in place on the table and she did something that surprised Hope – she spit. Pride towards the woman blossoming in Hope's chest, she nodded her respect to Crystal, recognizing that, despite the hopelessness of the woman's position, she continued to fight the bastards, refusing to allow them to crush her spirit as easily as they could her body.

Hope noticed how Xander looked away, bracing himself for what the guards would do. Maddy's words rang louder in her head – feigning weakness in effort to survive – the woman now locked onto the table was doing the exact opposite. Even though she was shown how her life would end, she fought – refusing survival by giving the men who tortured her dominion over her mind – she fought and she lost.

The guard stood behind her, and Hope focused on the side of Xander's face, tried to keep her eyes locked to something she could love – something that put an emotion in her other than the terror she felt. The drugs stopped fogging Hope's mind, the hormones produced by her body in reaction to the woman's terror and pain managing to wipe away the euphoric effects.

The guard approached her, and positioned the pole, intent on burying it in the woman from behind.

Her friend in the cage screamed and Hope covered her ears again, her skull crushed by the force of her own hands.

"Son of a bitch! Stop!" Patrick stood up and looked between the woman in front and her friend. Slowly, he stalked between the cages, his hands tucked casually behind his back. He stopped above the woman.

Kneeling down, he asked, "How the fuck am I supposed to enjoy the show with your annoying FUCKING SCREAMING!!" Once again, pulling the gun from the waistband of his pants, he aimed and fired.

Her body fell to the ground, blood splattered from the cage to land on Hope's skin. Hope opened her eyes, not able to keep from looking at what Patrick had done. She collapsed when she noticed the woman's face was gone.

Patrick stood up, brushing at the crimson splotches on his shirt. "Fuck!"

He walked back to his seat and looked over at Xander, "I apologize for the distraction. People have no fucking manners around here anymore." He smiled – the look unnerving in its insanity.

He turned his attention back to the front of the room. "Proceed."

The guard shoved his hands forward, the pole he held impaling the woman vertically until she choked on her own blood; her body jerking in Hope's peripheral vision from the stabbing, the tearing apart of her body from the inside. When it was forced fully through her body, her body went limp, a woman skewered like an animal on a spit.

The woman died on that table a whore, but Hope realized that she walked into the next life a warrior. She'd never stopped fighting, never given the bastard's the submission they sought. Hope laid her head against the bars of her cage imagining she could see the woman's spirit leave the room, finally freed from the madness and insanity of the house in which she'd been trapped.

244

The room grew quiet except for the heart wrenching sobs of the two women left alive in their cages.

"Well, that was – pleasant. Guess it takes practice to learn that you never force your dick into a bitch's mouth without removing the teeth first." Patrick stood from his seat, glancing at Xander before turning to glare in Hope's direction. "Remove her body and clean up the area." The tip of his tongue ran along his bottom lip, the look in his eyes cruel and calculating. When his lip curled at the side and a lewd grin stretched menacingly across his face, he continued, "It's time for me to take something that I've been wanting for the past week."

Hope's eyes widened. Locked to the blue and green of Patrick's, she attempted to move back in response to his stare – his words. Her body was lethargic and the cage in which she'd been trapped offered her no place to hide. The bastard stared down at her and grinned when he recognized that she knew she was next.

She saw Xander's body move, saw how he pulled against his own chains to realize what Patrick was about to do. He was discreet in his struggle, but Patrick noticed, smiling brighter to know that what he was about to do would destroy Hope and Xander both.

The guards moved about, dragging the woman's body away like nothing more than meat. They mopped up the area, leaving it wet and clean,

245

an empty canvas on which they could paint another portrait of pain, of misery and of malice.

Still staring at her, Patrick mused, "I was quite upset to hear you'd been caught, especially considering you promised me you'd return. I thought I'd chosen a professional by choosing you." He stepped towards her and all Hope could see out of the door of her cage was his approaching feet. "I seem to remember that you promised to play."

She stopped struggling to move away. Conserving her energy, she realized that while imprisoned by metal, she been rendered defenseless. When he reached her, he knelt down, peering in – a predator stalking his prey. "You have nothing to worry about. Unlike my guards, I don't feel a need to spill blood immediately; especially considering the fact that it will take days for me to do all the things to you that I've been dreaming up since our last encounter."

Hope looked at him, purposely blinking her eyes to appear dazed. Even though her muscles still protested movement, and the room still managed to spin around her, she could force herself to think clearly again.

"Clear the room!"

Hope couldn't tell who was more surprised by his order, the guards or her. When the men didn't move fast enough, Patrick stood, screaming his commands, the rage in his voice revealing the insanity contained within his psyche. He was mad,

246

a man overcome by demons – led by evil into becoming evil, into personifying the ugly truths of life.

His men removed the living women from their cages, leaving behind the women who'd died, the black shade of mortality already having freed them from the prison their life had become. She was jealous that those women had been granted the one thing fate had refused her for so long.

The dead were left behind, while the two who remained were led to a room and shoved inside before the men closed the door again and locking it. When the men had left and all who remained in the room were Hope, Xander and Patrick, she shuddered, the silence amplifying the threat of the violence to come.

Patrick didn't unlock her cage immediately, but rather, he walked casually away, stopping at a table across the room. Picking something up, he turned again to face Xander and tapped a syringe against his palm.

"The small amount of fluid in this is enough to kill a man." He took a few steps towards Xander and the muscles across Hope's back tensed, her fingernails digging into the palm with the growing fury inside her.

"I've been instructed to keep you alive – at least until we can obtain the information we seek. But, my partner and I disagree on whether anything you say would be beneficial or not." He stopped. "My vote is 'not'."

247

Stepping slowly towards Xander again, Patrict smiled deviously. "Is anyone up for a game of chance?" He kneeled down in front of Xander, "This amount could be enough to kill you – or – it could leave you just at that edge to allow you to know what death is, but not quite grant it. I'd like to find out exactly where it will take you."

The chains rattled on Xander's chair and the wood groaned and cracked as he struggled to move. Hope's head started to spin, but not from the chemicals floating freely in her body – no. It was fear, the same fear she felt for her sister, the same fear that meant she was losing something she valued. Even more debilitating than the drugs, her fear froze her muscles over her bones, made her throat swell to the point where it was difficult to breathe. She willed herself to calm down – to feel nothing. She needed the black space of violence and pain, she needed the clarity of having no thought inside her mind besides the idea that she was to kill or be killed.

Patrick chuckled, the sound hollow and heartless. Placing the syringe on the table beside Xander, he stood up again and moved to stand beside the metal table at the front of the room. The grating squeak of metal over metal resounded over the ceilings and walls – the sound scratching against Hope's mind when Patrick swiveled the table so that it faced Xander.

Hope could see the muscles flex and constrict beneath his clothes. He worked at the chains, but couldn't loosen them, no matter how desperately he fought.

248

"Even if I hadn't known already that you weren't truly intending to help my rebellion, I would have known by the way you fucked your *whore*. You see, it's the face that gives it away, the expression that reveals the truth about whether a woman hates what is being done to her, or if she likes it." His fingers idly played along the table, the tips walking along the cold metal surface as if they were a man's legs.

"In order to dominate, to control and to have power over another person, you must take something from them that they would not willingly give. To make it even more meaningful, you must break their mind by perverting their emotions, making them feel pleasure when they detest you for having done it. You must turn something good within them into something horrible. There is a distinct look in their eye when that happens, a true break in their spirit that is magnificent to witness." He smiled and Hope saw nothing but lunacy behind the green and blue of his eyes.

"I'd like to show you what that looks like."

Patrick moved quickly around Xander to approach Hope's cage. She remained completely still, hoping he would forgo caution because he believed she was too drugged to fight back. He knelt down to look at her. "I have a surprise for you – I kept her alive – your sister."

Her heart raced in her chest, the resultant sound like thunder in her head. Tears welled at the back of her eyes and she flinched at his words. Not knowing their truth, she was stuck in a vise between fighting the bastard when he removed her or playing the role to ensure her sister would live.

"Sometimes, it takes patience and cunning to free yourself...it might be the only thing that saves you and your sister's life..."

Maddy's words again, disembodied and floating through Hope's thoughts. She relaxed, breathing again to calm her body and her heart. The latch of the key in the lock made her jump.

Breathe in...breathe out...

She looked up at him, studied the cruel expression on his face, every movement of his body. She'd kill him, she'd sink to the same level of evil where he existed so that the 'look' he used to taunt Xander would be the last thing she saw in his eyes when he died. He pulled his gun again.

"You fight me, I kill you, and what I was about to do to you will be done to your sister instead. Considering you are identical, Xander will see what I want to show him regardless of which body is laid out across that table."

Hope blinked her eyes, pretending that she couldn't respond. It was obvious he knew she was no longer as helpless as when she'd first been drugged and caged, but she'd play the role anyway. At some point, Patrick would drop his guard and when that happened, Hope's true darkness would come alive.

"Let's go." He grabbed the leash that was still secured around her neck. Bringing her face

250

close to his, he said, "I'll have to thank Xander for the chain once I'm done with you." Yanking so hard, the bones at the back of her neck popped, he ripped her from the cage, replacing the gun in his pants, he grabbed her hair and dragged her to the table. She fought back feebly, pretending to not have the strength to protect herself. It was only half a ruse, she was not yet over the effect of the drug, but she had regained enough strength to know that in a few hours, she'd be in a position to end the bastard that held her.

"Bend over." She forced her body over the table, the razor sharp and stinging cold once again attacking her skin. She grit her teeth against it, used the painful temperature to awaken her body more and chase away the remaining influence of chemicals from her blood. One by one, the familiar clicks of the shackles sounded as they were closed over her ankles and wrists. Her chin fell into place at the notch cut into its edge. Her eyes aligned with Xanders and she died to see the torment, the anger and the pain that turned the sapphire blue into something resembling an angry sea. The tendons at his neck stuck out and he continue to struggle against the chains. She closed her eyes, hardly able to bear watching the emotions he was feeling play over the expression on his face.

Opening her eyes again, she locked her gaze to his. She studied him so intently; she could see her reflection in his eyes. Patrick's hands rubbed over her body, greedy fingers gripping at her skin.

"Oh yes, this is what I've been waiting for."

251

His voice disgusted her and she kept her eyes locked to Xander, noticed how his expression went blank – lethal. She'd seen it before when she attempted Aaron's life, knew that in his head, images of Patrick's death played out.

No, my beautiful boy...it won't be you that kills him...that privilege will be all mine...

She couldn't speak to him, couldn't do anything but look at him while Patrick readied himself to do revolting things to her body.

And then Patrick filled her; rutting against her like an animal, taking her body, but not her mind. Xander's hands gripped the armrest of the seat, the metal chains at his wrists pressed against the skin so tight, it turned white around the links. He was struggling to break his constraints and Hope looked at him, tried to convey to him that it was okay, that she wasn't hurt or broken by what the bastard did to her. She'd been trained, raped by her own network when she was young to ensure there wasn't one thing a man could do to her that would break her. She never told Xander the true extent of her training, didn't want him to know just how thorough her network had been. But now – now she wished she had told him because it could have eased the pain she saw swirling violently in his eyes.

"Scream for me, bitch."

She watched Xander and her rage grew more intense, clouding logic, demanding that she fight against the bastard that was inside her. She

252

knew she should play feeble, but she just couldn't give the asshole what he wanted.

"Oh, please, stop." There was no emotion in her tone and Patrick stopped suddenly when he heard her droll words.

Discreetly, Xander grimaced. It was a quick twitch across his face, but enough to make her realize she'd made a mistake. But she couldn't help herself and she didn't care what was being done to her, only what was being done to the people she loved.

After pulling out, Patrick shoved himself back in his pants and moved away from the table. She waited for him to hurt her, to force the reaction from her he wanted. Even if he were to slice her open, she decided she wouldn't give it to him. It was a decision she would soon regret.

"You want to play games with me, bitch? An ominous warning hung on those words. "Let's see if your sister would like to play as well."

Hope's fists clenched and the table shook when she pulled at the shackles binding her wrists and ankles. Fuck! She closed her eyes at how stupid she'd been to mock him.

"But first..." Patrick walked to where he was standing between Xander and Hope. Grabbing the needle from the side table where he'd placed it, he stabbed it into Xander's neck, and pressed down on the plunger, shooting the deadly dose into Xanders body.

253

"…I'll kill your fucking boyfriend."

Hope's mouth opened and a sound she'd never known was possible escaped her. It was the sound of loss, of heartbreaking pain and absolute misery. It felt like her body, her mind and her heart shattered and her eyes looked into Xander's, tears streaming down her cheeks when she watched the haze creep over his vision and his body, that had previously struggled against his chains, suddenly falling limp and loose against the chair.

Chapter Twenty-Five

A dark room now. Bursts of light when the door opens and closes. Food and water at Honor's feet. "Lap it up like a dog", they say.

He hasn't come back...her angel. They took her far from where he could find her. Far, far...but he will find her. As soon as she finds her way out from the darkness and into the light, he'll find her. And then he'll take her – away from the monsters, from their malicious hands and angry eyes.

Her stomach growls but she won't eat their food. They're making her crazy like them, so she doesn't eat or drink until her mouth is so dry, she has no choice but to swallow small bits. She hears the screaming still. The women he didn't choose. Only the screaming, the walls are too thick for their other sounds and Honor thanks the walls for making the other sounds go away.

The door opens and she looks up, her eyes desperate to see his large form fill the doorway, to know that he's found her, that he'll take her.

A man enters – not him – not her angel. She cries silent tears.

He grabs her by the arm, his fingers digging into the skin that hangs loose from her muscle. She can't fight and when he rips her to her feet, her knees fail, she falls, only to be ripped up again.

"I suggest you come with me. Your angel has a request."

Pounding...her heart is suddenly pounding and her body shakes because it pounds so hard. Her lips hurt when they smile, he's come for her, he's come.

She walks out of the darkness, the light blinding her eyes, but she blinks back the tears. So many people, and the bad sounds return – the crying, the women getting sick. The monsters surround her, the room terrifyingly bright. She looks for him, looks at each face – not him, not him, not him.

He's not there.

They lead her to the front. She looks up.

It's not her angel.

It's her mirror.

. . .

Hope...Xander tried to blink his eyes into focus, not comprehending that the woman they led out of the side room wasn't the girl he'd just seen strapped to cross on a wall. The drug Patrick had injected coursed through his system and he felt his skin become sticky with heat and sweat. His arms and legs wouldn't respond to his desire to move and his tongue swelled in his mouth and down his throat, making it feel like he couldn't breathe. His eyes opened and closed, the woman, Hope – no, her sister – being dragged to the front of the room.

After Patrick had drugged him, he'd called on his men to assist him in removing Hope from the table and securing her into a heavy wood cross. When she was secured, they'd drugged her as well. He moved his head to look up, to see that her hazy eyes still widened when she watched her sister come into the room. Tears fell along her cheeks and her body trembled where it hung. Her chest beat out with exhaustive breath and he knew her heart raced against her chest. She struggled against the effects of what they'd given her, but she was failing to remain alert.

Eyes opening and closing, he slipped away for brief seconds, the images playing out before him appearing more like still photographs than moving objects. In and out, he fought to remain conscious even when he felt his body shutting down. His heart split apart and he struggled against the chains, felt weak and defeated when he could barely move even his finger. When the men had approached Hope, holding her sister between them, he looked up at Hope's face, tears distorting his own vision to see what they were planning to do. When Hope finally comprehended what was being done, her expression fell - partly in response to the drugs and partly because she obviously knew that what was about to happen would destroy her.

Patrick approached Hope's sister, leaning in close to her to whisper something in her ear. Hope struggled in her chains behind them.

"My angel..." Her words were disjointed and Xander wasn't sure if she'd actually said

257

something or if his mind was succumbing to the poison coursing through his veins.

He faded out, caught in a wave of numbing intoxication. His breath hissed out over his lips, his eyes rolling back in his head and his teeth chattering against each other. His body began to shake violently, his stomach twisting over itself until its contents pushed their way up his throat. His head fell to the side and he retched – over and over until his abdomen cramped tight and he couldn't straighten his body.

"Disgusting...clean...hose..." Words, he was only getting words and they didn't make sense – didn't sound real. Forcing his eyes open again, he saw Patrick's face – angry, ugly, his features swirling and changing, evil made fluid and alive.

"Yes, your angel wants this." A demon whispering beautiful words, Patrick leaned over to speak to Hope...not Hope. The woman shook her head no, but after a moment, and after more words Xander couldn't understand, she reached out and took a thin metal chain from Patrick's hand.

Xander shook away his confusion, desperate to stay conscious, to remain sane. His eyelids were too heavy and they closed again, reality disappearing, replaced by starbursts behind his eyes. His throat swelled again, another wave washing over him and rendering him lost – suspended within a thick and soupy fog. He heard Hope cry out.

"Hit her harder, Honor. You can see how much she likes it." Patrick chuckled and Hope screamed again.

His eyes opened.

Hope's body writhed against her chains, unwanted pleasure revealed in the way her hips moved. His breath caught in his chest, his eyes trying to blink closed again when he fought to remain awake. Her sister stood in front of her, whipping her with the chain, leaving bloody trails along Hope's body and Hope responded to the pain, too drugged to resist, her nerves hyperaware and operating despite the fact that her mind knew getting off on it was wrong. Patrick stood back, the wicked machinations of his brain obvious in the distorted and liquid expression on his face.

"Tell us how much you like it, Hope. Scream for me now, bitch!" Patrick's voice and laughter rang out while Xander fought to train his gaze on Hope's face.

Tears rolled down her cheeks even when she was driven to a point of release. His eyes never left her face, he couldn't bear to look away. She didn't look back, staring instead out ahead of her, death sitting quietly behind her eyes.

And that's when he saw it. While he fought to stay with her, and while he slowly slipped away, he saw it. The look Patrick had talked about – the one that meant her spirit had broken, he recognized it and his soul felt like it shattered right there beside her.

259

Finally succumbing for the last time, he closed his eyes, his memory racing through images of his life – the look in Hope's eyes taking him back to the time he'd seen it before.

. . .

"Gregory Shipp. You've been caught stealing money from my network, from all of the men in this room, from my wife who sits beside me."

Xander looked up at the man on the stage. He was scared, his little knees knocking together as he attempted to move closer to his mother.

The man walked towards the front of the stage, his eyes locked to Xander's father. "You've been a member of my network for quite some time, Mr. Shipp, and as I'm sure you are aware, there have been three other occasions where some ignorant fool has attempted the same thing." The man paused and Xander fidgeted, not understanding what the man said. "Do you recall what happened to those men?"

His father looked up. "Yes, Joseph. The men were executed, they were shot." Xander's fear grew into absolute terror, scared that he heard his father's voice, weak and cracking – his dad was scared, and he'd never seen his father scared.

The man on stage nodded.

"They were. So I assumed, as someone who's seen that, you would have known better than to attempt the same thing. However, since I am obviously wrong for having assumed that, I realize that I need to step up the punishment. Shooting a man isn't enough,

260

is it? You still thought you could steal from The Estate. So, Mr. Shipp, I'll be stepping up the punishment tonight, hopefully deterring the next ambitious soul who thinks he can cheat the network."

The doors opened on the side of the large room. Everybody turned to look and Xander moved to grab his father's hand – the palm sticky with sweat. Xander squeezed tightly, shaking his father's arm, begging him to look down at him. He wanted to protect his dad, but his dad wouldn't look away from the man on the stage.

Looking up again, Xander noticed a beautiful woman moving quickly down the stairs, her eyes glancing over at him – filling with pain immediately when she saw him. He became more nervous as she looked at him, but then she turned and disappeared out the large doors.

"You have a very beautiful family, Mr. Shipp." The man looked over at Xander, an angry grin playing over his lips. "What a good looking boy. He looks to be my son's age. What is his name?"

"Xander." His father's response was choked and fearful.

The man on stage paused for a moment, the room became quiet and Xander's small heart was beating so fast he became dizzy.

"Aaron has been asking for a playmate."

His father squeezed his hand so tight, Xander grimaced to feel the bones rub together from the iron grip.

261

The man turned his eyes back on Xander's father. "Since you have stolen from me, I believe it's only fair that I steal from you. An eye for an eye. You took from me the one thing I worked so hard to gain — you took my money. So, I will take something that is important to you."

"You can have all the money in my account, Joseph, it's more than I took from the network; three times more. You can take it all, just please don't take my son."

Tears streamed down his father's face and Xander looked over to notice that his mother cried as well. She hugged his baby sister to her chest, shaking her head and attempting to back away from the large men that moved to surround them. He didn't know why the man would take him, didn't understand what was happening and why his parents were so upset.

"It's not just your son I'm taking, Mr. Shipp. I have a much larger acquisition in mind...your entire family, in fact. But first, I'll take your life."

When the blast sounded, Xander jumped and his father's grip released his hand. He felt something warm splash down on him, and he raised his tiny arms to see small drops of blood speckled over his skin. The sound of the large body falling to the floor surprised him. Turning he looked the dead eyes of his father.

His mouth opened and he screamed. Running to his mother, he wrapped his arms around her legs, felt her body shake with her own mournful cries. He was pulled away from his mother — held back to the side where he watched another man approach her,

262

silently stalking her with a mean look and ugly face. His mother took a few steps back, shaking her head in defiance, but she was stopped by another man, held still as the first man approached her.

Xander tried to pull away, desperately to free himself of the iron grip that held him, but he was too small. He couldn't do anything but watch and tears burst from his eyes.

When the man reached his mother, he stopped in front of her and smiled.

"Emory, we are not monsters here. Take care of it quickly." The man on stage laughed.

The man turned and ripped Xander's sister out of his mother's arms. She screamed and his sister screamed and Xander covered his ears to try and block out the terrifying sound. He saw the man's hand slip inside the blanket covering his sister, and with a flick of the man's wrist, his sister stopped crying – however, the shriek that tore from his mother's mouth was the most painful sound he'd ever heard. She fell to her knees, shaking and crying and the man who held his sister smiled again. He walked away and placed Xander's sister in his tiny little arms, smiling and patting Xander on the head. Sitting down on the floor, Xander held his sister in his lap. His mom was always afraid he'd drop her, so he placed her down carefully until his mom could come and help him hold her.

The men surrounded his mother, she fought against them and they tore at her clothes. Xander was so shocked – so scared – that he sat there quietly, too *afraid to scream or cry. He didn't understand what was happening.*

The beautiful woman reentered the room.

"Stop!" The man on stage yelled.

The men obeyed and stepped away from the table on which they were forcing Xander's mother.

"Arianna, so good of you to rejoin us. I need you to do me a favor." The man pointed down at Xander and his sister.

"Xander here is going to be staying with us for a while, I thought he could be a good friend to our son considering they are around the same age."

Xander's mom began to scream again, her body choking on the force of her sobs.

"Can someone please shut that woman up? I can't think with her screaming and crying like that."

They tied something around her mouth and Xander looked from his mom to the woman who'd reentered the room. His tiny heart pounded in his chest and he cradled his sister to him closer, glad that she'd fallen asleep and wasn't scared like him.

Smiling once that had been accomplished, Joseph turned back to his wife. "As I was saying, please take the child back to your suite. He'll be staying with us indefinitely."

The woman approached him and knelt down, he looked up at her not knowing if she would help him or hurt him. "May I take your sister from you, Xander, I promise I won't hurt her."

He didn't know if he could believe her, but she looked so nice that he nodded yes, his body quaking with fear as he reached up to hand her the small baby bundled in a blanket. She opened the blanket and he noticed that her eyes widened and a tear escaped to roll down her cheek. She closed the blanket again and placed his sister on the floor beside her. Looking back at him, she said, "Xander, your sister is going to be okay, my husband just wants you to meet our son, Aaron. You'll like him, I can tell already that you two will have a lot in common, don't be scared, okay?"

He nodded, his fear paralyzing him to a point where he wouldn't speak. His tiny hand in hers, the woman led him quickly from the room. He didn't know if he should go with her and he didn't want to leave his mom who continued to cry on the table. The woman tugged at his arm and he followed, worried about why they were leaving his sister behind. When the doors closed, he heard his mother scream again. He turned to go back, but the woman picked him up and ran down the corridor and away from his family.

The last thing Xander remembered seeing was the look in his mother's eyes when his sister had gone to sleep and when he was being removed from the large room. It was a look he'd never seen before and a look that scared him. He couldn't understand why, but he hated that man on the stage – hated him because of the look he caused in his mother's eyes.

. . .

265

Xander opened his eyes one last time, the sounds in the room were jumbled together, indistinguishable if they were words, or cries of pain, or pleasure or both. He looked up, barely able to see beneath the fall of thick lashes.

Hope hung limply from the chains, crimson trails streaking over her skin, forming a puddle on the floor beneath her. Her eyes said nothing – they didn't contain fear or pain or heartache – they were dead, lifeless, blank and no longer contained the spirit of the girl who'd longed to be broken.

Forcing his eyes to Patrick, his mind played cruel tricks and the face he watched shifted between that of Patrick – and that of another man who'd destroyed the people he loved. Keeping his eyes on Patrick, Xander realized that, although Joseph Carmichael had died years before, the evil he created was still very much alive.

Looking back at Hope, a tear escaped his heavy eye to find that she'd finally gotten what she thought she wanted all along – death had come to collect her. He closed his eyes again, his breath leaving him and his heart slowing down until it barely moved within his chest. He allowed the long dark tunnel to finally overtake him, dragging him away from the horrors and atrocities of his life and delivering him to a place where The Estate was no longer his prison.

Chapter Twenty-Six

The dark was disorienting. Waking up to what could be day or night, heaven or hell, death or life. She didn't know. Moving her limbs, she felt it – her skin shredded from a razor thin chain, areas that had barely begun to heal, opening again from her movement. Her eyes had opened first and she was delivered into nothing. No sound, no sight, no motion – nothing. Her chest hurt, the slices opening there from her intake of breath, from the stretching of her skin. Burning and sticky, she opened her mouth, desperate for any type of moisture but knowing she wouldn't receive it.

Her leg kicked out, her muscles regaining life and moving involuntarily over her bones. Striking against the metal bars, pain shot from her heel up her leg and her body jerked in response to the sudden sensation. The cage rattled from the strike and a small voice pierced the nothingness within which Hope had awoken.

"I thought you were dead."

Hope startled, the small voice unexpected. She blinked repeatedly, shaking her head as if that would chase away the thick sludge that was smothering her mind. Opening and closing her mouth, she finally found her ability to respond.

"Where are we?" It was a bare whisper against the silence.

"In a side room of some sort. I've been in here longer than you. They dragged you and the entire cage inside. I was surprised. They've never moved the cages in here before."

Falling back against the bars, Hope's head pounded, her skull feeling like it would split apart from the pressure inside. Memories rushed back at her, images of her sister standing in front of her – her eyes completely flat, without emotion or comprehension. Her breath rattled in her chest while her heart sped to suddenly remember. The fog lifted slowly, each image coming back and striking against her as razor sharp and deadly as the chain her sister had used:

Her sister's eyes...

Patrick's cruel grin...

The laughter of the men in the room...

And then – then she saw something that she couldn't stand to remember. She saw something that took the world she knew and twisted it, perverted it. Reality fractured and reformed, came back to life and left her stranded in a shadowed wasteland with her mind splintered and her heart broken.

She saw Xander – unmoving and lifeless in his chair. His hair was slicked back with sweat, his broad shoulders had fallen limp against his seat and his hands hung from the chains that encircled his wrist.

Her eyes suddenly burned when they struggled uselessly to forms tears. Her breath left her chest in quick, strangled gasps and her heart beat with pure rage. Twisted over itself, her stomach heaved, and every muscle in her body tightened when she lurched forward, retching so violently that she convulsed.

No....no....fuck...NO!

She screamed inside her own head, the sound ripping her insides apart, bouncing off her skull and drowning out the sound of her pounding heart and the rushing blood through her veins. She fell back against the cage, balling over herself and shaking – quaking – from the torrent of heartache and loss that consumed her. Desperately, she tried to breathe, but air was only entering her body in quick gasps, her throat closing from grief.

"Are you still with me?"

It was a disembodied voice that Hope couldn't understand. The waves of nausea returned and she rolled over, dry heaving to a point where the muscles of her stomach had cramped, leaving her locked in a fetal position on the floor.

"Are you okay?" The voice was quiet, but carried the small hint of concern.

Hope nodded her head, but couldn't voice her response. She lay still on the floor of her cage, curled around herself, hugging her abdomen in her arms and crying so pitifully, she hated herself for it. She was a murderer – a killer. She faced death

269

every day, never bowing or buckling at how ugly or soul crushing it could be. At six, she'd stared into the dead eyes of her mother when they'd found her raped and beaten in a dirty alley and she'd gone absolutely cold. She'd sought death, bathed in it and danced around it, never allowing it to touch her or affect her even though it was something she wished could finally take her.

And now that she was balled over herself, wallowing in her own sweat, blood and vomit, it finally did – just not in the way she'd always imagined it.

She wanted to shrink away, wither and melt into the rusted metal base of her cage. Every time she felt herself slip, felt her mind fall into a thoughtless void, her body worked to keep her awake and aware – trapped in the insufferable knowledge that the man she wanted so badly to despise had not only captured her heart, but crushed it when his own ceased beating. Her lip trembled and her face scrunched up when she thought about how he'd been the only one – he'd defeated her by taking her body, he'd defeated her by taking her strength, and he'd defeated her by taking the stone cold heart that existed within her chest, only to breathe life into it once again and leave it mangled and shattered, useless for anything else but to force blood through her body.

Hours – it could have been hours or days that she lay there catatonic. Every once in a while the other woman in the room would move or talk, her chains rattling from wherever it was that she sat.

She was falling into a void of resignation and loss. Eventually, the memories of Xander slipped away, replaced instantly by visions of her sister. The woman they'd brought out of that room, looked like Honor – but what Hope had seen in Honor's eyes made it frighteningly apparent that Honor was no longer the woman Hope had known. Her once vibrant eyes were dull, her voice weak and timid. She obeyed the men, didn't ask questions and would only talk about some fucking angel that couldn't have existed in the nightmare of The Estate. Tears finally forced their way free of her eyes when she remembered how she'd reacted to the pain her sister inflicted. It was wrong and it was sick – she was, for once, disgusted and afraid of the part of her that had always scared and repulsed the people who knew her. Her body found release while her mind splintered, small shards tinkling against one another like crystal broken and crushed. The only solace she had was that she couldn't remember anything but bits and pieces, the intoxicating waves once again stealing her from reality, only to replace her long enough for her to comprehend was happening around her.

Hope became angry and a spark burst inside her. From that small spark, rage ignited, building itself into churning fury against the man who'd broken Honor, who'd killed Xander, and who'd attempted to break her.

Pushing up weakly, her foot struck the side of her cage, the sound ringing through the dense silence of the dark room.

271

"So you are still with me." The voice sounded weak and bitter. "To be honest, I really couldn't care less whether you were rotting or still breathing – considering you're the reason I ended up here."

Hope was confused. "I don't know you, I'm not sure how any of this is my fault."

The woman laughed humorlessly. "You know me, although, our meeting was only for a second. I opened the door to peek outside and there you were – dressed in black, like a shadow. I didn't even have time to scream before you hit me and left me outside completely defenseless for the assholes who came along to find me."

Hope closed her eyes when she recognized the woman suddenly. She'd only seen her face, so she wasn't surprised that the woman's voice wasn't familiar. "You're the woman who let me into the mansion."

"Yes."

Shit. Hope let out a frustrated breath. She didn't feel bad for what she'd done because she would do it again if it meant she could save her sister; but at the same time, she'd never meant for the woman to end up in a place like this. "They've had you since that night?"

"Yes." She sniffled; the soft cry of hopelessness echoing softly throughout the room.

"I didn't intend for this to happen. They had my sister, I had no choice."

The woman laughed, the sound harsh and judgmental after hearing Hope's words. "You could have chosen to leave me inside."

Hope grinned, the futility of their situation finally driving her to a point of madness. "You wouldn't have turned out much better inside that mansion either."

"I may have turned out better if I'd remained conscious. At least, then, I could have run." Her words weren't bitter any longer, just an observation made without emotion or ulterior purpose.

It grew quiet between them, Hope thinking of all the innocence lost in the world in which she'd been raised. Her heart hurt, but she pushed the emotion aside and focused on the anger that had sparked within her just moments before. She wondered if her sister was still alive, wondered if Xander's body still existed so she could see him to say goodbye. Pondering how long she had before she joined him, she thought of the ways she could kill the bastard that had created this mess. Imagined his angry eyes, his lewd grin and his repulsive laugh. She allowed her anger to fester and grow, to awaken each nerve ending in her body and to replace the strength she'd lost by forcing adrenaline through her veins. She focused on her hatred and her deep-seated need for vengeance.

"Sometimes, it takes patience and cunning to free yourself…it might be the only thing that saves you and your sister's life…"

273

Maddy's words replayed – the same advice Hope had failed to take before. Her decision to fight, to mock Patrick while he attempted to break her apart – it was a decision that led to Xander's death and that almost destroyed her when Patrick used Honor in his sick games against her. But Hope wasn't dead yet. She remembered Maddy's words and she decided that there had been wisdom behind them after all. It wouldn't be easy – she'd never been the type who didn't fight back with everything that she had, but fighting had only ended in heartache. If there was any chance at all for her to, at least, save Honor, she'd have to endure the misery of Patrick's torture until the opportunity presented itself for her to finally end the bastard's life.

The decision renewed her, replacing energy in her body, and easing the pain of everything she'd lost.

"What's your name?"

The woman didn't answer her immediately, but eventually a small voice responded. "Erica."

Hope rolled her shoulders back and moved her limbs and neck to stretch out the sore and cramped muscles. "I promise you, Erica, I'll get you out of this place. If I have to kill every man in this house, you will escape."

Chapter Twenty-Seven

The door opened and a light was turned on above Hope's head. It burned her eyes, immediately destroying the darkness in which Hope had been trapped. She blinked to keep her eyes open, noticing the silhouette of a man enter the room and look between the cage and the two women who were chained in the room.

Erica shrunk back and Hope kicked her feet against the interior of her cage attempting to pull the man's attention to herself. He looked over and smirked. "You want to come out a play, bitch?" Stepping towards the cage, Hope glared up at him, bound and determined to distract his attention from Erica. Reaching through the cage, he grabbed Hope's hair, wrapping his fingers tight into the base and pulling her up so that her body was pressed tightly against the bars. His eyes looked black against the red rage in his face.

Hope smiled, the pain of his hold on her only driving more adrenaline into her body, waking her up despite how badly she was injured. She had no energy left – the lack of food and water only serving to weaken her further, but she used the adrenaline to keep her alert.

"Yeah, baby. Why don't you take me out of this cage and show me how a real man treats his whore." She winked knowing she would kill him if he pulled her from her cage.

The smirk on his face curled into a lewd grin. Her eyes flicked to Erica and she noticed how her body shook where she'd pressed herself into the corner of the wall. The man's voice brought her eyes back to his face.

"I'd love to, beautiful; but the boss man has other plans for you. I'd lose my dick if I touched you before he's done with you." He gripped her hair tighter and she hissed from the jolts of pain shooting across her scalp. "But when he gets tired and throws you to his dogs, you can bet I'll be at the front of the line."

His hand opened and she fell back to the floor of the cage, her bones striking against the metal base, more pain shooting up from her hips into the back. He turned and approached Erica, his boots hitting against the floor with portentous thuds. Her body convulsed, it shook so hard, and when he reached down to grab her arm, a small shriek escaped her. Lifting her from the floor, the man gripped into her small arm but her legs gave out beneath her.

She fell, her head falling back against the wall and the man laughed before reaching to grab her again.

The door opened.

"Get your ass to the upper level. We have a visitor and I want to the front room heavily guarded until he leaves." Patrick's blue and green eyes were rimmed red with anger.

The guard appeared stricken, obviously fearful that he'd been caught away from his post. "I'm sorry. I didn't know our guest would be arriving so soon."

Patrick moved aside from the door indicating that the guard should leave. While the man moved out of the room, Erica wept where'd he left her. Patrick glanced down at her and smiled. "Well, well, aren't you the lucky one." He chuckled. "For now, anyways."

His gaze moved to Hope and his hands folded in front of him. "I'm glad to see you are still with us Hope. I was concerned that you'd had a bit too much fun during our earlier game. I do hope you learned that being a *good* girl is in your and your sister's best interests. I'd hate to have to have you whipped again.

Biting the inside of her cheek to keep from telling the fucker where he could stick his whip, she forced herself to appear docile and afraid. She peered up at him through her lashes, allowed her bottom lip to tremble as if she were holding back tears. Her voice shook when she asked, "Where's Honor and Xander?"

Patrick's expression became mock sympathy. "Oh, I'm so sorry you haven't heard. Your boyfriend had an unfortunate reaction to the drugs we gave him."

Her heart fell into her stomach and smoldered in the vengeful fire that burned inside. "My sister?"

277

He grinned. "She's alive. We've been very impressed with her. She makes an incredible slave; especially now that her mind has been lost. She will do anything she's told; especially for *her angel*."

His words caused memories to trickle back and Hope remembered hearing her sister say them. "Who's her angel?"

"Tsk, tsk, Ms. Delacroix. You ask far too many questions." Kneeling down, he pulled a key from his pocket. "I'm taking you upstairs. We're going to clean you up and then I intend on having some fun with you. You're not going to fight me and you're going to do everything I tell you to do with a smile on your pretty little face. Any disobedience on your part will lead to punishment."

She blinked up at him, completely disgusted by every word he said.

Smiling, he added, "However it won't be you who is punished, do you understand?"

Nodding, she bit the inside of her lip again. She would have to play the part to get to her sister and she fought to control her instincts and not resist the man she knew she would eventually kill.

"Good to see you are learning to be more *cooperative*. I suspected you were an intelligent girl. It appears I was right." The metal key struck the lock followed by a small click. He opened the door slowly, the hinges groaning with the movement. "Crawl out to me. When you reach the door, put

278

your hands behind you and bend over so your forehead touches the floor.

Hope complied and felt where he handcuffed her hands in place behind her back. He slipped a leather collar around her neck and she recognized it as the one Xander had used. Clenching her teeth, she fought not to feel the devastation of his death. She needed to think clearly to escape and thoughts of him would only distract her from her task.

"I never did get the chance to thank Xander for this leash. It's a magnificent toy." He chuckled and her muscles tightened along her spine at the sound.

Pulling her from the cage, his shoes clicked against the ground in time with the pads of her bare feet. She struggled to stay upright and walk behind him. Focusing on her breathing again, she followed him through hallways to a back staircase. They climbed steps to the third floor and Patrick pulled another key from his pocket. He turned back to look at her, his mismatched eyes shining brilliantly against the tan of his skin. Black hair fell over his forehead and his cheekbones gave him the appearance of a cat. He would have been handsome if he wasn't so fucking psychotic.

"You'll love what I have set up for you. I must admit, I was extremely surprised to see how you got off on being whipped. It was extraordinary. It is rare to find woman so turned on by pain. People would pay good money for a woman like you." He ran the tip of his finger down

279

between her breasts, stopping just above her navel. "I always knew you'd be the more interesting twin." The tip of his tongue flicked out to run along his lip and Hope fought the urge to rip it from his filthy mouth.

Turning back, he unlocked the door and opened it to unveil a large room with a black tiled floors. Candles were ensconced on the walls, and were spread over every available surface – except for those surfaces that held the knives and other tools. She sucked in a deep breath, calming the rapid beat of her heart.

Patrick turned back to take in her expression. "Is that excitement I see glistening in your gold eyes? Because I'm sure you can see it in mine."

She didn't flinch at the implication. Remaining impassive, she trained her gaze over his shoulder, refusing to look the bastard directly in the eye.

His eyes traveled over her body, her skin prickling in disgust at the gesture. He tugged on her chain. "We'll need to clean you up first." He sniffed at the air around her. "I'm going to want you nice and clean for what I have planned."

She entered the room at his back, wishing her hands weren't bound so that she could grab a knife and shove it into his black heart. They moved to a side door that he opened to reveal a small bathroom. There wasn't much room to move once they'd entered and he shoved her in the shower stall and turned on the water. She cried out when the ice-cold water met her skin and her eyes watched the blood and dirt wash down the drain at her feet.

"Look at your beautiful skin." He traced his finger down a scar on her abdomen. "They show up so well against your natural tan. Are they battle scars?" His laugh was sickening. "Or, given your *perversion*, did you do these yourself?"

She flinched away from him, tried to appear timid and small. She needed him to drop his guard, to give her one second, one chance to kill him so she could find her sister.

He pulled his hand back to his body and stepped back, still gripping the chain. Reaching to the counter at his side, he grabbed soap and a cloth. "I'd tell you to wash yourself; unfortunately, you'll need your hands to accomplish that. That's not a luxury I can trust you with quite yet."

He wrapped the chain around his wrist a second time to secure it and moved back. He touched her everywhere, his fingers rough and crude above the cloth. After he'd finished, he dropped it to the floor, choosing to use his hand on her skin. He cupped her breast, pinching the tip, sending a jolt of sensation through her body. She bucked at the feeling, willing her body not to react, but losing against a man who'd discovered her weakness.

"I'm going to have fun with you."

Pulling her from the shower, he ran a towel over her body and walked her into the larger room. The table in the center was a smooth wood and there were no shackles stuck to its surface like the other table. He backed her to its edge. "Sit down."

She did as instructed. He kneeled at her feet and she fantasized about kneeing him in the face. When her ankles were secured by the chains attached to the table legs, he moved around her, locking her wrists to chains attached to the legs at the other end.

"Tell us what you know!"

The sound was faint, but a man yelled from another room. Her eyes widened to realize the space hadn't been soundproofed and she could hear somebody being interrogated on the other side of the wall. Patrick's expression grew annoyed.

"I wouldn't worry about that. Your screams will drown theirs out very soon." He pulled a black cloth off the table to his side. Folding it over itself, he held it out for her to see. "I'm going to blindfold you. It's more exciting when you don't know what toy I've selected."

Her stomach churned and bile shot up the back of her throat. She would kill him slowly when she finally had the chance. A quick death was too good for the vile piece of shit that stood above her. He tied the cloth around her eyes delivering her once again to darkness. Her other senses came alive when her sight was stolen. She listened intently to Patrick move about the room and she jumped when she heard a crash on the opposite side of the wall.

Patrick's phone rang a few seconds later.

"Yes...tell me you are fucking lying to me right now because I'm about to come in there and rip your balls from your fucking body if you are not lying to me right now!" His voice darkened, menace dripping from his words. "I'll be there in a minute."

He was suddenly next to her, walking so quietly that she'd not noticed his approach. "I'll be back for you shortly."

The door clicked behind him when he left and Hope was left bound and exposed atop the table. She heard more shouting from across the hall and she struggled to understand what was being said.

"Rebellion...The Estate...mansion...Aaron..."

Her heart leapt into her throat and she choked on her own intake of breath. She lay her head back on the table and listened carefully, couldn't allow herself to believe what she thought she was hearing. They were interrogating someone, alternating between screaming and silence. But she never heard another man answer and she wondered who they held. Tears formed in her eyes and slid down the sides of her face. Crystal blue eyes flashed in her thoughts, but she forced away the hopeless idea that he could still be

283

alive. She'd seen him die in that chair, the life leaving his eyes and body, the breath leaving his chest for the last time.

The door clicked open and her eyes opened beneath the blindfold. Her body tensed, her skin tingling from the anxiety coursing through her veins. Another click and footsteps, slow and heavy, approached. She braced herself for his touch and was surprised by the size of his hands.

She could tell immediately that he wasn't Patrick. There was something darker, more evil, rolling off his skin and she became physically ill when he ran his hands over her body. He didn't speak, didn't make a sound except for the brush of skin over skin. He moved slowly over her, as if he was studying her.

When he'd moved to her feet, she heard the sound of a latch before the table broke apart. Her legs spread to the side, held in place by the chains. A shudder rolled over her and she fought back the desire to fight. His large hands gripped her ankles, sliding up her legs, over her knees to squeeze around her thighs.

Her legs jerked beneath his hold, the tips of his fingers digging into the tense muscle. He was silent except for his breathing that was loud but even. A finger slipped inside her suddenly and she bucked against it. Another hand smoothed up her abdomen, pausing over her breast before moving further and encircling her neck. He pulled out of her and she heard belt unbuckle and his pants fall to the floor.

284

Within seconds, he was inside her; the width painful against dry skin. It burned and she clenched her jaw in reaction to the pain. The hand around her neck tightened cutting off her ability to breath. He moved inside her, skin slapping against skin when he sped his pace. It was strong, angry strokes – a man taking a woman freely. The way he moved made it obvious that this wasn't about sex; it was about having power over her, taking something from her against her will. The fact that she didn't know his identity only added to the insult. Laid out and bound, she was nothing but meat, a whore meant for every man's use.

She didn't react to him. Bile spiked up her throat that she would swallow back down refusing to give him any reaction to what he was doing. Eventually he pulled out, lifting her hips with one hand before shoving himself into her ass to finish himself off. She absorbed the pain, allowed the endorphins to wash her into a numb place and to fan the flame of rage that was building inside her. His other hand squeezed around her throat, and white noise boomed in her head when he'd pinched the arteries and blocked blood flow to her head. She struggled to stay conscious, coughing beneath his grip.

"...fucking your girlfriend now..."

It was Patrick's voice on the other side of the wall and the man pulled out of her suddenly, but squeezed her neck tighter. She struggled for breath, her arms and legs pulling against the chains that bound her. Her vision tunneled, her body

285

jerked over the wood, but her struggle was useless and consciousness was lost.

Chapter Twenty-Eight

His ribs were broken. Three men had held him, and the fourth beat him with every available surface of his body, eventually moving on to tools and heavy objects that now lay scattered across the room. He could feel blood dripping thick and wet down the side of his head and the skin of his arms felt like it had been shredded from the torture he'd endured.

He sat on the floor – his legs bent at the knees in front of him, his head falling heavily against the wall at his back. Shattered, splintered, broken and fractured, his body had been beaten, abused. Blood choked out his lungs, crimson coughs bubbling from his lips. But, he wouldn't talk. Despite how they beat him, despite the chains that bound him, despite the torment and suffering, the pain and the agony, he wouldn't give them the information they sought.

He knew they would kill him. They would toss his body aside as nothing more than a useless carcass, not worthy of reverence of respect. He didn't care, couldn't care because, despite the lies they spoke, he knew she was gone.

Hope. A woman he never imagined to exist, her name was a concept that was lost to the world in which he'd been raised. And just like the concept, she couldn't exist in this place, because there was no hope, no redemption, no honor and

287

no deliverance. There was nothing left but the obliteration and annihilation of anything good. Morality didn't exist and only pain remained.

His eyes were heavy, his breathing slow and his body protested the simple motion of his lungs expanding and contracting. He was left lying in a puddle of his own blood and sweat.

Even more tortuous than their fists were the words – the lies – that they spoke.

"She lives..."

It was impossible. He'd seen her eyes left empty and dull, her body cut and broken, hanging from a wall. Her sister, the one thing she'd cared to save, becoming the person who'd delivered the blows that took her life.

He heard her scream, the memories – hazy and crude – the drugs still working their way through is system delivering back fragments of images, the spark of light off the chain, her tears that fell, the blood that ran in rivulets down the scars across her body. She'd lost control of herself, her body finding a release from the pain, her mind being torn apart to take pleasure in the depraved act of the men that held her.

The scream echoed in his thoughts and his heart pounded to hear it, blood curdling and strong.

"You're screaming now, bitch, aren't you?"

The sound was muted, unreal. He never said that – Patrick never said that. Hope had never given him what he wanted, but then...

The scream. Anguish and pain, heartache and loss, it went on for what felt like forever and it tore at his heart. It couldn't be real. She never gave it to him. She fought until the end. Even when her body was forced to act in opposition to her mind, when the one bit of light she had was used to deliver her to darkness, she never gave in. But the scream he heard – whether it was memory or reality – it was the sound of her soul shattering, of her limits finally being pushed.

Xander's blue eyes opened. Crusted blood blocked the clarity of his vision and he reached up to wipe it from his face. His heart pounded harder, his wounds aching under the sudden pressure pushing through his veins. The wet trails that dripped along his skin, seeped harder and faster, the puddles beneath him rippling from the drops falling from his skin.

"Show me how much you like it, bitch! Fight against me now!"

Another muffled phrase and he shook his head to chase away the confusion.

The scream again, louder – even louder and his fists clenched, his jaw ticked, his entire body came alive to hear it. It had to be impossible. It couldn't be true.

The sound of a table moving, a rhythmic pounding against a wall; he looked up.

"Fuck you, you sick son of a bitch!..."

His heart stopped, his entire body froze, but his spirit was reborn. That sound – those words – it couldn't be, but it was.

Hope still existed – she lived – and she was fighting against the bastard still. How long had it been?

Chains shook when Xander moved his arms and legs and he felt around his body. His guns had been stripped, every weapon removed and taken. He slipped a finger along the inside of his belt and smiled to feel the thin bit of steel that still remained hidden beneath the thick strap of leather. Hope's blade – the one she'd used to stab him when he'd first captured her. It was tiny, unnoticeable, a weapon so easily concealed that even searched, they hadn't found it. She'd told him it was her favorite – a hidden surprise that had saved her ass in countless fights and now, it remained tucked away and within his reach.

He pulled the blade from beneath the belt, still listening to her screams. Anger raced through his veins, feral rage exploding within his heart and mind.

The pounding, it was angry and raw. The walls shook from the other side, the guttural moans of one person satisfying every vile and depraved urge that his bloodthirsty mind had dreamed up.

Pulling his hand over his body, forcing the broken bones to still work within his fingers, he used the thin blade to pick at the locks on his chains.

Click…

It released the metal shackle slipping from his wrist – her screams driving him to keep going.

Click… The second shackle fell.

"I'll fuck you bloody bitch – just how I know you like it!"

Xander's eyes widened. His body shaking with unbridled fury. She screamed again – this one punctuated by the shame of her orgasm. He knew she absorbed it, gathering the energy inside her, combining it with years of abuse, years of training, years of turbulent wrath. He worked faster at the chains, the links clattering against each other, his body jumping when the broken bones moved – but he wouldn't stop.

It was faint when he heard it: men screaming, shouting and arguing. He stopped for only a second and when the gunfire erupted, his breath caught in his chest. Hope's screams stopped and it was quiet for a moment.

And then hell broke loose.

Down, two stories below him, but so loud, it sounded like it was in the hallway on the opposite side of the door: men dying, torn apart by bullets and blades. Shot after shot after shot, guns were fired. Screams and cries, madness and chaos.

291

Xander smiled.

A door opened and slammed closed on the other side of the wall. Hurried and heavy, the fall of boots on the floor, running. The sound of another door and the room was left in muted symphony of the war taking place below him and laughter – Hope's laughter. He laughed to hear it and worked harder at the chains, desperate to free the shackles at his ankles. The blade cut into the tips of his fingers, but he wouldn't give up. He needed to reach her. He needed to place his hands on her and find that the warrior was still alive inside her.

Click...

Metal falling against the tiled floor, one more.

Footsteps up and down stairs, walls shaking from the bodies hitting against them. They'd reached the second floor. He worked faster, blood now dripping along the blade he used to pick the lock...

Click.

Relief flooded his body. He pushed up and fell back to the floor. His body was weak, electric pain shooting along his nerves with his movement, but he pushed up again until he was standing on unsteady legs. Using the walls to support his weight, he moved through the room, reaching the door and finding it unlocked. His breath rolled over his lips, hot and heavy, his blood pounding through his head. A thundering rush of adrenaline finally forcing its way through his body and he was out the door.

Chapter Twenty-Nine

Hope lay on the table, chained down, the crimson drips and trails sliding along the links, flooding the ground below her. Death teased her, sitting closely, watching her, but not approaching, refusing to grant her oblivion.

Her skin was scored, the cuts not deep enough to bleed her out entirely. Wounds made to damage but not kill. She stared the beast down as he hurt her – the blindfold removed when he'd returned. He wanted to see her pain – her fear. She didn't give it to him.

But, even in her abject refusal, he pulled her screams from her body, bathed in the pleasure of a woman who couldn't resist the bite. Her body betrayed her, but her mind remained strong. She focused on his death, kept the image of his body ripped apart and bloody in her mind. It pushed her through the worst parts, created a barrier behind which she could escape his loathsome amusement.

Her throat was raw and her muscles would twitch randomly across her body. Waves of euphoria flowing through her, pouring over her, delivering her to the darkness, awakening the demon inside her. One focus – one objective - she vowed to make his death slow.

She heard the gunshots, felt the tremors in the walls of the house from a fight transpiring beneath her. Patrick face turned white when he finally heard it as well – when he recognized the sounds of fighting. She laughed when he ran, half in satisfaction, half from insanity; her laughter followed him out of the room and down the hall where he ran scared from what was coming into the house.

The door opened, the blinding light from the hallway pouring in. A large silhouette broke through, bent over and practically dragging. She couldn't see his face. The skin around her eyes swollen from where her cheekbone had been broken. She blinked her eyes, forced them to acclimate to the light. He stepped forward and the light from the candles reflected in his eyes.

She couldn't breathe suddenly, and her heart raced while her entire body froze. Tears streamed down her cheeks and she pulled at her chains, not because she sought freedom but because she was desperate to go to him - to touch him – to know that it was possible that he still lived.

He reached her, his face bruised and bloody, his eyes as swollen as hers. The warmth of his palm was immediately on her cheek and her body shook violently with her sobs. Reality splintered again, but came back into focus. The sounds beneath them disappeared, nothing existing outside of the room. His touch was the only thing she could feel; each broken bone, each slice across her skin, each and every wound silenced by the warmth of his hand.

"You're not real. You can't be real. I watched you die." It was a breathless whisper that pushed past the fire in her throat and over her broken lips.

He grinned. "No, sunshine. It's you who's not real." The candlelight caught a tear that ran down his cheek and she cried harder, overtaken by emotions she never dreamed she could feel. He leaned down and brushed his mouth over hers – the simple touch sending her spirit soaring. Redemption was held in that kiss, a wish finally come true. Fate had never been so kind and she smiled against his lips.

When he finally pulled away, he pulled something from his sleeve and held it up. She grinned to see her blade held in his hand, the same one she used to hurt him, the same one she'd demanded he carry on him when they first walked into this nightmare.

"It's very useful for picking locks." He grinned back at her.

One by one, he removed her chains and helped her sit up on the table. He examined her wounds, ensuring himself that she would survive each and every one. "Can you walk?"

Moving her arms and legs to see if they moved, she pushed herself off the table, testing their strength. Her gold eyes met the deep blue of his. "Yes."

The sounds below them grew louder and she noticed the satisfaction that flitted across Xander's expression.

"Please tell me that the cavalry has arrived."

He grabbed her, pulling her body against his. Looking down at her, he responded, "It appears that Aaron has found us."

A short burst of elated laughter escaped her. "It's about fucking time."

She pushed away from him and turned to pick through the knives and tools that only moments before had been used to torture her. Selecting a few blades, she turned back to Xander. "We need to find Patrick. Aaron better not kill him before I have the chance to do it myself."

Xander chuckled. "If you're intent on killing him, then you'll have to get to him before me."

Her swollen eyes narrowed at his words, the skin on her face protesting the motion. He laughed while reaching over his head and slowly pulling the shirt from his body. With each movement he made, she saw him grimace, pain obviously shooting like lightning through him.

"How badly are you hurt?" It was her turn to look over the different bruises and wounds that covered his once perfect skin. Cuts ran across the broad expanse of his chest and down along the muscles of his abdomen. Bruising blossomed out over his ribs and swirled with angry green, red and

297

blue marks. She was surprised that he could still move with the injuries he'd suffered.

"Bad, but I can still fight." He held the shirt out to her. "Put this on. It's sweaty and bloody and nasty, but I can't stand to let another man see you."

Taking the shirt from his hands, she pulled it over her body. "And here I thought you were more concerned about allowing me my modesty."

He smirked. "Modesty is the last thing a woman like you worries about. I'm not a fool." He leaned over and kissed her again. "However, I don't have time to stab every man's eyes out who looks at you when we cut through the crowd."

The walls shook again, more footsteps climbing the third flight of stairs. Xander turned his head towards the sound. "We have company."

They could hear the doors being thrown open as the men poured down the halls. Gunfire still punctured the air, the sound of metal against metal, the rattle of men choking on their own blood. The door opened and Hope readied the blades in her hand, her body falling into a fighting stance despite her injuries.

"Aaron! He's in here!"

Their heads swiveled in the direction of the door to see Aaron stalk in, his expression blank and unreadable. He stilled when he entered the room and Hope noticed the blood that ran over his face, dripped from his hair; the blades held in his hands that were stained in a glistening crimson.

Nobody spoke, three people staring at each other as if they were ghosts. Suddenly, Aaron's feet moved, heavy boots falling across the tiled floor and his arms surrounded Xander, pulling his friend into an embrace that was flooded with relief and concern. Xander flinched from the pain and Aaron released him immediately, holding him by the shoulders looking over the wounds that Hope had earlier examined. "Can you fight?"

Xander nodded, his voice deep and gritty when he responded, "You better fucking believe it."

The corner of Aaron's lip turned up and he pulled a gun from the back of his pants. Handing it to Xander, he said, "Well, then – let's do this."

Aaron turned to walk out the door and Hope yelled after him, "If you find Patrick, don't you dare fucking kill him. That asshole is mine."

Aaron looked over his shoulder and smiled. "I'll be sure to let my men know."

Surprise overtook her. Xander grabbed her hand and squeezed it to get her to look at him. "Stay at my back."

She squeezed his hand in return. "No, you stay at mine."

Entering the halls, Hope allowed the numbness to cover her, pulling from the pain of each injury on her body, she rushed into the fray, twisting and weaving through the men, her blade catching their throats or burying itself in their hearts. The blood sprayed from their bodies, spreading across her skin, bathing her in vengeance and reprieve. She came alive, each small movement of her body an instinct to survive and to destroy. She could feel Xander behind her, could hear the sickening crunch of their bodies broken by his fists. The sound of gunfire blasted behind her and she felt his back against hers, men falling to the floor around them as they turned.

The strong iron scent of death and destruction wafted around her, men bleeding out and writhing on the floor. She'd become a machine as she cut threw them, her eyes open and searching for the one man she wanted most of all.

When they'd cleared the hallway, Hope and Xander followed Aaron and his men down the stairwells, throwing open doors and tearing apart any man they found inside. Hope searched the faces of the dead, not recognizing most of them. Her body was tired and the pain became too much as she continued to move. Xander dragged at her side, and when enough of Patrick's men had been slaughtered, Aaron and his team took over, allowing Hope and Xander to follow behind. They held onto each other providing support when the other became too weak to move forward. If not for her rage, she wouldn't be able to walk, but she had to find the sick and depraved bastard who'd enslaved her sister and who sliced up Hope's body while he raped her.

Reaching the bottom floor, the house had become eerily quiet. Dead bodies littered the floors and Hope had to step over them and between them to look at each face and determine that Patrick was not amongst them.

Calling out to Aaron and his men, she asked, "Have you found my sister? Any of the women that they held?"

Aaron looked over at her from where he knelt down, graciously ending the life of some poor bastard whose stomach had been split open in the fight. "No.

Xander commented, "You need to check the basement. Most of the captives were held there. From what I saw when we arrived, not many of them will be alive."

Aaron nodded and stood up. Looking at Jason, he motioned towards the back of the house that led into the dark and dank basement beneath. Jason followed without question, but both men stopped suddenly when Hope shouted, "Wait!"

Their heads swiveled in her direction, watching as she stood up and walked over to join them. "If there are men hiding downstairs, can I trust you two to kill them and watch our backs while Xander and I search for the women?"

Aaron's brow arched over his eye and he smirked. "You are either very brave or very stupid for the way you think you can speak to me."

She shrugged. "You're not royalty."

Xander grabbed her arm and forced her to step back from Aaron and Jason. "You'll have to excuse her, she's had a bad couple of days."

Aaron's blinked.

Xander grimaced. "Let's go finish this." His fingers dug into her skin, holding her still to allow Jason and Aaron to enter the room first. She heard fighting almost immediately when they passed the doors.

She attempted to move forward but Xander pulled her away from the door. "I want to know if you're ready for what we might find in there. I know your sister was kept in one of the smaller rooms downstairs. It has to have been two days since..." His expression fell and it was obvious to Hope that he was remembering what had occurred when they arrived.

She nodded her head, swallowing down the lump in her throat that had formed from her fear. He kissed her on the forehead and placed an arm around her shoulders, his chest glistening with sweat. "After you."

She moved forward and after descending the stairs, she stepped over the bodies of the guards that Aaron and Jason had killed when they'd entered. Hope looked down at their faces, once again searching for one particular man.

"Hope. Get in here!"

. . .

302

Xander moved behind Hope towards a small room to their right. He recognized the room instantly as the one they'd led her sister out of earlier. Aaron and Jason stood by the door and Hope ran inside, immediately shouting her sister's name when she found her on the floor.

"Honor?" Her voice fractured when she spoke her name.

Xander moved to kneel down beside her, helping Hope lift her body and cradle her. He was still surprised at how identical the two women were. It looked as if Hope held her own broken and spent body in her arms.

"Honor?" Tears ran in streams down her face. "Baby, wake up. I'm here Honor, please wake up." Hope's body trembled over her sister and Xander had to shake away how familiar the scene was that played out before him. Images of Joseph on that stage and Emory taking his own sister from his mother's arms – a quick snap and the baby he'd only known for a few months, was gone forever.

"Honor..." Hope smoothed her palm down her sister's face, and when Honor blinked her eyes open for a split second, Hope's expression changed from despair to a hesitant smile. "Hey, little sister, wake up, I'm here."

The way Hope held Honor was tender and loving. Xander sat back, ready to help them in any way, but also not wanting to get in the way of them. He feared Honor's reaction to the three men in the room when she regained full consciousness. She smiled brighter when Honor stirred and moved.

"My angel…"

Xander flinched back at the reaction on Hope's face to Honor's weak words. They were spoken out of confusion and it appeared Honor didn't understand what was going on around her. Hope shook her gently, attempting to rouse her fully. Honor's eyes closed, her body going limp in Hope's arms, and Hope immediately moved to check her pulse.

"She's gone back to sleep. She's breathing and her pulse is strong." Her shoulders dropped in relief and she continued to hug her sister to her body.

"Do you want Jason to carry her upstairs for you?"

Hope turned to Aaron, distrust flickering across her expression, but only for a brief moment. Aaron held up his hands in mock surrender, "I only ask because Xander and you are injured, it will be difficult to carry her yourself."

Looking between Jason and Aaron, she let out a deep breath and nodded her head. Jason approached her and kneeled down beside her. He looked her in the eye when he promised, "I won't hurt her."

Hope appeared hesitant even though she'd already agreed. Breathing out another breath, she opened her arms and allowed Jason to lift Honor's body. Once he'd moved away, Xander reached out and helped Hope to her feet. Honor's eyes flicked open again and she looked up at Jason.

"My angel…" A small smile crept over her face and she was lost to sleep once again. Jason pulled her closer to his chest, looking down on her with caution and concern.

"Who's her angel?" Aaron's menacing voice growled.

Hope sneered, "Patrick, I assume. Is there any possible way he was able to escape this house?"

"Not alive." Aaron responded. "I have men posted at every exit."

Leaning against Xander for support, she nodded, "Well, then he has to be around here somewhere, hiding like a fucking coward."

"Have you checked all the rooms in the basement?" Her thoughts instantly went to Erica. "There's another woman trapped here that we need to find."

Aaron's expression fell. "I've found the women. None of them survived."

Hope shook her head. "All the rooms? You've checked all of them?"

They left the side room to walk into the main space of the basement. Aaron motioned

305

towards the cages. "No. I've haven't checked them all; but, from what I see here…"

"They were dead when we got here," she interrupted.

Hope moved quickly towards a side door, Xander following closely behind her. Both limped heavily, their bodies wearing down now that the adrenaline from the fight was slowly dissipating from their veins. He tried to hold Hope up, tried to remain the strength she needed to finally end this.

They reached a door to what Xander believed was only a small closet. However, when Hope opened the door and reached over to turn on the lights, a much larger space opened up before them. One body remained shackled to a wall, eyes that had gone grey with death staring out. Hope rushed through the room, completely distraught at her inability to find what she sought. Xander approached her, noticing the tears that streamed down her cheeks.

"She has to be somewhere!" Hope tried to break away from him, but he held on tighter.

"Who?"

"Erica; the woman who let me in the mansion. They have her because of me. I promised her, I'd get her out."

A muffled scream sounded from within the room, and Hope's body spun in the direction from which it had come. A bookshelf stood empty and

Hope rushed over, grabbing the side of to knock it over, but finding that it swiveled out, revealing another doorway. Hope pulled at the door to find that it was locked.

She looked back at Aaron and Xander. "Break this fucking door down, please."

Xander chuckled as Hope stepped away. He looked at Aaron and motioned towards the door. "Be my guest."

Grinning, Aaron responded, "Fine. But only because I don't think there's an inch of your body not already injured."

Aaron approached the door and kicked out at the handle. The wood splintered almost immediately and the hinges squeaked as it slowly opened into the hidden room. Hope ran in front of it and stopped in her tracks.

Xander stepped up behind her to look in over her shoulder. He smiled when he saw who was hiding inside.

Chapter Thirty

He sat against the wall of the tiny room, Erica held in front of him, a knife held to her jugular. Hope eyes met with Erica's and her heart caught in her throat. Erica's eyes were barely open, rolling back closed and open again as she held on desperately to consciousness. Blood seeped from where the tip of Patrick's blade dug in at the skin. He sat completely motionless, his eyes locked to Hope's face.

"Take one more fucking step, and I kill this bitch."

Hope hesitated and felt Aaron and Xander position themselves at her back. "I'll kill you, Patrick." Hope spoke slowly – purposefully. "I will fucking flay you when I get my hands on you."

He let out a humorless laugh. "And kill your little friend here? He motioned his head up towards the ceiling. Hope turned to look and saw the camera. When she looked back he smiled.

"I saw what you did for her – when the guard came for her. I also heard the little promise you made her. You'll get her out of here alive? That's highly improbable." Another sick chuckle.

Hope's eyes flicked to his hand, noticed how the blade shook in his grasp. Looking back at his mismatched eyes, she teased, "Don't piss yourself, Patrick. You look nervous."

He pressed the knife against Erica's throat, her face not reacting to the pain. Hope looked down, noticed a crimson trail along the ground where Erica had been dragged, it puddled beneath her body where Patrick held her. Hope watched her arms and legs, noticing the trembling as her body grew cold from blood loss. When Erica's eyes opened, they were hazy and unfocused.

Oh, God...no...

Tears burned at Hope's eyes, and she shook her head in denial. "What did you sick bastards do to her?" Her voice cracked, rage returning and creeping along her spine as she watched an innocent woman become lost to the evil and vehemence of Hope's world.

"WHAT DID YOU SICK BASTARDS DO TO HER?" Hope screamed, the sound tearing at her already shredded throat. She felt Aaron and Xander tense at her back, felt Xander's hand touch her back in an attempt to calm her.

Erica's eyes flicked open in response to the scream and moved over the room, finally settling on Hope's face. She gasped for air, her body shivering violently in Patrick's arms. Her jaw moved and, at first, Hope had thought it involuntary. Erica coughed, a thin trail of blood slipping down from her mouth, bright red against the pallor of her skin.

309

"Do...." She coughed again, the tip of Patrick's knife drawing more blood from the movement of her head. "Do me a favor."

Hope blinked, the room seemingly slowing down. Reality altering so that every minute movement or noise was large with meaning. Hope nodded, unable to speak over the agony in her heart.

"Kill him."

Patrick held the tip closer, the crimson trail dripping stronger down her neck. "Shut up, bitch!"

Erica jumped at the sound of his voice, but locked her eyes to Hope's once more and her voice found strength and courage one last time. "And when you do..." She coughed, fighting to say what she needed to say. "When you do – make it slow."

The slow motion in the room, the stillness, the anxiety and tension – it was gone, replaced instantly with dizzying speed. It was unexpected and Hope couldn't move fast enough, couldn't react quick enough to do anything about it.

Closing her eyes, Erica threw her head forward, forcing Patrick's blade into her neck, finishing off what he and his men had started.

Hope fell to her knees, her eyes wide with shock, her jaw opened wide on a silent scream. Her eyes remained locked to Erica's face, Aaron and Xander running past her to grab Patrick; but, Hope couldn't look away. They pulled Patrick up between them and Hope crawled forward, reached out to grab Erica's hand, staying with her until the light had been extinguished from her eyes.

The anger that had simmered inside her just moments before, exploded into pure hatred and wrath. She placed Erica's hand down and turned, pushing up on her feet in one fluid motion and locking her gaze with the mismatched eyes of a dead man. Patrick stared back, his arms bound at his sides by Aaron and Xander.

Hope sunk when she looked at him, fell into a darkness where she floated away from all feeling, where a numb madness drove her. She was a machine, one intent on destroying the man that was held in front of her.

"Take him upstairs; to the room where I was held." Her voice was mechanical and cold.

Xander smiled and Aaron eyes narrowed; but, they didn't ask questions, simply turning to drag Patrick out of the room and up the flights of stairs. Hope walked behind them, her feet falling heavily up the stairs, a clock ticking down the minutes Patrick had left to live.

His feet slammed against the stairs from being dragged, his bones crunching against the edges, his face grimacing with each step. Hope smirked.

When the entered the room, she instructed, "Put him on the table. Hold his arms out to the sides, I'll lock his ankles down. Xander eye's widened and his brow furrowed in concern.

311

"Hope?"

She raised her hand up, stopping him in his thought. Her bottom lip quivered and images flashed through her head: her sister as a child, the bright smile and barrettes morphing into the woman at the end of Patrick's chain and the woman with a chain in her hand, whipping Hope because she her mind had been lost to the madness Patrick had created within her.

"My angel..."

He'd broken Honor, made her worship him despite the abuse and he made her mind fracture because of it. And for what? The look that he'd described to Xander? Or to simply break someone so thoroughly that he could feel powerful for having done it?

She snapped. Her body shook from the hatred and anger inside her and she saw red. All she wanted was to give back to him the pain he'd delivered to the people she cared about and all the other helpless victims he'd tortured and killed.

Her voice was eerily calm when she said, "It's your turn, Patrick. Now, you get to scream for me." She grinned.

Hope knelt down to secure Patrick's ankles before moving to a side table to select a blade. She was suddenly thankful for the level of Patrick's depravity —happy that it'd left her with a wide selection from which to choose. She grabbed a small, thin blade, one that would slice the skin, but not damage the muscle beneath. Her eyes fell on another blade; serrated and thick, it was designed for intimate torture, and she reached out relishing the feel of its handle on her palm. Turning back, she saw the concern on Xander's face. She looked away, not able to handle any emotion or to witness the disappointment in Xander's face at what she was about to do.

When she looked to Aaron, she was surprised. He smiled – his approval of her actions written clearly in his expression; a darkness in his own eyes that mirrored her own. He would enjoy this, and he wasn't ashamed of it like her. She stared at him and he nodded at her before she looked down at Patrick and stalked towards him, the knife spinning over her palm as she approached. Patrick started to scream and Xander reached for a rag on the table beside him and shoved it into Patrick's mouth to silence him.

Hope shook her head. "No. Let him scream. I want to hear him scream."

Xander removed the cloth, replacing on the side table slowly, eyeing Hope as he did so.

She broke his stare, hatred festering inside her, she kept the images of the women he'd killed in her mind.

Reaching for his pants first, she used the blade to cut away the fabric, exposing him, limp and flaccid now that he was the victim on the table. "Not hard now, are you Patrick?" She placed the knife at the base of his genitals. "This…is for Erica." She pulled the knife up, sawing through the

313

skin with the serrated edge of the knife she used. Slowly, the skin split and tore over the steel, blood rushing over her hands and she kept her progress painfully slow until the flesh had been torn completely from his body.

The sound that came out of him was inhuman and unholy. She could hear the tissue in his throat being shredded from the horrifying volume of his scream. It was unnerving, but Hope breathed slowly, kept her mind focused on the task.

Aaron smiled and Xander grimaced from pain when Patrick struggled against them.

Hope wasn't finished.

She looked around the room for anything she could use to turn this bastard into the *angel* he'd demanded to be with Honor. Spotting some rope, she moved to grab it, throwing it over her shoulder before moving to his side. Bringing her face down so that the tip of her nose touched his, she whispered, "You want to be a fucking angel? Let me help you with that."

Patrick's eyes rolled in his head from pain, but he still managed a whispered response. "I'm not her fucking angel."

Hope didn't believe him. "This…is for my sister."

She cut into the skin of his chest, flaying him open so that the flaps could be pulled aside.

""Scream for me Patrick. Every angel needs his wings!"

Patrick screamed again, his voice so loud, it gave out and his body went into shock. Hope reached up, tapping him on the cheek. "Don't go to sleep on me yet, it's not over until I say it's over." Pulling the skin out at his sides, she used two smaller knives to pin the skin to his arms, the muscles, bones and organs of his chest and abdomen left open and exposed.

Moving quickly to unlock the shackles from his ankles, she looked up at Aaron, not able to look at Xander and see the concern she knew he was feeling for her. She needed to stay numb – to feel nothing – so she could finish this.

She wasn't surprised to find approval in Aaron's expression when she met his eyes.

"Carry him out of the room and to the railing." There was no emotion in her voice and she didn't wait to see if they'd follow her instruction. She knew they would – knew that they could no longer be surprised at the horrors hidden within a killer.

When they reached the banister, Hope tied the rope to the thick wood rail. She fashioned a noose from the other side and slipped it over Patrick's neck pulling it tight. He continued to struggle feebly against Aaron and Xander, but his body was losing blood quickly and shutting down.

Looking into the eyes that were losing life, she smiled. "This Patrick – is for me."

315

Shoving out with her palms, she struck his shoulders and knocked him over the banister. The railing cracked, but held his weight and she looked over and watched as his body convulsed at the base of the rope. Only when he stopped shaking, and only when it grew so quiet she could hear the creaking of the rope as it swung back and forth, did she breathe out the remaining anger that she held. It was over. She'd paid the bastard back for the cruelties he'd committed. She left him swinging; a macabre, carved monster, hanged and displayed over the death and carnage of his men beneath.

Her eyes closed when she felt a hand fall on her shoulder. Opening them again, she looked up and she was surprised to see approval in Xander's eyes, something she feared she'd lose the minute he witnessed the true monster inside her.

He stared at her for a few minutes before he leaned close, his lips brushing her ear when he confessed, "We all have darkness inside us and, sometimes, it's necessary to release our demons. You are no different and he deserved what you gave him."

He pulled back, but she reached up, her heart pounding against her ribs, and she kissed him - slow and deep. She felt his body jerk, his pain obvious and she hated to have to let him go, but she did, not wanting to damage him any more than he already was. He straightened, but looked down at her and smiled.

Aaron disturbed the silence when he mused, "I think that just turned me on."

316

Xander's eyes shot over to Aaron. "What?" Every muscle in his body tensed despite his injuries. Hope turned around to find Aaron looking over the railing at Patrick's body.

"That was an impressive kill."

Xander sighed in frustration. "Aaron, if you ever say anything Hope does again *turns you on*, I'll kill you for it."

Aaron smiled.

Hope eyed him. "Actually, if you ever say I've turned you on again, I'll kill you for it – on behalf of Maddy."

Aaron smiled brighter and nodded his agreement.

Refocusing on the rebellion, he looked up at Xander and asked, "Were you able to discover how many units are involved in this?"

"Patrick said there were three total, that *his partner* was working on more."

Hope's mind flashed back to the silent man who'd raped her. "Did you find out the identity of his partner?"

"No. All he told me is that their reach is farther than we think, as if there was someone feeding him information from the inside. He knew I wasn't actually on your list of executions."

"It could be a number of people – any man on my personal guard knew about our plans, especially once I had to organize the attack. We checked the warehouse, but when it was discovered to be empty except for a few cages, I came here. I hoped the bastard would be stupid enough to bring you back to his house. Jason scouted before we arrived and confirmed what I'd hoped." He paused. "Jason was able to identify three units based on the guards who were here. They will all be eliminated."

Xander breathed out heavily. "Let's go."

They made their way from the house and approached Jason who was standing guard over Honor's sleeping body. Hope moved to her side and reached out to hold her hand.

"Jason, place Hope's sister in my car. Xander, I want you to drive Hope, her sister and yourself back to the mansion and go to Maddy immediately. I want all of your wounds cleaned, disinfected and the bones set. Maddy might also know what can be done about Hope's sister. If we have to call in doctors, we will."

When they moved to the car, Aaron also instructed, "Jason, once they've left, I want the victim's bodies removed for proper burial, but leave the rest inside. The entire fucking house needs to be burned to the ground. Once that's done, barricade the men into the houses of the other two units and burn them alive. This ends tonight."

Chapter Thirty-One

"Is there any part of your body they didn't touch?" Maddy worked over Xander's skin, cleaning away the blood and surveying the damage inflicted when he'd been interrogated by Patrick's men.

Hope sat back in a shadowed corner, her eyes locked to his, refusing to let him out of her sight now that they'd escaped the horror of Patrick's house. His heart melted for her, his mind replaying the images of her face when she'd ripped Patrick apart, when the look in her eyes was that of a demon instead of the woman he'd known.

When they'd returned to the mansion, they'd worked together to carry Honor inside. Completely passed out and oblivious, they'd placed her on a bed in Aaron's suite before leaving the room in search of Maddy. They found her in the bedroom she shared with Aaron, silently staring out a window, watching the fire rise in the horizon mimicking dawn in its intensity. Maddy turned when she heard them, the expression on her face revealing the depth of her relief to see them both standing in her doorway, beaten but alive.

Maddy moved instantly to them, her hands reaching up to run over their skin, exploring and surveying the injuries on their bodies before she dragged them both into the bathroom and into the shower. "The water is going to hurt, but we need to clean you quickly." Maddy turned on the water and Hope and Xander clung to each other; their bodies shuddering against the liquid washing away the blood and dirt from their skin. Hope had helped Xander remove his clothes and he stripped his shirt from her body in return. The water gathered brown and pink in puddles around them and they both had sunk to the floor, exhaustion overtaking them. They held on to each other, refusing to let go, to risk being once again torn from the other's arms.

And now that Maddy had forced them apart in order to tend to them, they still clung to each other from across the room; their eyes remaining locked to the other.

Maddy pushed against the flesh around his broken bones as she searched for signs of internal bleeding. Finally satisfied that his injuries weren't life threatening, she stitched up the open wounds and wrapped gauze tight around his abdomen to keep the ribs from moving where they'd been broken beneath his skin.

"There, that's the best I can do with you. I think some of your fingers are broken, but if you're able to move them, I'll leave them alone. If they get worse, we can make a splint." Her voice was shaking, the memory of the night Joseph died was obviously on her thoughts – the hours spent in Aaron's suite stitching and cleaning the wounds on Aaron's body, on Xander's and on hers.

Her blue eyes looked up from his hand, a haze apparent from the mist of tears. "Will it ever end?"

Hope frowned in the background at Maddy's words. Xander looked away from the gold of her eyes finally to answer, "It takes time." He reached up, cupping her chin and kissing her on the forehead. "But yes, Maddy, it will end."

She nodded, her next works spoken weakly. "Go get dressed. I'll tend to Hope."

He looked back at the girl hidden amongst the shadows. "No. I'll wait if you don't mind, I've been separated from her enough for one night. I'm not letting her out of my sight again."

Hope's eyes widened.

Maddy turned around to look at her. "You're up."

She shook her head in response. "Not me – not yet. I want you to look at my sister. She's in another room."

Maddy opened her mouth to object, but Xander interrupted knowing that Hope would fight against being cared for until she knew her sister was okay. "She's in the spare room, Maddy. I'll go with you."

They all stood, Hope holding a towel around her body, hobbling past them, leading them down the corridor. They entered the room and she moved to the side of Honor's bed, reaching out immediately to run her palm over her sister's cheek.

"Honor." Gently, Hope patted her sister's cheek. "Wake up, beautiful. You're safe."

Maddy approached the bed, looking to Hope for approval before touching Honor. Hope moved just enough to let Maddy close. Xander watched Maddy place her hand on Honor's head, only to run her hands across her face and down her body looking for any sign of injury or illness. Honor's eyes blinked open, confusion sitting heavy in the gold of her eyes. She opened her mouth and she screamed.

Maddy jumped away and Hope picked Honor up from the bed, desperate to calm her sister's nightmare. Xander's heart fractured and he stepped forward, anxious to help, but not knowing if his presence would do more harm than good.

"Get out!" Hope screamed out her command.

He felt Maddy's hand on his arm and forced himself to turn away from Hope. Maddy nodded her head in the direction of the door, silent tears sliding down her cheeks to see Honor's reaction to the touch of another person. Xander looked back, every instinct in him demanding he go to Hope, that he shelter her from the ugly truth of what had become of her sister.

He didn't move for a few seconds; but, eventually he followed Maddy, leaving Hope to tend to her twin.

Closing the door behind him, he shut his eyes against the sad reality of Honor's fate; her body freed of captivity, but her mind still lost to the men who'd held her. The screaming didn't end and he heard Hope quickly speaking over the screams, her voice torn and frantic as she pled with her sister to calm down, to recognize that Hope wasn't one of the monsters.

An hour passed, then two, and it went quiet. Xander sat on the floor, his body pressed up against the wall where Hope sat with her sister on the other side. The door opened, Hope stepped out.

She fell on her knees and Xander was immediately by her side.

"She didn't make it…"

His heart felt like it stopped.

"She's still trapped there, in that fucking house with those bastards…She won't see me, she doesn't know me!" Her voice finally broke from the tears that flooded from her eyes.

Xander breathed deeply. "She'll improve. She has to. We won't give her any other option."

Hope looked at him, her eyes red from crying. "She sees the demons inside me, Xander; she always has. She used to look past them, love me despite the beast that hides inside me – but now – I'm the same as the men who destroyed her."

324

A door slammed in the front room followed by the hurried fall of boots across the floors. Their heads turned in unison to find Aaron and Jason standing in the entryway of the corridor. Maddy rushed out from their bedroom, running quickly down the hall to wrap her arms around Aaron. He stepped back when she reached him, Jason stepping forward to keep her from approaching.

Xander pushed up and moved quickly down the hall, angry at how Jason had steped into Maddy; but Aaron stopped him in his tracks when he demanded, "Ballroom. Now."

Tension, anxiety and fear exploded over Xander's body to hear those words.

Aaron looked at Maddy. "This is not for you to witness. I want you to stay here in the suite until I return. Do NOT disobey me."

Her tiny body shook and she backed up into Xander where he stood behind her.

He knew he had to diffuse the situation, sensing the executioner running in Aaron's veins, he knew that no emotion was contained in Aaron except for the need to feed the darkness inside.

Bending down, he spoke softly to Maddy. "I'll go with him. Please stay here and watch over Honor while we're gone."

She looked up at him, fear heavy in her eyes, but she nodded and turned to walk back to her room.

Hope stood up and he watched her approach. She took his hand and turned towards Aaron. "Let us get dressed and we'll go."

. . .

After exiting the suite and walking to the ballroom, Xander saw the procession of Estate members flooding in between the large doors. Releasing a shuddered breath, he willed his legs to move, tightening his grip on Hope's hand when they crossed the threshold into the large room.

The Estate members took their seats amongst the tables arranged on the side of the room, their voices murmuring out, each individual voice adding to the tension of the sudden meeting. Pulling Hope behind him, Xander climbed the stairs to the stage, memories washing over him, his stomach twisting at the familiarity of the proceedings.

Aaron stood at the front of the stage, his stance reminiscent of the man who'd raised him. The iridescent light of the crystal chandelier sparked against his blood soaked skin, his expression indifferent as two unit leaders, locked in chains, were led in by Jason.

Blood pounded through Xander's veins, his head swimming in white noise and pain. His eyes shot to Hope. She was fixated on what played out before them.

"Thank you for joining us on such late notice gentlemen." Aaron's voice boomed out over the large space; the building tension from just

326

moments before becoming a suffocating blanket over the room. "We are here tonight because three men believed they would attack The Estate by attacking me."

Spinning a blade in his hand, he began to pace the stage. "Tonight, I personally executed and burned each and every member of this network who thought they could outwit me. At this very moment, they are becoming nothing but ash, the houses they were given on the compound burning around them." He stopped and looked up into the bright lights of the room, crimson trails dripping along his skin. Looking back down he said, "I've brought you here tonight, gentlemen, to remind you what happens to a person who attacks The Estate!"

Whispers burst throughout the audience, followed by laughter and sudden applause. It had been years since executions had played out inside these walls and Xander fought to restrain himself from stepping forward and stopping what was about to occur.

"These men took innocent women, bound them, raped them and left them for dead in direct disobedience of my orders as leader of this network. I could have ended their lives quickly, allowed them a death free of the pain and torment they caused. But, I decided other methods would be more appropriate."

Aaron laughed and Xander's stomach turned – the sound eerily familiar against his thoughts.

"Adair and Charles..." He looked down at the unit leaders, his eyes slowly traveling over them as he spoke their condemnation. "Since you found so much pleasure in the suffering of the women you killed, I think it's only fair the same is done to you." Aaron looked up at the audience. "Wouldn't you agree?"

The men cheered, boisterous laughter punctuating the approval in the air.

The men were led to the center of the room and tossed to the floor, still bound in chains.

Aaron stepped back. "It's time to teach these men what happens when you FUCK WITH THE ESTATE!" Holding his hands out to his sides, he smiled. "Gentlemen, do your worst!"

Screams punctured the air when the estate members fell on the men, ripping their clothes from their bodies, violating them in ways no person should have to endure. Xander fell back into his seat, his eyes closed against the carnage that played out before him and his mind reeling against the realization that Joseph's insanity was still alive in his son. He attempted to pull Hope closer, but she stepped away trying to approach the front of the stage. Looking up at her, he noticed how her eyes were locked to the men, her hands fisting and her shoulders straightening. Her hand slipped from his, their fingers sliding along each other, resting at the tips until separating from him entirely.

She walked forward, stopping when she reached the front. Xander grew still, looking between Aaron and Hope, noticing how they both were lost to a madness from which he could not pull them away. They stood still, the lights of the room playing across their bodies and their expressions completely indifferent to the rape and death of the unit leaders. They were two monsters bred by crime, by violence, and by torment. Two people, born with demons, who were trapped in nightmares for so long that eventually, they became lost within the very thing they fought against.

When the men's bodies were torn apart and when their screams dissipated from the room, the men slowly exited, leaving Aaron, Xander, Jason and Hope standing on the stage looking down at the strewn body parts across the floor.

No person spoke. The promise of redemption lost instantly within the blood that now ran in rivulets across the floor.

Epilogue

She was the epitome of grace, the way her body twisted and spun, the muscles straightening when she moved, only to curl skillfully and strong when she dodged in a different direction. Xander reached out for her, smiling to watch her dance artfully around him. Her instinct was razor sharp, almost as if she knew exactly what he would do next.

Her eyes were focused on his, the gold swirling with playful opposition. He lunged, and she volleyed, springing back, her body arching away, weaving around his arms like she was liquid and impossible to hold.

"Oh, come on, you're not even trying," she teased.

Xander smirked. "I'm a little tired. You've been keeping me up late." He winked.

Her cheeks blushed red. "I've been staying up with you, so that's not an excuse."

Lunging forward again, he caught her and pulled her quickly into his body, sweeping his foot beneath hers and dropping her heavily to floor. The wind was knocked from her chest on a loud huff when she went down, and he fell over her, pinning her arms to her sides and pressing his body tight against hers.

She moaned, her breath catching again when he leaned down, nipped at her ear and growled, "Do I need an excuse now, sunshine?" He pressed into her again and her lips parted, her eyes closing in reaction to the feel of his body against hers. A growl shook his chest, quickly losing patience with their game.

Bringing his face to hers, he rubbed the tip of his nose along her jaw. "I believe I win this round."

She struggled against him, her body falling limp beneath him once she realized he wouldn't budge. He chuckled in response before stripping her of her clothes, forcing her submission even when the light of rebellion still shown in her eyes.

It had been a year since Patrick was killed. Following the events of the ballroom, Hope and Xander had returned to Aaron's suite long enough to allow Maddy to tend to Hope's wounds. Aaron had paced the living room while Maddy worked and her eyes would flick over to him every few seconds, her fear of what he was becoming evident in her eyes. Once Maddy had finished, Xander grabbed Hope up from her chair, leading her immediately to the front door to leave. He felt guilty for leaving Maddy alone with Aaron when he was so enraged, but Xander feared what he'd seen on the stage that night: Hope and Aaron lost to the madness, both becoming part of the thing they hated their entire lives.

He'd taken Hope back to his room, laid her down on his bed and crawled beside her. They

331

must have slept for days, only waking up to drink water or use the bathroom.; their minds struggling to process what they'd seen and survived. Only when Maddy arrived and insisted that they get up did they finally leave his suite.

Within weeks, their bodies had healed, but Xander lived with the knowledge that The Estate was infectious, that it had somehow buried itself so far inside Hope that she didn't notice when she'd become lost to it.

However, he wouldn't give up on her - wouldn't allow himself to believe that she couldn't be brought back from what dark depth to which she'd fallen.

Every night Hope woke with nightmares, her voice screaming into the stillness of his room and every morning he brought her in the gym. They fought daily – her against the threat of losing her mind and him out of refusal of letting her fall. Much like Maddy and Aaron, Hope and Xander needed each other to survive – but the tables were turned and it was Xander who dragged Hope into the light each time her heart and mind were covered in shadow.

When she found her release and when he body fell against the floor sated and spent, he joined her. They lay with each other on the floor of the gym, their bodies loose from the fight, their minds lost to the connection that held them together.

When it had grown quiet between them, Hope spoke, her voice nothing more than a whisper across his skin.

"Thank you."

He leaned up, placing his weight on his elbows so he could hold himself while looking down at her face. "For what?"

"For taking care of me. I've been a terror these past few months with the nightmares and my mood swings. "I just..." Her voice was frustrated and strained. "I feel so lost sometimes, so helpless without her."

He sighed and rested his forehead against hers. Locking his eyes to her stare, he smiled, "Don't worry. We'll get her back."

Hope's smile was hesitant, but she nodded. "I know."

. . .

Hope sat on the edge of Honor's bed. Reaching over to a table, she poured a glass of water and brought it to her sister's lips encouraging her to drink. Honor's eyes were blank, her mind trapped in nightmares that Hope worried would never let her go.

"There you are little sister. Are you hungry."

Honor looked back, her face a perfect mirror of Hope's. She nodded, still not speaking even though it had been a year since she'd been freed of Patrick's hold. Hope turned to grab a plate of food from the bedside table. Taking Honor's hand in her own, she assisted her as she ate, encouraged her to continue living despite the events of the past.

Her heart split apart when she looked in Honor's eyes. Every day she walked in this room hoping to see her sister's spirit healed, hoping to find that the monsters had released her, finally letting her out of that house and away from the torture and abuse they committed against her.

And every day it was the same disappointment when she walked in to discover that Honor was lost to something she couldn't fight against. She was trapped by something intangible and cruel, evil that Hope couldn't destroy, memories gathered like cobwebs in her mind, keeping her buried and tangled inside.

After Honor had eaten, Hope sat with her for several hours, telling her stories of their youth, reminding her of the days before their mother had died. Honor would smile sometimes and Hope's eyes filled with tears in those moments, relishing the light inside her twin if even for a brief second that she got to see it. There were moments when Hope swore her sister recognized her – moments when the life she'd always seen in her sister's eyes returned to let her know that Honor still existed within the cage of her body.

Standing up, Hope pulled the blanket up to tuck her sister into bed, to make sure she felt safe.

She knew it was pointless, that Honor comprehend what was going on around her. "Okay, baby sister, I'm going to leave you to get some sleep, I'll be back tomorrow to see you. Maybe tomorrow will be the day you finally come back to me." A tear slowly traveled down her Hope's cheek

"Hope?"

Hope's head swiveled and her eyes locked on her twin. "Honor?" The question was spoken in a whisper, disbelief stealing away the strength of her voice.

Honor blinked a thick fall of mahogany lashes over the metallic gold, and looked around the room. Confusion settled over her brow and she pushed herself up into a sitting position, allowing the blanket that Hope had just used to cover her to bundle at her waist. She went to speak again, but her words caught in her throat, coming out scratched and broken. She cleared her throat.

"Hope, where are we?"

Hope stood dumbfounded and her heart pounded against the walls of her chest. Realization settled in that her sister had just spoken and, quickly, her palms were against Honor's cheeks and she looked into life behind the eyes that of the woman she'd missed for so long. Tears poured faster from down her cheeks and she pulled her sister into a warm embrace – strong, protective, and relieved. "Oh, baby...we're at The Estate mansion, we've been here for a year."

335

Honor's body tensed and shook with quiet fear. "Oh God! They took you? How....How did they get you too?! We need to get out of here!" The words flew out of her mouth, her body struggling to be freed from Hope's grasp. "Hope, we need to get out of here!"

Letting go so she could look in Honor's eyes, she gripped her sister's arms and attempted to calm the terror of her sister's words, "Honor, baby, we're not being held here. They don't have us anymore baby girl, I got you out! You're safe. Please, please calm down, please believe me, Honor, we're safe – I promise you that no one will hurt you again."

Honor stop fighting, eventually relaxing her body as she slowly comprehended what Hope was telling her.

When Honor had finally calmed to a point where Hope could look her in the eyes, Hope asked, "What's the last thing you remember?"

Honor blinked again, her cognition slow to return. Her eyes kept searching the room, her own tears welling in response to Hope's. "I remember being taken. They..." She cried harder, her body shaking from the force of her sobs. Hope pulled her closer, her tears joining that of her twin. "They... I was walking to my car from an art class, my hands were full and I tried to stop them – I did – but they were too strong. They shoved me in the trunk and when they let me out we were at some house I'd never seen before. I don't know what happened after that, I..." She cried harder and struggled for breath. Hope shushed her, stroking her hand over her sister's hair, calming a woman who'd just waken from a nightmare. "I don't know what happened. All I know is I woke up in this room. I was so scared the first time, I didn't recognize anything and I panicked and would wake up again."

Hope closed her eyes against Honor's words – angry with herself for not staying in the room day and night in case Honor pulled through. But it had been a year, twelve long months where Hope had allowed herself to believe her sister wasn't coming back. "I'm sorry. I should have stayed in here, I shouldn't have left you alone to wake up in a strange place. That's my fault, Honor." Tears fell harder, her eyes burning from the effort. "I'm so sorry."

For what felt like hours, Hope hugged her sister, hushed words of encouragement and love spoken between them as Honor slowly regained her place in the world that, for a year, had continued on without her. Even when Honor pulled away, and had been stricken by the details of what had become of her life, Hope wouldn't let her go, wouldn't stop touching her in desperate need to know that her sister had, in fact, recovered. She knew it would take time, knew that trauma like her sister had endure could not easily be forgotten. The hours ticked by until, finally, Honor had fallen back to sleep tucked safely within Hope's arms, the promise of a new day breaking with the soft hint of sunlight on the horizon. Hope was surprised the see that she'd spent the entire night holding her twin, but she didn't feel exhausted from having done so. Her spirit was once again alive, her mind spinning with the pure joy that she felt. She was somehow stronger again, more determined than ever to break down the walls of The Estate, to destroy it for all that it had done.

Begrudgingly, she tucked Honor back under the blanket before standing up and walking across the room. Turning back once more to look at the beauty of her twin, she flicked off the lights, closed the door, and left Honor's room for the first time not feeling defeated as she always had before. A smile tugged at the corners of her lips and she stared at the wall opposite where she stood. She was dazed, but ecstatic – hesitant, but hopeful.

A throat cleared in the distance disturbing her reverie and her head swung to glance down the hall. All she could see was his silhouette, the broad width of his shoulders cutting down to a thin waist. He leaned his shoulder against a wall, staring down at her for a few minutes before pushing up and walking slowly in her direction.

Her feet moved below her without conscious thought, carrying her down the hall to join him. When they approached the light from above caught his face, the beauty of his features coming into view. Her heart felt like it stopped for a brief second and a broad smile spread across her face. For once in her life, she felt balanced. It was the first time that something wasn't missing, that there wasn't an empty spot inside her aching to be filled. She didn't care that she was living inside the network she feared – didn't care that in the coming years they would still have to fight. As long as she had Xander and her sister beside her, she'd fight forever if it meant that all three would eventually banish the shadow of the evil that had always existed within their lives.

He returned the smile, his face lit with confused elation when he searched her eyes. "You've been gone all night." He wasn't angry. His words were spoken in concern, but not condemnation. "I've been worried about you." His voice fell over her like satin, love spoken by a man she'd fought so hard not to need in her life. The realization struck her that he'd told the truth that night in the cave – he'd held on to her as much as he did Aaron - refusing to let them sink into the hatred and rage bred by the evil that surrounded them.

When his arms came around her, she sank into him, melting against the heat of his body when his hands moved over her in comfort. The smile never left her face, when she softly confessed, "She's come back. Honor...she..." Tears threatened her eyes again – but not ones bred of sorrow or fear. It was relief that poured from her eyes when she spoke. "She's talking again. I was leaving and then she called for me. I couldn't leave her alone after just getting her back."

He tightened his hold on her, his own relief coming out in a shuddered breath that vibrated through his chest. Hope huddled close to him, her arms locked around his body, her cheek pressed against his chest. "She doesn't remember anything after she was taken."

339

She felt Xander's hand beneath her chin. Lifting gently, he brought her eyes to his, grounding her as he gazed down.

"That's a good thing. Maybe her mind is just protecting her from the worst of what happened in order to give her time to heal. We'll take good care of her and she'll continue to improve."

"To be trapped here forever?" It was a passing thought, but one she couldn't keep from escaping her lips on a whisper.

He held her gaze, strength and determination hidden behind the sea blue of his eyes. "It'll take time, but, one day, this place will burn around us, it will become nothing but a memory. When that finally happens, we can walk away, finally freed of the one thing that has destroyed us all." His lips brushed against her mouth – the soft kiss sealing the promise he'd just spoken.

She smiled, the belief finally settling within her thoughts that with Xander beside her, she'd be strong enough to conquer anything that threatened to tear her apart.

Hope had entered The Estate a warrior – and despite how much she despised it, she choose to remain behind its walls in order to tear it down from the inside. Taking comfort in Xander's words, she was reminded that she no longer fought alone. Finally, letting go of all her pain and fear, she looked up and smiled at the kindness she saw in him; once again allowing herself to look into the crystal blue eyes that revealed to her the blinding truth that, even inside the darkest corners of a living hell, there was still the promise of light.

THE END

Coming in Spring 2014

Honor Bound (The Estate, #3)

Synopsis:

She was meant to be his perfect pet.

Innocent, naïve and easily shattered.

Yet her mind was too fragile for what he'd imagined.

As Honor struggles to regain herself,

She becomes the one thing that could tear The Estate apart.

Honor Delacroix was raised in a rival network. Always looked after by her twin sister, Honor was an artist who lived her life in the ever-present shadow of The Estate. However, the life she'd always known ended on the night she was abducted.

Jason Arrington is an Estate Member who is working his way up the chain of command. Silently, he watches over Honor inside the mansion. Hopeful that she will improve, Jason sets out to help Honor remember the details of her captivity.

After being held by depraved men for four weeks, Honor has to put the pieces back together. Watched over by the members of The Estate, she fights to remember what happened when she was a slave. When Jason offers to help her, will Honor's demons be too much for him to handle and will Jason be the man who can finally help her break free of the nightmare?

Prologue of Honor Bound:

The greatest fabrication of fairy tales and romance novels is the idea that 'happily ever after' is a place within the light. A place where love or friendship can disperse the shadows of a difficult past, where a person can rest knowing they can overcome and that they'll find peace in the end.

But, not every ending finds itself where a person expects.

Raised in a rival network, she chose to see beauty despite living under the ever-present eye of The Estate. She was an artist, her life spent capturing the world through the point of a pen or the brushstroke across canvas. But like anything of innocence or purity, it was only a matter of time before evil finally found her and stole her away from all that she'd ever known.

This is a story where happily ever after sits cushioned within darkness – where everything we think we know about love is challenged. It's a place where a person becomes trapped inside - a place where they seek out others who are willing to join them in the suffocating hold of their shadowed past.

Her angel. He was a man who'd imprisoned her, who'd terrified her until her mind had shattered around her, sparkling down like crystalline shards of the fantasies and dreams he'd destroyed. And after doing so, he'd picked her up again to rebuild her, to teach her, and reform her into the perfect pet.

He was her tormentor and protector, her enemy and lover, and her darkness and light.

Her name was Honor Delacroix, and she never imagined that when she was taken to The Estate to be enslaved...

She would choose to never leave again.

343

M.S. Willis

If you are interested in reading additional books by M.S. Willis or would like to know when new books are being released, M.S. Willis can be found at:

Website: http://www.mswillisbooks.com

Facebook:
http://www.facebook.com/mswillisbooks

Join the Mailing List!!!

If you are interested in receiving email updates regarding additional books by M.S. Willis or would like to know when new books are announced or being released, M.S. Willis can be found on the website or Facebook page.